Lady Germaine Elizabeth Olive Eliot was born in London on 13 April 1911, the daughter of Montague Charles Eliot, the 8th Earl of St Germans, and Helen Agnes Post.

She twice married—first to Major Thomas James in 1932, then to Captain Hon. Kenneth George Kinnaird, the 12th Baron Kinnaird, in 1950. Both marriages ended in divorce. She apparently applied for American citizenship in 1971. She published five novels, the first of which, *Alice* (1949), was a Book Society Choice. Her non-fiction *Heiresses and Coronets* (1960, aka *They All Married Well*), about prominent marriages between wealthy Americans and titled Europeans in the late Victorian and Edwardian period, was a success on both sides of the Atlantic.

Elizabeth Eliot died in New York in 1991.

WORKS BY ELIZABETH ELIOT

Fiction

Alice (1949)*
Henry (1950)*
Mrs Martell (1953)*
Starter's Orders (1955)
Cecil (1962)*

Non-fiction

Portrait of a Sport: A History of Steeplechasing (1957)
Heiresses and Coronets (1960, aka *They All Married Well*)

*available from Furrowed Middlebrow/Dean Street Press

ELIZABETH ELIOT

HENRY

With an introduction by
Elizabeth Crawford

DEAN STREET PRESS

A Furrowed Middlebrow Book

FM27

Published by Dean Street Press 2019

Copyright © 1950 Elizabeth Eliot

Introduction © 2019 Elizabeth Crawford

All Rights Reserved

Published by licence, issued under the UK Orphan Works
Licensing Scheme.

First published in 1950 by Cassell & Co.

Cover by DSP
Cover illustration shows detail from *30 Regent Terrace* (c.1934),
by Francis Cadell

ISBN 978 1 912574 61 2

www.deanstreetpress.co.uk

For

SYLVIA and FREDERIC CAUNTER
at Commonwood

INTRODUCTION

REVIEWING Elizabeth Eliot's debut novel, *Alice*, for the *Sunday Times*, C.P. Snow noted in the author 'an astringent sympathy, a knowledge from bitter experience that life is not easy' while the *Times Literary Supplement* review of her second novel, *Henry*, mentioned her 'light-heartedness, delicious wit and humanity lurking beneath the surface'. Comparisons were drawn with the work of Nancy Mitford and Elizabeth von Arnim, although Snow observed that 'Alice was set in the world of the high aristocracy, loftier, though less smart, than the world of Miss Mitford's "Hons"'. This 'high aristocracy' was, indeed, the world into which, on 13 April 1911, Germaine Elizabeth Olive Eliot was born, her birth registered only as 'Female Eliot'. Time was obviously required to select her full complement of names, but by the time she was christened decisions had been made. 'Germaine' does not appear to have been a family name, although it echoes that of the earldom – St Germans – of which, at that time, her great uncle, Henry Cornwallis Eliot, the 5th earl, was the holder. 'Elizabeth' was the name of her maternal grandmother, Elizabeth Wadsworth, whose grandfather, General James Wadsworth, had been military governor of Washington during the American Civil War. Transatlantic connections were to prove important to this 'Female Eliot'. No hint of an 'Olive' appears in either her paternal or maternal line, so that may have been a mere parental indulgence. Of these three forenames 'Elizabeth' was the one by which the future author was known.

At the time of Elizabeth's birth her parents were living in Marylebone, London, the census, taken just ten days previously, giving us a glimpse into the household. At its head was her 40-year-old father, Montague Charles Eliot, who, with a script replete with flourishes, completed the form, listing also her 26-year-old American mother, Helen Agnes; a butler; a lady's maid; a cook; two housemaids; and a hall boy. Doubtless a few days later a nursemaid would have taken up her position in the nursery. Montague (1870-1960) and Helen (c.1885-1962) had married the previous June. Helen (or 'Nellie' as she was known), although American-born and of American parentage, had, in fact, spent most of her life in the United Kingdom. Her father had died when she was four-years-old and her mother had then married Arthur Smith-Barry, later Baron Barrymore of Fota House, near Cork, Ireland. As Elizabeth Eliot's novels reveal a knowledge of Irish estates and relations, she probably had on occasion visited Fota.

In the newspaper reports of his marriage no mention was made of Montague Eliot's connection to the St Germans earldom, so far was he at that time from inheriting. However, tragedy has long hovered around the St Germans family and in 1922 the death in a riding accident of the 6th Earl meant the title and estate passed to Montague Eliot's elder, unmarried and childless brother. On his death in 1942 Montague Eliot became the 8th Earl of St Germans and his daughter Elizabeth acquired the title of 'Lady'. Montague Eliot had joined King Edward VII's household in 1901 and at the time of Elizabeth's birth was Gentleman Usher to George V, later becoming Groom of the Robes. He held the latter unpaid position until 1936 and from 1952 until his death was Extra Groom-in-Waiting to Elizabeth II.

The 8th Earl's heir was Elizabeth's brother, Nicholas (1914-88) and the family was completed after a long interval with the birth of another son, Montague Robert Vere Eliot (1923-94). Around this time Elizabeth and her family moved to 111 Gloucester Place, a tall house, one of a long terrace on a canyon of a road that runs north-south through Marylebone.

While it is on record that her brothers were sent to Eton, we know nothing of Elizabeth's education. Was she taught at home by a governess; or did she attend a London day school, or an establishment such as 'Groom Place', where we first meet the two young women in *Alice*, or 'Mrs Martell's 'inexpensive but good school on the south coast of England'? Elizabeth's mother, certainly, had had a governess, 70-year-old Miss Dinah Thoreau, who took rat poison in December 1934 and killed herself in her room in Paddington. Lack of money was not a problem for the Eliots, unlike the Pallisers, whose daughter, Anne, narrator of *Henry*, remarks that her family had been 'too poor for my sister or me to be properly educated (although Henry, of course, had been sent to Harrow)'. Naturally boys had to go to school in order 'to have a good answer when people asked where they had been at school. That was why Henry had been sent to Harrow.' The fact that the young women in her novels invariably received an education inferior to their brothers may indicate that Elizabeth did indeed feel that she had not been 'properly educated'. Whatever the reality, a review of the US edition of *Alice* revealed that Elizabeth 'Like many authors, has been writing since she was 10'.

Nor do we know anything of Elizabeth's relationship with her parents. What is one to make of the fact she dedicated *Cecil*, the story of a loathsome, manipulative mother, to her own mother? What is one to make of the tantalising information contained in the publisher's blurb for *Cecil* that the book is 'based on fact'? Which strand of *Cecil*'s plot might have been developed from a factual base? For the novel, quite apart from placing a 'veritable ogress' of a mother centre stage, also deals with drug-taking, murder, and impotency. *Cecil* was published in November 1962, a couple of months after Nellie Eliot, Dowager Countess of St Germans, committed suicide in a hotel room in Gibraltar, having arrived the day before from Tangier where she had been visiting her son Vere. Whatever their real-life relationship it is fair to say that in Elizabeth Eliot's novels mothers tend to be seen in a somewhat negative light, while fathers are noticeable by their absence.

In 1922 the elevation to the earldom of St Germans of her unmarried uncle brought significant changes to Elizabeth Eliot and her family, with visits to Port Eliot becoming more frequent. In 1926 Elizabeth had the honour of opening the St Germans parish fête, held in the grounds of Port Eliot, and made, according to the *Western Morning News*, 'an effective and amusing speech'. Port Eliot, an ancient house, shaped and reshaped over the centuries, is so extensive that, its guidebook confesses, not once in living memory has the roof been completely watertight. If not so ancient, similarly large houses, often in the west-country and sometimes decaying, certainly play their part in Elizabeth Eliot's novels. When Margaret, the narrator of *Alice*, visits 'Platon', Alice's Devonshire family home, she sat in 'one of the drawing rooms. There was no fire, it was bitterly cold, and everything in the room, including the chairs and sofa on which we sat, was covered with dust sheets.' 'Trelynt', the west-country home of Anne Palliser is, post-Second World War, similarly large, damp, and servantless.

Naturally Elizabeth Eliot's position in society meant that in due course she 'did the Season' as a debutante, her presence recorded at hunt and charity balls and even in a photograph on the front of *Tatler*. In *Alice*, Margaret admits that 'The basic idea was rational enough. When a girl reached marriageable age, she was introduced by her parents into adult society, where it was hoped she would meet her future husband. There are many examples of such practices in *The Golden Bough*. Only somehow by the nineteen-thirties it had all got rather silly.' Margaret is presented at court, her Uncle Henry, like Montague Eliot, being a member of the royal household, and observes that this connection 'meant that we had seats in the Throne Room, which was fun, as there was always the chance that someone would fall down. Not that one would wish it for them, but should it happen, it would be nice to see it.'

Elizabeth's 'Season' produced the desired result and in January 1932 her engagement to Thomas James (1906-76) was announced in the press on both sides of the Atlantic. The wedding took place barely two months later in St George's Hanover Square. Thomas James' father, a former MP for Bromley, was dead and his mother too ill to attend. The bishop of Norwich gave a particularly didactic address, much reproduced in press reports, stressing the seriousness of marriage. Were the words of the cleric tailored specifically for this flighty young couple?

After a honeymoon in Rio and Madeira in early 1933, delayed perhaps until after the death of Thomas James' mother, the young couple settled down to married life. Tended by five servants, they occupied the whole of 4 Montague Square, a five-storey house, five minutes' walk from the Eliot family home. In the years after the Second World War Thomas James was employed by BP, but it is not clear what his occupation was during the years he was married to Elizabeth. On the ship's manifest for their 1933 trip he is described as a 'Representative'. Was fiction imitating life when, in *Alice*, Alice and her new husband Cassius sailed to Rio where he was 'to represent a firm of motor-car engineers'? Despite both Elizabeth and dashing, Eton-educated Thomas James having family money, rumour has it that during their marriage they ran up considerable gambling debts, a contributory factor to their divorce in 1940.

On the outbreak of war in 1939 Lady Elizabeth James, now living alone in a flat in St John's Wood, was registered as an ambulance driver with the London County Council. However, nothing is known of her life during and immediately after the war until the publication of *Alice* in 1949. A few months later, in March 1950, she married the Hon. George Kinnaird at Brighton registry office. When asked by the *Daily Mail* why they had married 'in strict secrecy', Kinnaird replied 'We are both too engrossed in our work'. The *Daily Mail* then explained that 'Lady Elizabeth is authoress of Book Society choice *Alice*. Mr Kinnaird is a literary adviser.' Kinnaird was at this time attached in some capacity to the publishing firm of John Murray. This marriage ended in divorce in 1962.

For some years in the 1950s Elizabeth Eliot lived in Lambourn in Berkshire, a town renowned for its association with horse racing. This was clearly a sport close to her heart for during this period, apart from *Henry* (1950) and *Mrs. Martell* (1953), she produced two books devoted to horse racing, one, *Starter's Orders*, fiction, and the other, *Portrait of a Sport*, non-fiction. In *Henry* the narrator's much-loved but feckless brother, the eponymous Henry, is a haunter of the race track. As he observes, 'I can always reckon to make quite a bit racing, and then there's backgammon. Backgammon can be terribly paying if you go the right way about it.' Of Elizabeth's brother, thrice-married Nicholas, *The Times*'s obituarist wrote, with some circumspection, that he was 'a supporter of the Turf in his day, as owner, trainer and bookmaker'. On inheriting the title and estate on the death of his father in 1960, Nicholas Eliot, 9th Earl of St Germans, made the estate over to his young son and went into tax exile.

After her second divorce Elizabeth seems to have spent a good deal of time in New York, mingling in literary circles, and in June 1971, while living in Greenwich Village, at 290 Sixth Avenue, applied for US citizenship. Thereafter she disappears from sight until *The Times* carried a notice of her death in New York on 3 November 1991. For whatever reason, detailed facts of Elizabeth Eliot's life have become so obfuscated that even members of her own extended family have been unable to supply information. Fortunately for us, her mordant wit and powers of social observation survive, amply revealed in the four novels now reissued by Dean Street Press.

Elizabeth Crawford

ONE

THE HOUSE we lived in was too large for us. In a book published in 1829 it was described as being a plain and neat structure standing amidst picturesque grounds. 'Trelynt,' the book said, 'had been erected about the year 1760. It had been the property of various families until it was purchased in the year 1812 by Captain J.P. Pallisser, R.N.'

The mansion was no longer plain, for a piece had been added to the side, in the late 'eighties, by grandfather and there were straggling back premises which the authors of *Devonshire Illustrated in a Series of Views* had neglected to notice. Also, it was no longer at all neat and it stood amidst grounds which could be described as being extremely neglected and overgrown. It was reached by a long damp drive.

'You may walk down to the end of the drive, but you are *not* to go in the road.'

'Not as far as the village?'

'Don't be silly,' my sister had said, for the village was more than three miles away and in those days there was no bus. The end of the drive and back was quite a long walk and I was not an energetic child.

'And don't forget to put on your outdoor shoes.'

I stumped down the drive, an ugly scowling little girl, my hands in the pockets of my overcoat, and in the pockets there was half a crown (mostly in pennies and threepenny bits); perhaps after all I would change my mind and go to the village—perhaps after all I would disobey Sophia. I would get a lift in the postman's van or the greengrocer's; but when I reached the end of the drive there was no sign of the postman. I stood under the dark dripping trees and wondered why it was so very seldom the summer, the summer with clouds of dust and long hours spent on the beach and the sun burning the back of one's neck. Suddenly there was the sound of a motor-bicycle. Not the postman, not the greengrocer, just a dull man on a motor-bicycle.

Life was very unrewarding. And then the motor-bicycle, with a fine sweep, turned in at the gate.

'Henry,' I screamed, and again, 'Henry,' for here was something really exciting; it wasn't the holidays, Henry shouldn't be here at all and he shouldn't be riding a motor-bicycle when he hadn't got one. He stopped the engine and I ran towards him; how beautiful he was, more beautiful even than I remembered him and he was laughing as I came up to him.

'Hullo, Anne, what are you doing?'

'Take me to the village,' I said. 'Oh, please take me to the village.'

'Why not,' Henry said, and I clambered up on the pillion.

The rest of the afternoon was a long and golden enchantment. We went to the village. I spent my half-crown and Henry treated me to tea in one of the beautiful teashops which were so much deplored by mother. I sat and ate yellow cake and thought how lucky I was to have Henry for a brother, so wonderfully old and so very good-looking, although it was only lately that I had noticed just how good-looking he was; the fact had been pointed out to me by the housemaid.

Darling Henry, whom I loved so very much and who had now fulfilled all my hopes for him by running away from school.

Oh, it had been an enchanting afternoon, and for once Henry had really listened when I talked to him, and had answered all my questions, but when we had finished our tea, he had said that we must go home.

'Are you going to live there always now?'

But Henry was busy starting the bicycle and he didn't answer, or anyhow I didn't hear the answer.

We arrived at Trelynt. Feeling extremely happy and important I accompanied Henry into the drawing room and there the row had started; half-way through it I had been told by mother to leave the room, reluctantly I had done so. I didn't see Henry again for several years; and it was several weeks before Sophia had told me what exactly had happened.

Mother, it seemed, had been very cross. Father disliked being cross, so, instead, he had washed his hands of Henry. That had been a good idea. It meant that he didn't have to give Henry any more money.

Mother doubted whether the authorities would receive Henry back.

Henry had said that he wasn't going back in any case. He had a job and the man was expecting him to report the following day; he had only come to Trelynt to collect some clothes.

Mother had said that at seventeen Henry was too young to have a job, and what about Oxford?

Henry said that if they liked they could send Sophia to Oxford instead of him. She was much cleverer than he was, anyhow, and personally he was going to work in a circus. It was at that point that father had left the room. Mother said that Henry was too old to begin work in a circus. 'Their parents start bending their backs about before they can walk; I was reading about it in the paper only last week.'

Henry said that that was acrobats and he wasn't going to be one.

'What are you going to be?' Sophia asked.

'A lion tamer, I should think,' Henry said, but obviously he didn't really care.

Father came back into the drawing room to say that there was a motor-bicycle outside the front door, and had Henry stolen it? Whereupon Henry had taken great offence and had flung out of the house without collecting the clothes for which he had come. Sophia had had to send them on to him later at a poste-restante address in Reading.

The strange thing about all this, of course, was not that Henry had run away from school in the morning and had a terrible row with his parents in the evening (for that has happened in varying circumstances to several people whom one knows), but that he did actually join a circus, and spent several delightful years as an assistant to a man who was the owner of a troupe of performing dogs.

'You, if I may say so, are one of the few truly adult people I know.' Pamela Merritt peered anxiously at Lawrence who sat at the other end of the sofa. He smiled at her encouragingly. He did not offer to contradict her and I was impressed, for according to my conventions he should have said: 'Not at all, really,' or even: 'Oh, do you think so?' in a pleased bright voice. That is what I should have said, but then, nobody had ever suggested that I was adult. Grown up, of course, and old enough to know better, but never specifically adult.

Lawrence agreed gravely with Pamela, and their conversation soared grandly over my head. A few moments later and they were discussing Rimbaud.

Rimbaud didn't write *Les Fleurs du Mal*. That was all I could remember about Rimbaud. It wasn't enough. One would have to know more than that to meet Pamela on her own level. Tomorrow I would look up Rimbaud in *Les Poetes Français Contemporains*.

In the meantime, I continued to sit in front of the fire and look complacently around the room. It was a highly intellectual room, with oilcloth on the floor, and rather ugly curtains. There were a great many books, both in bookcases and on shelves which sagged in the middle. Besides Pamela and Lawrence there were several other people. They talked together in low modulated voices, and when they asked a question they waited for the answer. As far as I was concerned it was all most unusual and charming and these people were quite obviously superior to the ones I had hitherto known. I envied them, and I longed to be like them.

My eyes strayed to a large engraving which hung on the wall. The young Victoria on the day of her coronation. The maple frame was much decorated with gold and at the top there was a carved gilt crown. Not a very big crown, but then neither was the one on the queen's head. 'Such a little neck,' no, that was Anne Boleyn, but it was all extremely touching. The queen was very young, the mantle of royalty weighed heavily, too heavily, on her young shoulders. She looked rather tall in the picture, but that hadn't been so, she had been quite tiny, and later on she had turned into the widow of Windsor.

'Anne,' Stephanie Marsh called from the other end of the room, 'will you go and make some tea?'

I jumped to my feet. Of course I would make tea for these delightful intelligent people. It was a privilege, and in the end I would be so useful that they would find me indispensable—and in the end they might discover that I had a certain intelligence of my own.

I hurried to the basement, lit the gas-stove and put on the kettle. While I waited for it to boil I laid the tray. I remembered that Stephanie liked the tray to look nice. That meant decanting the milk into a thickish earthenware jug, and using the cups that were the least chipped. Then teaspoons, the ones that had been the least recently used for egg. Tonight, with seven people to be provided with tea, there was not much choice. It was this scarcity of the most ordinary kind of equipment which had surprised me on first coming to live with Stephanie. I could understand that china got broken, and that silver was liable to get dents in it and become scratched; what I could not understand was the china not having been nice in the first place, and the silver not having been silver. I decided that these things were a mark of a superior mind. Only inferior people, like my mother, would fuss around trying to match up cups and saucers, going into Exeter for them, and when that failed, writing to London. It did not occur to me that it could be a question of money, for since my childhood it had been impressed upon me that we were extremely poor. Too poor for my sister or me to be properly educated (although Henry, of course, had been sent to Harrow), and too poor for us to have decent clothes or be able to hunt. Father hunted, but that again was different; father was father, and he was a man.

At length the kettle boiled. It didn't seem to be a particularly good kind of gas-stove. I made the tea and carried the tray carefully upstairs. When I got to the sitting room everybody was too busy talking to notice me. I put the tray down on a stool made of woven string and went back to fetch the kettle. Back in the sitting room they still hadn't noticed the arrival of the tea, so I poured it out, keeping for Stephanie and myself the cups that were definitely known to leak. Then I sat down on the floor near the fire and prepared to listen to the nearest conversation. It did not occur to me that there might be one going on in which I was qualified to join. I was quite right.

Much later, the visitors were leaving to catch their underground trains. I was left alone with Stephanie, Lawrence and Pamela Merritt. Pamela lodged in the house, and Lawrence (I had been given to understand) was either married to Stephanie, or shortly would be. For the moment, though, they had their own surnames, Stephanie Marsh and Lawrence Smith-Jackson.

'Brilliant,' Lawrence was saying about one of the departed guests, 'quite brilliant.'

Stephanie leant back on the sofa and lit a cigarette. 'I shouldn't have said he was sound.'

'Unsound' was their worst criticism.

It went without saying that no one could actually be stupid, and I never heard them accuse anyone of being unkind. People were boring. This was the only quality which they deplored equally with my mother, but naturally they and my mother would find people boring for different reasons.

Lawrence closed his eyes, lay back in his chair and said he was tired. It was the most intelligible thing he had said for some hours. He was a large man with dark untidy hair. He wasn't young and he didn't seem yet to be middle-aged. He was a scholar and a writer. Two of his books had been published. They were novels, but they weren't the kind of novels I was used to. Probably that was because they were significant. Lawrence's presence in the house enabled me to tell them at the office that all the people I lived with were writers and artists. It was true that Stephanie painted; sometimes she sent her paintings to an exhibition, but usually they were returned to her without having been displayed. Pamela, like Lawrence, was a scholar, but she wasn't a writer. She was a doctor of medicine, and held appointments at various clinics; most of them had to do with birth-control, and I hoped that she would tell funny stories about them, but she never had.

I had met these people through an advertisement in the *New Statesman*. Stephanie had advertised that she was congenial, and that the person who answered the advertisement could have bed and breakfast and an evening meal. I had gone to see Stephanie and found that the room she offered was clean, although not particularly cheap. We agreed to give each other a month's trial. It was the easel in the sitting room which had really decided me. Then I wrote to my mother telling her that I had seen the advertisement in the *Spectator* and that I wouldn't be staying any longer with Aunt Mary, who had been patiently doing her duty by me until I should find suitable lodgings. I told Aunt Mary about Stephanie, and she said I would enjoy the young companionship.

It was fun living in London, almost anywhere in London.

Until now my life had been spent almost entirely in Devonshire, helping mother to match the teacups and helping Sophia with the hens.

Neither Sophia nor I had been to school. We had had a governess, who, until she left to be married, had made herself very useful to mother. I was about twelve when she left and after that I did lessons with Sophia. As Sophia at that time was twenty-two she was considered to be old enough to teach me, and anyhow there was the library. An intelligent child could learn more in a well-stocked library than in all the schools in England, anyhow if the child was a girl; for boys, of course, it was different. They had to play football, and they had to have a good answer when people asked them where they had been at school.

That was why Henry had been sent to Harrow.

Sophia and I had never been expected to earn our own livings. We were expected to make ourselves useful at home and, more vaguely, to get married. With this project in view we were sent, every year, to spend a fortnight at Cowes with Uncle George and Aunt Emily. Aunt Emily was one of my mother's many sisters, and she was the only one who had married money and it must have been quite a lot of money, for Uncle George owned a steam yacht and he was a member of the Royal Yacht Squadron. That was not a question of money, it was a question of being elected, and it was a great honour.

Sophia and I always enjoyed going to Cowes, but so far we neither of us had got married. For this omission mother, in her more querulous moments, would blame Aunt Emily. Aunt Emily had clearly not tried, and, with Sophia, she had had years of opportunity. I had only been to Cowes twice, then the war had started. That was no excuse. Twice would have been quite enough if Aunt Emily had really tried.

On the outbreak of war I had gone into the W.R.N.S; mostly because I wanted to leave home anyhow, and my mother said that the W.R.N.S. were nicer than the A.T.S. (She may have been right, but I didn't particularly like the W.R.N.S.) Sophia stayed at home and took the place of the servants, who had left immediately. Our servants usually left anyhow, but my mother explained that this time it was because of the war. My mother was furious when she found that one of them had gone into the W.R.N.S.

When the war finished I was still not expected to earn my living, and my mother said I could come home now. So I went home and it wasn't a success. I decided that I would go to London and become a secretary.

'But wouldn't they expect you to *know* something?' my mother asked.

I told her that I had done quite a lot of typing in the W.R.N.S., when I wasn't driving a lorry, and that I would learn shorthand in the evenings.

'The papers are full of advertisements for secretaries and junior typists. So I don't expect people will be as particular as they used to be.'

Mother said that standards were certainly going down, and that 'they' were forcing 'us' out of existence.

And my mother had looked mournfully round the drawing room. 'They' had prevented her renewing the faded chintz covers, and also, presumably, buying a new castor for one of the armchairs.

'I cannot, of course, make you stay in your home, but I hardly think you are being fair to Sophia.'

I didn't answer. I knew perfectly well I was being unfair to Sophia. I only wished that Sophia would start being unfair to mother. Then we could both have gone away.

'Sophia has been very much tried by the war. As well as doing so much work in the house, she had her V.A.D.'s.'

I nodded in sympathy, and remembered that before the war Sophia had also done a lot of work in the house, and had had her Girl Guides.

'And there are the hens,' I said.

My mother said that she didn't know how they would have got through the war at all without Sophia's hens. 'You needn't think that you young people in the Services were the only ones who were doing anything. Of course, it was different for the men, they were fighting.'

'Some of them weren't, some of them were just going round with the milk, like Henry.'

My mother said that was not a nice way to speak of my brother, and that the Royal Army Service Corps was a very important part of the army.

'Only one shouldn't dance with them,' I said, recalling advice given me in the past by Aunt Emily.

Mother said that Henry would have been the first person to have welcomed being sent abroad. Being kept in England had been a terrible disappointment to him.

I said that I hadn't meant that at all, and fortunately Sophia had come in to say that she was bicycling to the village, and did either of us want anything? I offered to go instead of her, and mother said that whoever went might just go to Mrs Yeo's who had half promised her a duck.

Later I had talked to Sophia about going to London and being a secretary.

Sophia had sighed, and said that she supposed staying at home wasn't much of a life for a young person.

'Then why don't you come, too?'

'I couldn't possibly leave mother, and anyhow I don't mind it. I *like* the country really,'—and Sophia had looked out of the window at the dripping laurels which obliterated the view from the drawing-room windows. Not that there would have been much of a view even without the laurels, for on the other side of them was a high bank.

The drawing room was in that part of the house which had been built by grandfather. The room was large and badly proportioned. The windows were contained in a bay which was the segment of an octagon. The middle window went down to the ground and in wet weather water would seep in from outside.

'But, Sophia, you can't like it, *nobody* could.' I was being utterly selfish. If I urged Sophia to come away, I should feel less guilty about her when I was in London. 'You said yourself that this was no life for a young person.'

'But I am no longer young.'

'Nonsense, you're only thirty-five,' I said briskly, and wondered how it would feel to think of oneself as no longer young.

When Sophia was my age she had been giving me my lessons, and looking after the hens, and helping mother. I wondered if Sophia had ever been in love, and realised I didn't much care.

The only member of my family whom I had ever really liked was Henry, for Henry, as the Irish housemaid had not been slow to point out, was so very good-looking. And he was brave, worthy to rank with Casabianca and the Major in the army whom the dentist had told me about. The Major, so the dentist had said, had had a piece of bone grafted on to his jaw without having an anaesthetic, and the Major had never moved and never murmured.

Only once had I seen Henry in the least frightened.

We had driven over to Torness. Mother, and the picnic basket, and the governess, and Henry and me. I was eight years old and Henry was sixteen. It had been a cold damp day, and we had sat on the sands. I remember the tiny grey pebbles clinging to my toes and to the edge of my spade. Henry said he would climb the cliff, and I had got up to follow him; but mother had said, no, I would only fall. I said I could go part of the way.

At the base of the cliff there were rocks which were covered at high water. Henry scrambled over these easily enough, but they were too high and I was defeated by them. I scraped some skin off my foot, and sat down for a little, not to cry, but to feel sorry for myself. I watched Henry who had now reached the cliff proper. It looked fun up there, with the scaling grey rocks and sea pinks, and those other plants which looked as if they would be useful to hold on to. I imagined how it would have been if only I could have got past these smooth steep rocks. Beside me there was a little pool with green seaweed and anemones, and if I put my hand under the ledge, I would probably find winkles. But who wanted winkles when one might be climbing a cliff? I watched Henry going up and up and I admired his strength and his long legs. If only my legs had been longer, I should not have been sitting here on the rocks. But now Henry had stopped. He was spread-eagled against the cliff-face and he did not move.

The governess was sent running for help. Mother climbed up as far as my rock pool, from where she shouted encouragement and directions to Henry who could not hear her. In the end he was rescued and hauled to safety by two young men who wore khaki shorts; one of them had a red handkerchief tied round his head. Mother and I climbed to the top of the cliff by the path. The young men stood over Henry who sat on the grass looking white and shaken. Mother thanked the young men, who said it was nothing and that they couldn't imagine what had come over the chap.

'It started to give way,' Henry explained to mother, 'and then I caught at one of those blasted plants and that didn't hold either.'

The young men were very sympathetic, and the one with the handkerchief said that some people couldn't stand heights, no head for them, and Henry had looked up and smiled and called himself a fool.

It seemed that I had been right when I told mother that the lack of secretaries was now so great that it would be possible, without any very great difficulty, to find someone who would employ even me. On my second day in London I found Lady Merton. An employment agency, which specialised in finding positions for gentlewomen, was responsible for my introduction to her. The gentlewoman who ran the agency told me that Lady Merton was very nice and that all her secretaries had been extremely happy.

'Has she had so very many then?'

The gentlewoman became vague and gave me a card to give Lady Merton. The card had my name and age and lack of experience typed on it. At the bottom the gentlewoman had written '£4 10s. 0d.' in red ink.

Lady Merton had an office in a large building off Victoria Street. She was in when I arrived and I was surprised to see that she was quite young. She was dressed in some kind of a uniform. That also was surprising. I had imagined that that sort of thing had gone out with the war.

Lady Merton smiled at me and said she was glad to see I was an ex-Service woman. As I wasn't dressed in uniform I wondered how she knew, then I remembered it was written on the card. Lady Merton began to explain about her interests. It seemed that she ran a chain of canteens for ex-Service women in England and the occupied countries. Lady Merton felt that at all costs ex-Service women should be 'kept together'; after all, with everything so unsettled, one never knew when they would be next required; and what better way is there of keeping people together than by herding them into canteens? Canteens had been very popular during the war, especially with the ladies who ran them, and who were able to wear uniforms and explain to their friends how very essential their particular canteens were and how very grateful the troops were to them. During the war, when there weren't always enough troops to go round, some of the ladies ran canteens for policemen and for dockers and even for the out-patients of hospitals. It was the dockers who were the most startled.

'It must be interesting,' I said, thinking drearily of N.A.A.F.I.

'It will be when we get going,' Lady Merton said heartily, 'and I shall be away a great deal, of course, inspecting our different branches. What rank did you hold when you were demobbed?'

'I was a Wren,' I said.

'Not an officer?'

'I was a Wren rating,' I said. 'I was a Wren rating for five years.'

Lady Merton said it was extraordinary and showed how the Services had wasted good material. 'An educated girl like you.'

'But I'm not educated. I explained that to them at the agency. Didn't they put it on the card?' I had decided by now that I didn't want to work for Lady Merton.

'You know what I mean,' Lady Merton was saying, 'a lady and all that. Of course they should have made you an officer. Sheer waste of material.'

I reflected that if that was the way Lady Merton's mind worked, there was no point in her being young.

'You'll be able to start on Monday, I suppose?' Lady Merton was saying. 'Four pounds and a uniform allowance.'

'It says four pounds ten on the card.'

Lady Merton said that the ten was a mistake and that really the agency was too sickening.

'I didn't know one had to wear a uniform.'

Lady Merton looked hurt. 'You don't have to, but you will find it an advantage, make you more efficient.'

I accepted the explanation. I hadn't been made at all efficient by my Wren uniform, but perhaps Lady Merton's would be different. It was rather a pretty one, now that I came to look at it, but as Lady Merton was about six feet tall she would probably have looked quite good in almost any uniform.

'I don't type very well,' I said, making a last bid for freedom.

'Typing?' Lady Merton said airily. 'You won't find there's a terrible lot of typing. As long as you're neat and accurate, that's all that will be required. I want you to think of yourself more as my P.A. than anything else. You can drive a car, of course?'

'I can drive a lorry,' and added, 'in all weathers,' so as to make it sound more friendly.

Lady Merton said that that was perfectly splendid and that she counted on me to be punctual on Monday. 'Nine o'clock sharp, and if I'm not in you can start on the post.'

The interview was evidently over, so I went away. Outside Lady Merton's door I dared myself to go back again and tell her that I didn't want the job. I dared myself the whole way along the passage and while I was going down in the lift. I dared myself for the last time on the pavement outside the building. Then I realised that it wasn't any good and I went into a bookshop to cheer myself up. I walked round and round that shop and there didn't seem to be a single book that I wanted to read. I went downstairs to their second-hand department, and bought a mathematical text-book. If I was going to have to work for Lady Merton in the daytime, I would teach myself arithmetic in the evenings. I reminded myself that Lady Merton had said that she would be away a great deal. If that were true, I might even be able to teach myself arithmetic in the office. I remembered that, having got a job, I must now find myself somewhere to live. I bought a *New Statesman* and discovered Stephanie. The rent that Stephanie asked was more than my salary. If I counted in my allowance it was the same as my salary and I would have nine shillings a week for everything else. I began to see the point of a uniform. Fortunately, I still had the two brooches left me by my grandmother, and a rather nasty ring which had belonged to an aunt who was now dead. I supposed it would be possible to pawn them and perhaps get them out if my mother ever came to London. Perhaps if I got really good at typing I could take some in in the evenings, or perhaps I could make just a little money by betting.

I bought an evening paper and looked for the racing page.

It was on a Monday in late September that I began to work for Lady Merton. The next day I moved from Aunt Mary's to Stephanie's.

Stephanie leant back on the sofa and lit a cigarette. 'I shouldn't have said he was sound.'

Lawrence said that the departed guest was sound enough.

Pamela echoed that he was quite brilliant.

I didn't say anything, as I wasn't sure which of their guests they were discussing.

Stephanie yawned and said that it was time for her to go to bed. She went out of the room and Lawrence followed her. He paused in the doorway to ask Pamela if she would put out the lights.

Pamela watched them go.

TWO

'PALLISSER,' Lady Merton said to me one morning after I had worked for her for about a month, 'you're not smart.'

I shifted from one leg to the other. Experience had taught me that it was a good idea to get up when Lady Merton came into the room. Sometimes we pretended that I was her personal assistant and sometimes we played at my being her aide-de-camp; in either case it was better to stand.

'I'm sorry,' I said, and looked down at my silly pale grey uniform, 'but I've never been smart, never.'

'But don't you take a pride in your personal appearance?'

'Would you take a pride,' I asked, 'if you looked like this?'

'You'd look all right if you'd only smarten yourself up.'

'I wouldn't,' I said, 'really I wouldn't, I've always looked silly in uniform.'

'Well, you must do something about it. Later on when I make my tours of inspection I may have to take you with me.'

'I thought I was going to stay here and keep things going.'

'Somebody from the outer office will probably be able to do that; we shall have an outer office by then, you know. Frankly, Pallisser, I like having you here, we talk the same language, but if you don't pull yourself together I shall have to make a change.'

Weakly, I said I was sorry and sat down again. 'There are two new applicants for canteen workers this morning.'

'Any good?'

'I don't think so, they're both over fifty and one of them says it won't be inoculated for anything ever.'

Apparently this pleased Lady Merton and she was in a good temper for the rest of the morning.

Working for Lady Merton was not as bad as I had imagined it would be. For one thing it made me quite popular with Stephanie and the others, who were always asking for the latest Lady Merton, and there almost always *was* a latest. The occasions when I had to invent something preposterous for her to say or do were extremely rare.

There was a time when I might have felt that I was being disloyal in thus gaining popularity by making fun of my employer, but five years of strict discipline had taught me that authority was there (anyhow partly) for my amusement.

There was no doubt that Lady Merton was funny; but Stephanie and her friends, although they were more than capable of enjoying her, couldn't, I soon found, enjoy her straight. They had to mix her up with a lot of sociological significance. As far as I could make out Lawrence thought that she did a lot of harm, mostly because of her good humour, and Pamela thought that she did a lot of good, because she epitomised decadence, and after decadence had gone on for some time everything always got better by way of revulsion.

'Or revolution,' I said, remembering some pamphlets I had been lent by a friend in the W.R.N.S.

Pamela said that nobody now believed in revolutions; they were, it seemed, hopelessly out of date.

'I know some people who believe in them.'

'They are probably drawing-room pinks.'

I was furious with Pamela, for I believed in revolution myself and wished I was brave enough to say so.

The next morning Lady Merton didn't tell me I wasn't looking smart; she asked me instead about Henry.

I admitted he was my brother. He, I said, had been an officer, for I didn't see why he shouldn't be made to do me as much credit as possible.

'I met him last night.'

'Oh, did you,' I said, and wondered if Henry had found Lady Merton as funny as I did.

Lady Merton said that she thought he was terribly attractive and awfully amusing, what?

So then I knew that Henry must have quite liked Lady Merton, and concentrated on her, for when Henry didn't notice people they often didn't realise that he was attractive.

'Where did you meet him?' I asked.

Lady Merton said it was at one of those little clubs. Rather an amusing one actually, and they give you a damn good dinner as well, all black market, of course.

'Of course,' I said politely, and remembered that at Stephanie's we were shocked by the black market.

'I don't know how it first came up about you,' Lady Merton went on, 'but he was awfully amused when he realised that you worked in my office. He's very fond of you, isn't he, Pallisser?'

I said that I hoped so and was rather pleased.

Lady Merton said that Henry had said that we must all go out together soon.

I said that that would be very nice and wondered if 'all' was going to include Henry's mistress with whom he had been living for about a year now. I supposed not, but you never knew with Henry.

Henry's mistress was what Lady Merton would have described as a lady and all that. Henry's wife hadn't been and it was one of the things mother had had against her.

Mother also said that Henry's wife was a model and that she had caught Henry. As a matter of fact, she was a film extra.

Their married life, which had lasted a very short time, had been gay, inconsequent and filled with drama.

Mother, I think, felt that Pat's not being a lady made Henry's treatment of her, which admittedly had not been good, perfectly permissible. If they didn't get on, and if Henry was so unfaithful to her, it must be Pat's fault. When Henry finally left her and they were divorced, Pat was, for a time, very unhappy; but fortunately the war was going on and she was discovered and married by an American officer whom she described as being so nice and dull, darling.

On the whole Sophia and I liked Pat and we were sorry when she went out of our lives.

We had only met Henry's mistress once or twice and we hadn't cared for her. Mother, who had never met her at all, never referred to her except as 'that woman.'

The telephone rang, I answered it, and it was Henry. He was very friendly and advised me what to have on a horse in the two-thirty. If it won, which it was bound to unless something went wrong, I was to put the proceeds on another horse which might be running in the three o'clock. It sounded very complicated and I wrote it all down and then Henry asked to speak to Lady Merton.

Their conversation was fairly short, but Lady Merton managed to get in a good deal of laughing and smiling and gesticulating.

She rang off and told me that we were all going out together on Thursday evening.

'Your brother says you're to get hold of a boy friend.'

'I haven't got one,' I said.

'Don't be ridiculous, Pallisser!'

I tried, not very hard, to think of someone. A party with Henry was always fun, but I didn't want to spend an evening with Lady Merton, it was bad enough having to put up with her all day, and I couldn't think of one man I knew who would truly have enjoyed her company, or who was rich enough not to mind paying for his share of a party at a black-market club. Fortunately whatever happened it couldn't possibly be Thursday for two whole days. Perhaps by then I should have a rich admirer who, for the sake of my company, would be willing to overlook Lady Merton; or perhaps I should have influenza. Come to think of it, I didn't feel too well and I gave a tentative cough and felt my neck for the glands which usually came up when I got influenza, or even a fairly bad cold.

'Shall I do the filing?' I said, and admired myself for the way I carried on in spite of influenza and a high temperature.

Lady Merton, who was now in a very good temper, said that I had better start a card-index system for the people who had applied to us for jobs.

I said, all right, but what would we do with it when it was finished?

Lady Merton said it would help us to keep a check on things generally and that I could grade the applicants according to suitability. 'You know, H for hopeless and A for aged.' So I went out to the stationer's, and bought a little box with cards in it and spent the rest of the morning filling in the cards from the correspondence file, and making a glossary of the abbreviations and initial letters, so that Lady Merton and I would be able to understand the cards. V.V., I remember, stood for varicose veins, and V.V. followed by a capital S enclosed in brackets meant varicose veins suspected. It was rather fun and in the afternoon, Lady Merton being away from the office, I took some more money out of the petty cash and went and bought another card-index system for the people who were already working for us.

This was rather more complicated and I came to realise that it is easier to make out cards about people if you don't know anything very much about them.

At four o'clock Henry rang up to speak to Lady Merton.

I told him that she was out and he told me that the horses had done what he had expected of them and I calculated that he had been the means of winning me five pounds. If this would only go on for another day or two I might be able to afford to bribe someone to take me out to dinner with Henry and Lady Merton.

I asked after Henry's mistress and Henry said that as far as he knew the little woman was cooking his supper.

'But surely it will be awfully overcooked by the time you get back this evening?'

Henry said, 'Well, doing the shopping then,' and rang off.

At five o'clock I left the office and went back to Chalk Farm. Nobody was in but Stephanie who was in the sitting room with a naked model—a rather anaemic-looking young woman. Stephanie, in front of her easel, was painting a picture of a very pretty girl who wasn't anaemic at all.

Stephanie called out that if I wanted some tea would I have it in the kitchen? I didn't want any tea, but interpreted this to mean that Stephanie and the model did, so I went down to the kitchen to make it. Presently I was joined by Stephanie and the young woman, who was now wearing a mackintosh. When she sat down I noticed that she was wearing all her clothes under the mackintosh, so maybe she was cold.

As she stirred her tea, Stephanie asked me for the latest Lady Merton, so I told her about the card index and about Henry.

'You never said you had a brother.'

'Didn't I?' I said.

'How extraordinary you are.'

The model suddenly came out of a trance to say that she had *two* brothers.

So I said that I had a sister as well, and the model said that she had three sisters. Stephanie, very wisely, had dropped out of the conversation. When we had finished our tea, Stephanie told the model that she looked tired and that they wouldn't do any more today, but would the model come again tomorrow afternoon? The model looked doubtful and said that it was really her day for the post office but that she would do her best. Then she looked unhappy and Stephanie asked her how much she owed her? The model said how much it was. It seemed a very small sum, and then we both helped Stephanie look for her purse. Stephanie paid her, and she went away, and then Stephanie and I went up to the sitting room.

Stephanie stood for a long time looking at her picture. I looked at it, too, and said I liked it. Stephanie said that it wasn't right, something had gone wrong with the balance. So I looked again, but I didn't see what she meant.

'Perhaps,' Stephanie said, turning away from the picture, 'you will have Lady Merton for a sister-in-law.'

'I hope not,' I said.

'Well, Thursday ought to be funny anyhow.'

'I was rather planning not to go.'

'Oh, but you *must* go. Lady Merton in action ought to be simply wonderful. Will she wear her uniform?'

'I don't know.'

Stephanie became restless. She said that Lawrence ought to be back by now. She said that Lawrence was worried about his new book. She said that Lawrence could be incredibly selfish.

I nodded in sympathy.

Then Lawrence came in. He seemed very tired and the ends of his trousers were splashed with mud. He looked for some time at Stephanie's picture and said that the balance was wrong.

Stephanie said, 'Oh hell!' and what was the use of trying to do anything new.

Lawrence said he often wondered, and began to fill his pipe.

By Thursday morning I still hadn't got a rich admirer; nor had I got influenza. I went to the office determined to tell Lady Merton that in no circumstances whatever was I prepared to spend the evening with her.

'Besides, I haven't been able to find a boy friend so I'd make you the wrong numbers.'

Lady Merton said, 'Oh, rot!' and surely I hadn't *tried* to find anyone.

'I told you at the time,' I said, 'I don't know anyone.'

Lady Merton said, 'Oh, rot!' very crossly indeed.

'Anyway,' I said, 'I've got a headache, so it's probably all for the best.'

But it wasn't for the best at all, because Lady Merton was determined, for some reason, that I should go out with her and Henry that evening. She made me give her Henry's telephone number and herself rang him up immediately; and that wasn't a success, because the telephone was answered by Henry's mistress.

At half-past eight, wearing what might be considered to be evening dress and my grandmother's brooch, which hadn't so far gone into pawn, I arrived at the club at which Henry had first met Lady Merton.

The club was like all clubs of its kind, but this one was cleaner than some, as it had only just been opened. It occupied a house in Bourdon Street, which must originally have been a stables. There was a doorman in the hall who said that he thought Henry was in the bar. I thought he probably was too, and the doorman handed me on to a man in a black coat. I was handed on a few more times and eventually I arrived in the bar which was almost empty. Henry with two men was at one end of it, leaning up against the counter, and with them was Henry's mistress. One knew before one started that Lady Merton wasn't going to be a bit pleased about that.

Henry seemed quite pleased to see me, ordered me a drink and introduced me to the two men, and then became remote and far away and detached. Henry's mistress and I smiled rather nervously at one another.

They were all talking about racing and for a sentence or two I joined in the conversation.

I wondered what Lady Merton was going to think later on when she arrived. I wondered what Henry was thinking now and I silently admired the fur stole that Henry's mistress was wearing. Henry came down to my end of the bar.

'I couldn't help it,' he whispered. 'She insisted on coming.'

He was now looking rather pleased with himself but at the same time apprehensive. It was the cat who has eaten the cream and waits to see what will happen. Before I had time to say anything Lady Merton arrived. I was rather glad to see that she was not in uniform, as she had threatened earlier in the day.

'Really, Pallisser, I don't think I shall have time to change. I've got this conference, you know, and I promised the Wing-Co I'd drop in on him afterwards and let him know how it went.'

Lady Merton was always keen that the War Office, and the Air Ministry, and, if possible, the Admiralty, should take an interest in her work and she enjoyed conferences. One person talking to another person was a conference as far as Lady Merton was concerned.

One had hoped that in spite of the conference she would have time to change, and I had had to suppress a desire to tell her that myself I should be wearing black and my grandmother's unpawned brooch, because the Field-Mar had especially asked me to. But evidently the Wing-Co had not been there when Lady Merton had dropped in, for she appeared in a lot of tricky pre-war brocade. She had fine athlete's shoulders which I had not noticed before.

Henry was very pleased to see her, Henry's mistress less so, which was only to be expected. Henry addressed Lady Merton as Angela, which was going to make it sound rather silly if she was going to go on calling me Pallisser. Perhaps she would call Henry Pallisser, too, which would make it sillier still.

We went upstairs to dinner, and were again passed from one black-coated attendant to another. This club must be expecting to pay most awfully well if it could afford so many servants. The dining room was large and white, with cushioned leather seats round the walls. The room was almost empty; what members were there seemed to be mostly tough men like Henry's friends or tough rich women who were dining together.

We were given a table in the corner, and there was a slight difficulty as to where everyone was to sit. We were hovered over by a lot of waiters and I began to think out a remark that I might make to one of Henry's friends, after they had decided on what they were going to eat.

Henry was talking loudly to the waiters and Lady Merton was abetting him and smiling up at the waiters as if they were so many Wing-Co's or Air Marshals.

I became uncomfortably aware of Henry's mistress. She was talking pleasantly enough to the man who sat across the table from her; but she was blindly, furiously angry.

'Of course,' the dark man was saying to me, 'the 1928 isn't what it was, you'll come across an occasional bottle of course.'

He *must* have said something before that. Nobody could start a conversation with that remark.

'How about the '37?' I was guessing wildly. Was '37 a vintage year or wasn't it? I couldn't remember.

'Those high-up Service women are all the same,' Lady Merton was saying. 'No sense of humour at all.'

Henry was leaning across the table, looking into her eyes and smiling. 'But how terrible for you,' he kept saying, and, 'We had a Colonel just like that when I was in the army, no sense of co-operation.'

I glanced again at Henry's mistress; wasn't there something rather ominous in her assumed brightness?

Lady Merton, oblivious of everything but her own effects, went on talking to Henry, and now she was drawing the dark man into her orbit. That, anyhow, was a relief, I shouldn't have to try and concentrate any longer on vintages.

The dinner, probably because it was black market, was extremely good and the wine was delicious. I began to enjoy myself.

A very sophisticated woman dressed in black satin started to play the piano; the sound made a pleasant accompaniment to the conversations. Henry was laughing a great deal now, so was Lady Merton, so was the dark man, whose name was Ambrose.

How pleasant everything was with the dim lights, the damask tablecloths, the rich folds of the curtains, and the gold candelabra which stood on pedestals in the corners of the room; and how far removed from the cups of tea splashed on the surfaces of deal and marble-topped tables. Whoever owned this club knew what he was doing.

There was another burst of laughter from Henry's end of the table. 'When you are asked out to tea you must try and join in with the others'—that had been mother. 'You are not paid to sit and do nothing—you are not here to enjoy yourself'—but that must have been someone else. Rather belatedly I joined in the laughter, but I had not heard the remark which had occasioned it.

I thought of Sophia alone at Trelynt with mother and father. She and mother would be sitting in the drawing room, not talking to each other, probably not doing anything very much. I had been unfair to Sophia; but if I had stayed at home would Sophia have been any better off? 'It doesn't seem right really, everything always done for the boy and nothing for the girls'—that had been someone who had not appreciated Henry. But Sophia had never had Henry's dazzling good looks, his dark curling hair. 'It doesn't seem right really, hair like that ought to have gone to the girl.' Who was the speaker? I couldn't recall her, only a whining voice which came back to me out of the past.

'But you can get them in Soho,' Henry's mistress was saying, 'and only four and ninepence a pound.' Her voice was triumphant. She was imparting a precious piece of information, but who would be interested?

'It's all very well,' Lady Merton was saying, 'but the girl was jolly well *for* it. I mean, you can't go around just *marrying* people and never getting a divorce.'

'Horribly vulgar,' I heard Henry's mistress say, 'but what can you expect. . . .' and then she lowered her voice.

'Marriage can be all right in its way,' Henry said, 'but you don't want to let it tie you down, do you?' he said to the wine waiter who had just arrived with another round of brandies.

'Indeed not, sir.'

'Oh, I don't know.' Lady Merton was prepared to be open-minded. 'Discipline can be a very good thing; now that's what this girl I was telling you about hadn't got, you know.'

'Ill-bred.' Henry's mistress was talking quite loudly. There was no doubt that it was Lady Merton whom she was criticising.

'You've been married, of course,' Henry said confidentially to the wine waiter.

And Lady Merton said that she was sure he had.

'Loud-mouthed,' Henry's mistress said, and then again, 'vulgar.'

It was no longer very easy to ignore her. Lady Merton didn't even try to. Henry, who had obviously been thinking about something completely different, or not thinking at all, suddenly realised what was happening.

'What's the matter with you?' He sounded very angry.

Henry's mistress was understood to say that there was nothing the matter with *her*.

'Then don't start criticising other people; it's extremely bad manners, isn't it?' Henry turned for further corroboration to the waiter; but he had gone away to another table. 'Isn't it?' Henry said to Ambrose.

Henry's mistress said that it was not Henry whom she had been criticising.

'Oh, shut up,' Henry said, 'you've been as dreary as hell the whole evening.'

'I say, that's a bit much, isn't it.' Lady Merton in her public-school traditions was rushing to the defence of the weak.

Henry's mistress was understood to say that she was surprised at Henry.

'Oh, shut up,' Henry said wearily.

Whereupon Lady Merton said that that was no way to speak, and that he was being jolly rude.

Henry's mistress said something about vulgarity. She was furious with Lady Merton; but she was also furious with Henry; between the two hatreds she became somewhat incoherent.

Henry looked from one to the other of them, bewildered, and evidently aggrieved. He called to the waiter, ordered another round of drinks, and said that women could be the devil when they started to quarrel, couldn't they?

The waiter smiled diplomatically. Probably he had seen a good many quarrels in his time and was no longer interested in them.

Henry's mistress broke off her tirade and smiled a refined sour little smile.

In the moment's silence that followed, I looked across at Henry. He was still looking aggrieved.

THREE

The next morning at breakfast I was very sleepy. Mrs Omrod, the charwoman, was late, so it was Stephanie who had made the tea and put the kippers under the grill. Pamela was already dressed for her clinic; but Stephanie and Lawrence and I sat round the table in our dressing gowns. Mother would not have approved. At home there had never been any question of coming downstairs unless one was fully dressed.

'What sort of an evening did you have with Lady Merton?' Lawrence asked.

I said that it had been fun on the whole and I began to describe it to him. I toned it down a little and I left out the part when we had gone to a night club and Henry had been turned out for trying to start a fight with a man at another table. At least, the man had *said* that Henry was trying to start a fight. But Henry had said that he was only offering the man a drink.

I got involved trying to explain to Lawrence about Henry's mistress.

Lawrence said it didn't sound as if she had had a very amusing evening.

'I'm glad Lady Merton had a good time,' Stephanie said inconsequently.

Lawrence looked thoughtful and I wondered if he was going to put Henry and Lady Merton and Henry's mistress into his book.

Stephanie said did those people ever think about anything at *all*? And I said, yes, they thought a great deal about racing.

Stephanie sighed and said that probably they had the best of it in the end. 'At any rate, they're happy,' Lawrence said.

But I knew that Henry wasn't happy. Henry's mistress seemed happy enough, or anyhow self-satisfied, which might be the same thing. But she wouldn't be self-satisfied if she really thought she was in danger of losing Henry; and if she was going to make scenes in restaurants she probably would lose him.

Why did she go on being so fond of him when he wasn't always nice to her? I decided that it must be something to do with sex. Sex was responsible for so many things which were otherwise unaccountable. It was a pity in a way. It made it dull when there was only one answer to every question.

Owing to the absence of Mrs Omrod I had a tepid bath, and I was late for the office; but Lady Merton was later. When she did arrive she was very bright and cheerful and said that late nights agreed with her.

'Anne,' Stephanie said to me that evening, 'we're going to have a party and you must ask Lady Merton.'

'I don't think you'd like her,' I said hurriedly. 'She's much nicer to hear about than to actually meet.'

'How do you know we wouldn't like her?'

'I can guess,' I said.

'And your brother,' Stephanie said. 'We want to meet your brother.'

I tried to imagine Henry as he would appear at Stephanie's. I wondered uneasily what sort of drinks Stephanie was going to provide. 'I'll ask him,' I said doubtfully. 'I mean, thank you very much. Who else is going to be at the party?'

Stephanie told me the names of a great many people I didn't know and some, who being celebrities, I had heard of. Then there was another smaller category who were being invited, either because they would play the piano or because they would bring champagne.

So it wasn't, after all, going to be the sort of party I had expected.

It was about this time that I first noticed Gerald Ross. He had detached himself from the people who were always in and out of Stephanie's, because he was one of the few that seemed inclined to talk to me.

Gerald wrote detective stories which, of course, put him out of the class of the intellectuals. But they read his work, which gave him something in common with Rimbaud, if you looked at it one way; but, unlike Rimbaud, Gerald was very clean. Not neat, but clean, and he was apt to tell one that he never left the house without having a bath. I thought myself that it was a pleasant habit, but Lawrence said, no, it was merely evidence of the guilt complex. 'Like Pontius Pilate always washing his hands?' (I saw what Lawrence meant, but I still thought it was better to be clean.) Anyhow, not washing *enough* was far worse, it meant that you were going mad. I had read an article about it in one of the Sunday papers.

Gerald had started to write detective stories when he was in the army. Before the war he had had a badly paid, though interesting, job in the ceramic department of a museum. He was not proposing to go back to it.

Lawrence said that Gerald was an opportunist, and had no business to be writing detective stories.

I said, 'Why not?' and Lawrence said, 'Well, look how well he did at Cambridge.'

Which I shouldn't have thought was the answer to the question.

I asked Pamela what she thought about it; but her answer was too complicated, and I didn't even *begin* to understand it.

I didn't ask Gerald what he thought of Pamela. But one evening he began discussing her with me.

We were sitting together in a corner of the sitting room. Around and about us the intellectuals were discussing subjects which were beyond the range of my education.

I heard the word, 'Plato,' and remembered that Plato had said that human souls had once been round and that at a given moment they had broken into two and spent the rest of their existence looking for their other half; like in a cotillion.

'A strange girl,' Gerald said as Pamela went out of the room.

'What's strange about her?' I asked, and remembered that Pamela was given to unaccountable fits of crying and to moods of depression.

'She's very good-looking,' Gerald was saying, 'wonderful eyes—have you noticed? But somehow she always seems to be terribly dissatisfied with herself.'

'I don't know why she should be,' I said. 'She's a most intelligent woman doctor.'

'Perhaps it is that she hasn't really got anything of her own,' Gerald said. 'Not that that would matter particularly, if one didn't feel all the time that she was wanting it so desperately.'

'Lots of people haven't got anything,' I said.

'Perhaps not, but they've got more than Pamela. Take Stephanie, for instance. She's got the house and Lawrence, and most people have got a family and a settled background. Why, even I have got my mother in Northamptonshire.'

I wondered what Gerald's mother was like; but I couldn't agree with him that a family and a settled background were invariably assets.

Pamela had no family. When they had been alive, they had been municipal councillors and had lived in Birmingham. Also, I think that they had at some time been school-teachers. Pamela was always very particular to state that she was a member of the working classes, and she may have been, but she wasn't my idea of them. Added to everything else she had been a hockey player and at the age of thirty she could still run faster for the bus than anyone else in the house.

She always seemed to be full of theories about life and living and it seemed to me that she was extremely sentimental.

She made heavy flat-footed jokes which were difficult to understand.

'My brother doesn't like settled backgrounds either,' I said to Gerald. 'At least, I don't think he does; but maybe it was just home he didn't like.'

'I'm sure he's charming,' Gerald said politely.

I hoped that when he did meet him Gerald really would find that Henry was charming or, at any rate, interesting. Of course, Henry was a human being and human beings were always interesting.

People were quite different. They overcrowded the buses and they created queues.

Lady Merton, rather to my discomfiture, had accepted my invitation to come to Stephanie's party.

'Rather fun, Pallisser, what? See how these highbrows live.'

'They don't like you to call them highbrows,' I said. 'They're intellectuals.'

'Same thing,' Lady Merton said shortly. 'Can't think what *you're* doing among them, though.'

'They were an advertisement,' I said.

Lady Merton was understood to say that those sort of people were all very well, but that you couldn't imagine them at the races.

'You could,' I said, 'if you put them on the other side of the course.'

Lady Merton said, 'H'mm,' and that my brother didn't seem to have very much time for them.

I wondered how much time Henry was having for Lady Merton. Rather a lot, I imagined.

I decided that I wouldn't invite Henry to Stephanie's. It would be rather awful if he didn't like my new friends, especially Gerald, and I realised I would hate it if they didn't like Henry.

The decision didn't do me any good because Henry himself rang me up on the day of the party and told me he was coming. I rather hoped that by the evening he would have forgotten about it.

Stephanie had made no particular rules about what anyone was to wear. It was supposed vaguely that people who had evening dress would take this opportunity of wearing it, and those who hadn't would be understood to have come straight on from meetings. This I felt was perfectly right and proper: clothes, when compared with the things of the mind, were not important. All of which made the fact of Pamela's evening dress even more surprising. For at half-past eight Pamela came downstairs in a flame-coloured frock decorated with pink ostrich feathers. She had an evening bag. She had satin shoes with *diamanté* buckles; and she had brushed her hair. Her face was flushed and she skipped about making those difficult jokes.

One felt embarrassed for her.

Lawrence came into the room wearing a blue suit and a shirt with a soft collar. It was affected of him not to have put on a dinner jacket. One knew quite well that he had one.

Stephanie, who I had expected to be 'arty,' came out of the kitchen wearing a black evening dress. Over it she had, for the moment, a white linen pantry apron. It was very becoming and I was sorry that later she would probably take it off.

The house seemed to have undergone a complete change. It had been filled with flowers by Stephanie's rich friends. In the kitchen there was a professional cook to help Mrs Omrod, and in the dining room there was someone's butler arranging the glasses which he had brought with him. I stopped wishing that

Lady Merton and Henry would not come. Why had I thought that Stephanie would give a party with beer and sausages? She was intelligent; if she gave a party it would be a good one. It was a pity about Pamela, but perhaps when people began to arrive she would quiet down.

The first arrivals were a middle-aged couple whom I had often heard described as brilliant; with them was a lady photographer. She was brilliant, too. I happened to be in the hall when they came in. They were much encumbered with mackintoshes, plaid scarves and galoshes. The butler had difficulty in disentangling them from all these. Instinctively, I looked for their thermos flasks. I wondered if he did, too. When they were ready to be presented in the drawing room he caught my eye and winked. I was much shocked.

Soon the sitting room was full of people. They were being given champagne, they were being taken into corners and talked to. One of the young men who was to play the piano had arrived. He was playing it quietly, as if not wishing to interrupt the conversations which swayed around him. I went over to his side of the room and listened. He was playing all the latest dance tunes and playing them extremely well.

Soon it would be time for supper and Lady Merton and Henry had still not arrived.

A small-sized man, who wore his arm in a sling, came into the room with great assurance. It was Stooks, whom we knew as 'Pamela's professor.' Stooks was one of those professors who specialise in making science and philosophy quite simple for ordinary people to understand. Other scientists might work for years to produce the atom bomb, for instance, and just as soon as it was invented Stooks would write a short paragraph in the *Sunday Post* explaining the whole thing and all but giving directions for running up atom bombs in the potting shed. Or take philosophy. The republic, the pathetic fallacy, or a categorical imperative; Stooks could, and did, make mincemeat of all these, by explaining them week by week in his lucid little article. But whether his explanations were right I was not in a position to know.

Stooks took three paces into the room and stood quite still. His eyes were half-closed against the possible assaults of flash-lights. Nothing happened, of course, so he opened them again. Pamela rushed forward, but nobody else took any notice of him. He looked round the company with gentle forgiveness, his moist underlip protruded. Pamela took his arm and they started on a tour of the room.

Obviously Pamela was proud of knowing Stooks. She liked it when we referred to him as 'her professor.' I didn't blame her. It must be nice to be the friend of someone whose name was continually in the papers, who was, in fact, a celebrity, even a public figure. I thought what a pity it was that Pamela couldn't marry Stooks. They could have talked about science together in the evenings. But Stooks, they said, wasn't a marrying man. He was very fond of women but he wasn't the marrying type.

'Anne,' Pamela said, 'I don't think that you have ever met Stooks?'

I tried to be equal to the occasion. I shuffled my feet and grinned. There was a pause.

Then Stooks pointed to the sling that supported his left arm. 'Hockey,' he said. 'I did it playing hockey.'

'How awful,' I said. 'Is it broken?'

Pamela, at Stooks's other side, was propelling him onwards. The moment was over. I felt it had been a failure. The trouble with meeting celebrities is that one has to have something to *say* to them. I had not yet learned that unalloyed admiration, however clumsily expressed, is all that is usually required.

Warily I began to stalk Professor Stooks. I wanted to hear what other people found to say to him. I went and stood behind Stephanie. Stephanie knew Stooks quite well. I had even heard her mock at him a little. Stooks was fundamentally sound, but it was allowed that he played to the gallery. But now Stephanie was exerting herself to flatter him. She had drawn him aside from the crowd. She was asking his advice. My mother would have approved of that. She had recommended the asking of advice as part of the behaviour I was to pursue at Cowes. I was to smile, I was to ask to be advised. Then someone would marry me. It was as simple as that. If only Aunt Emily would first introduce me to the right people.

But Stephanie didn't flatter people because she wanted them to marry her.

Some of these women must want to get married; but they would scorn the use of tricks which dated from the time when women were inferior to men. In *this* world men and women came together as equals. Or did they? I noticed Pamela who still hovered beside Stooks. Her expression set bright and eager, she was ready to pick up any crumb that should drop in her direction. I saw Stooks's words as little dry dusty crumbs.

It occurred to me that Pamela was jealous that Stooks should spend so much time talking to Stephanie. Pamela was not being a disinterested comrade. She was just plain jealous, as people had been when mother was a girl.

'The trouble with you, Anne, is that you're always imagining things.' Who had said that? Probably mother. Or the governess before she had left to get married. How disagreeable, and it was all the fault of the sub-conscious. It was the sub-conscious that was always making one remember things that were better forgotten. Why didn't the sub-conscious ever turn up things like: 'Anne, how beautiful you are looking today.' Or even: 'That's a good girl finishing up all your dinner.'

We went down to supper, which was very good.

Lady Merton and Henry arrived. Henry appeared remote, and disassociated from these unfamiliar surroundings. Lady Merton managed to make it clear that she was there as an interested sightseer.

She asked to be introduced to Stooks. She was sympathetic about his arm. When it was quite better he must come and play hockey with some of her canteen workers. Lady Merton would lead one team and Professor Stooks the other. It would be jolly good, put some life into them, what! She turned to me for confirmation. I said that perhaps I could blow the whistle.

Lady Merton said nonsense, I was jolly good at hockey, and I said, 'Oh, really, not a bit.'

Lady Merton and Stooks began to get rather technical about hockey.

'What an extraordinary man!' Henry spoke quite loudly and several people looked round.

An anonymous girl murmured that it was *the* Professor Stooks. She was looking at Henry with some curiosity, he turned and smiled at her. He did it quite automatically; he was used to the admiration of women. Men, on the whole, didn't care for him so much. This evening I was struck again by the way he stood out from the people who surrounded him. He was so much better-looking than most of them and he looked so friendly. Perhaps Lady Merton was going to be good for him. Mother was always hoping that people were going to be good for Henry, and at the beginning they nearly always were. This had led mother to the belief that somewhere in the world there existed a woman who would be good for Henry all the time. This led on to its not being Henry's fault that he drank.

'I say, is this going to be any fun?' Henry looked gloomily at the small dining room, crowded now by Stephanie's forty or fifty guests. Apparently they held no interest for him, and he had withdrawn into himself. It was this power of Henry's of being able to detach himself from his environment which so irritated father.

'It depends what you mean by fun,' I said.

'Well, there doesn't seem to be much to drink, and nobody,' he added as an afterthought, 'to talk to.'

I looked round for somebody who might amuse Henry. I hadn't wanted him to come; but now that he was here I felt responsible for his entertainment.

Pamela was beside us. She had been separated from Stooks by Lady Merton, so it seemed that she was probably having rather an unsatisfactory evening. I introduced her to Henry and felt that I was doing well by her. Then I went and talked to the butler. He must find some whisky for Henry; for Henry didn't like champagne.

* * * * *

It was nearly an hour later when I came across Pamela and Henry again. Then, with quite a lot of other people, they were seated on a divan and Pamela was teaching Henry the words of a song which started: 'Oh, our cricket first eleven is the finest in the land, It's the one above all others we admire on every hand.'

Henry and Pamela sang it together with the pianist accompanying them and several admirers joining in the chorus: 'We've Marjorie for captain and Bruce for play, Our glorious first eleven is unbeatable and brave.'

Henry looked up and saw me. 'They used to sing that quite seriously at Pamela's school.'

They went on and on. Pamela's old school songs were certainly very extraordinary. There was one in honour of a headmistress who had released them from shame and from wrong.

Gradually the whole party became centred round Henry and Pamela. They were so obviously enjoying themselves, and somehow Pamela's flame-coloured dress didn't look so terrible any more.

Afterwards one saw that that party had been responsible for a great deal and yet it was only by chance that Henry had been there at all. And until he met Pamela he had been quite apart from it. It was Lady Merton who had persuaded him to come; and there was no very good reason why he should ever have known Lady Merton.

It was the sort of chain of events that encouraged one to believe in fate. But, of course, one didn't believe in fate really, because it didn't make sense to believe in evolution *and* fate both at the same time.

It was from Lady Merton that I first gathered that things were changing a little. There had been no signs of it at Chalk Farm. Stephanie and Lawrence continued to find each other difficult and overworked. Pamela was just as usual; very secretive and taken up with Plato or whichever philosophy was worrying her at the moment.

Lady Merton remarked during the course of a morning that my brother really was impossible.

I said that that was what father had always thought.

'He doesn't know his own mind from one minute to the other.'

So I guessed that Henry had made a date with Lady Merton, and then, at the last minute, put her off, or even not bothered to put her off. That was quite likely, too.

'Of course, he's your brother,' Lady Merton said resentfully, 'but I do think that the way he goes on is a bit too much.'

I said that father thought that as well.

Lady Merton told me that I was a good child and patted my shoulder. She seemed to think that I needed sympathy for something.

To change the subject I showed her a letter from the head of one of the canteens. It wasn't a very lucky letter to have chosen, for after a long list of requested supplies the letter ended by announcing chattily that in the opinion of the head of the canteen one of their workers, a really very nice girl indeed, was probably pregnant, and what did Lady Merton think ought to be done about it?

Lady Merton said, Good God, people really were impossible, and I got out the card index and marked the worker's card with 'H.A.B.?' in red ink which stood for 'having a baby?' There was really nothing else we could do about it, and Lady Merton spent the half-hour which remained to lunch-time in telling me what an awfully nice girl this girl *was*, and what an awfully nice family she belonged to. 'Ladies and all that; every one of them.' In the end she was persuading herself that the head of the canteen was a sex-starved old busybody and that the suspicion probably wasn't true. I then copied out the list of stores and sent it to the appropriate Service Department.

Henry's interest in Lady Merton had waned, that was obvious. I supposed that Mrs May had succeeded in disentangling him, for Mrs May was patently of the bulldog breed; as British, so they tell us, as the flag. Once her teeth were firmly embedded, one would not expect her to let go, and the scene in the black-market club had shown that she was not hampered in any way by a sense of pride.

For some reason it never occurred to me that Henry had found Pamela attractive. She had been fun at the party singing those songs; but that wasn't the same thing, or perhaps it was. Mother, long ago, when she had been explaining to me about life, had told me that one never could tell which women would turn out to be attractive to men. It was quite mysterious and had nothing to do with being pretty. All you could do was to watch and see who got married, and who managed to have a great many admirers. Pamela didn't seem to have a great many admirers. There was Stooks, of course, and the Hungarian about whom Pamela had told me one evening when we had sat late over the fire drinking the black coffee that Pamela was always making. It was one of Pamela's peculiarities that she always spoke of this coffee as being strong and hot, thus apparently taking it for granted that other people only drank their coffee when it was stone-cold.

The Hungarian, Pamela said, had been a political refugee; and she had met him at one of those meetings which are, or were, supposed to promote European peace, without in any way going too far. The Hungarian, it appeared, had fallen deeply in love with her, and one evening when she had invited him back to the basement flat, which she occupied at the time, he had gone a very great deal too far. Pamela had not been expecting anything like that, she had been expecting that they would drink strong black coffee and be friendly, on an intellectual level, about the state of Europe. The whole thing had upset her very much indeed; and the affair had not flourished. Soon he was being cruel to her; one gathered that by that she meant unfaithful.

After Stephanie's party, I didn't see Henry again until the day before father's funeral, when we travelled down to Devonshire together. Nobody had been expecting father to die. He had been eccentric and a recluse for so long now, as long as I could remember, and one had got into the way of considering him as an institution rather than a person. People die, institutions go on for ever; at least one expects them to. If they ever come to an end one is shocked, and that's how one felt about father.

The business-like unemotional telegram from mother, surely that had been composed by Sophia, and anyhow it didn't make sense. Father couldn't possibly be dead. One was tempted to get in touch with the office of origin for the free repetition of doubtful words. Dead, yes, dead could be doubtful; but funeral, there was nothing doubtful about funeral. In the end I rang up Henry.

Henry had just received a replica of my telegram. He was in a very good temper.

FOUR

THEY HAD SENT a car to meet us at the station. It had come from a garage in Exeter and we didn't know the driver. I was glad. If it had been Mr Bethwick from the village we should have had to talk about father, and I didn't want to do that. As it was we achieved the journey in silence. In silence we drove along the long damp drive, with the two gates which Henry and I took it in turn to open, and up to the front door. Never had the drive or the house looked more utterly dreary. As we got out of the car, I looked up at the house. I supposed that it would be sold. Henry had always said that he would never live here, and Trelynt now belonged to Henry. It had been entailed on him, before his birth, by my grandfather. That had annoyed father, and as time went on, and it became more and more obvious how Henry was turning out, father's annoyance had progressively increased. One saw why. Henry wasn't at all the sort of son that father had wanted. I don't think he was even the sort of son that father had deserved.

In the hall we were met by Sophia, looking gaunt in her black clothes. I glanced at her legs. So the stockings from her Red Cross uniform had come in handy, after all. Poor Sophia, would she be glad to leave Trelynt, or would she become sentimental about it? In any case she would probably miss the hens. Or perhaps, if she and mother went on living somewhere in the country, she could take them with her. Hens always looked so pathetic when they were travelling. It was the only time one was sorry for them.

'Hullo, Sophia, how are the hens?'

Henry did better, he asked after mother, and Sophia kissed him; then we all went into the drawing room together.

Today the drawing room seemed terrible, especially for some reason, the mantelpiece, which was monumental and heavy and made mostly, I imagine, of cast iron. On it were silver photograph frames, for mother was no slave to fashion. The photographs were mainly of her children, and there were two of the minor princess to whom mother had for a short time been lady-in-waiting.

There were bulbs in bowls. Their long tangled leaves drooped despondently. Why must mother grow bulbs indoors when she had a whole garden in which to grow them?

'Mother is really bearing up wonderfully.' Sophia smiled at us brightly.

Mother came into the room. She kissed Henry and me in a manner which reminded me that we were orphans. Then she put up a hand to the back of her neck and settled the thick hairpins more firmly into place.

Sophia went out to get tea.

It was the day after the funeral. Again we were together in the drawing room, mother and Sophia and Henry and me.

'We must talk,' mother had said. She turned to Henry. 'Of course, you will arrange to sell the house?'

She looked round the room and I realised that she hated it. How extraordinary. Mother had lived here for nearly forty years and she hated it. Why had she never said so? But perhaps she had? Perhaps she had said so to the aunts?

'Why should I sell the house?' Henry asked.

'You always said you would,' Sophia reminded him.

'Well, I'm not going to.' Henry looked defiantly from mother to Sophia. 'What's the point, when I'd be obliged to invest the money?'

'But what will you do with it?' mother asked. 'You know you can't afford to live here.'

They went on wrangling over it. I ceased to listen. It was none of it any concern of mine. And apparently, although the whole argument was about him and his house, it was no concern of Henry's either. For glancing across at him I guessed that he too had withdrawn into some dream of his own where mother and Sophia could not follow him. In a few days I would go back to London, to Stephanie and Lawrence and Lady Merton; and to Gerald Ross. Gerald thought I was very nice; he must, or he would not spend so much time with me.

'Anne,' mother said sharply, 'you'll have the leg off that chair in a minute.'

'I'm sorry.' I looked at mother expectantly, waiting for her to tell me that the talk was now over and that the plans were made.

'It is near Westminster Cathedral,' mother said. 'It is quite a large flat; you will be perfectly happy there.'

'But I'm not a Catholic.'

'I was not suggesting that you were.' Mother sounded annoyed. I remembered that she disliked any reference to religion. 'Aunt Emily writes that it belongs to a friend of hers who is moving to the country. We shall be very lucky if we get it. It is an old-fashioned flat and there will be room for the furniture.'

So I was to live in London with mother and Sophia. But I didn't want to; I wanted to stay at Stephanie's. I had a vision of mother in the Army and Navy stores and she was buying teacups. I saw Sophia walking down Victoria Street and she was wearing her gum-boots.

'I don't think it will be a good idea at all,' I said. 'I mean, us all living together. I'm very difficult to live with now, worse than I used to be.'

Mother didn't take any notice, she went on talking to Sophia about what furniture they would be taking to London. It seemed that most of the furniture at Trelynt belonged to mother.

Sophia said that Pemberthy Mansions would be handy for Lady Merton's office. 'You will save your bus fares and you will be living more comfortably.'

Impossible to explain to Sophia how very uncomfortable I should always be living anywhere with her and mother. Impossible, too, to explain the utter squalor of a saved bus fare. And their plan was so reasonable. A widowed mother living with her two unmarried daughters. Suitable and economical. It was ridiculous to feel such panic. I was over twenty-one. *Years* over twenty-one. I didn't have to live with mother and Sophia. I didn't have to feel like a rat in a trap. But how did a rat feel? One didn't know. Anyhow it didn't feel that it had to be polite. So I wouldn't be polite to mother. I would tell her that nothing would induce me to live with her. I would rather be dead. But I mustn't say I would rather be dead, for only yesterday there had been the funeral.

Anyhow it couldn't be yet, for first there would be arrangements. Leases would have to be signed. Linen would have to be packed away with lavender bags. Or maybe the linen would have to be unpacked. Either way it would take time.

Henry was standing with his back to the mantelpiece. His hands were in his pockets. He hummed to himself a little, under his breath, and he seemed to be practising some dance steps. He was not listening to mother and Sophia and the discussion about the furniture. He was utterly remote.

'You might let the house,' mother said suddenly. 'You could put the rest of the furniture in store and let it unfurnished.'

'Or I could put some more furniture in, and let it furnished,' Henry said. 'Or I could leave it just as it is and call it partly furnished.'

Mother told him not to be silly. She said irrelevantly that it was sad that he wasn't married.

'You used to say it was sad when I was. It was one of the reasons I got divorced.'

Mother sighed and said nothing.

'Perhaps I shall get married again,' Henry said. He executed a particularly complicated step and inadvertently kicked the fender.

'Are you thinking of it?' mother asked.

'I hardly ever think about anything else,' Henry said.

Mother repeated that it was all very sad.

I wondered if it was. It was sad to die, and it was sad to be divorced. Sometimes it was sad to be married.

I looked round the room and wondered if Henry would really live here. It seemed an extraordinary thing to want to do. He would live here and grow old and eccentric as father had done. He would have a wife, a new wife whom we didn't know. I imagined her with grey hair, looking rather like mother; but probably he would marry his mistress. I tried to imagine Henry's mistress as she would appear at Trelynt. She would wear softly coloured tweeds and a pearl necklace. I was almost sure that she would wear a pearl necklace. But what would they do? There were no race courses near Trelynt; there were no black-market clubs, there were no bars. Unless you counted the pub in the village, but that wasn't what Henry's mistress would mean by a bar. And anyhow she and Henry could not afford to live here. Mother had said they could not and I was prepared to believe mother. The Pallissers had hardly any money at all now. Once, years ago, they had been comfortably off, not rich but comfortably off. They had lived in this house and their sons had gone into the Navy, and usually they had become Admirals. Admiral of the Blue, Admiral of the Red, it sounded pretty and it made them not quite real, like the characters in *Alice in Wonderland*.

'Anne,' mother said, 'you will have the leg off that chair.'

Father's death and funeral had coincided with Christmas. Afterwards Henry and I went back to London. In the train Henry said that he was determined not to sell Trelynt. It was, after all, he said, his home.

I was surprised, even rather shocked. I had been prepared for Sophia to be sentimental; but not Henry.

'One has to live somewhere,' Henry said defensively, 'and I think a change is always rather to the good, don't you?'

He fell silent, staring out of the window. He looked tired and rather worried and presently he said that life wasn't very easy. One could only agree with him; life for many people was very difficult. It had been difficult for my nurse who had had two invalid sisters to support—and a deaf-and-dumb nephew into the bargain. It was difficult for Stephanie when Lawrence got on her nerves. It was difficult for Sophia when mother nagged at her; and it must be difficult for Henry, who never seemed to concentrate on it properly.

'I used to get awfully sick of being told I was unsatisfactory,' Henry said. Obviously he was thinking of father, for father had never stopped saying that Henry was not satisfactory; and quite probably they had said it at Harrow too, and that was why Henry had run away from it. I hoped they hadn't said it in the circus. I liked to think of that time in his life as having been extremely happy, a short bright interval in the weight of years.

'Did you like the W.R.N.S.?' Henry said presently. 'After the first excitement about the uniform I simply hated the army.'

'I liked the uniform, too, at the beginning,' I said.

'Perhaps I ought to have had a profession,' Henry said. 'Perhaps I ought to have been a lawyer and gone to the office every morning in a bowler hat.'

'But you did have a profession,' I said. 'You had those dogs in the circus.'

'There was no future in it,' Henry said. 'But it was interesting.'

'But the people must have been fascinating.'

'When you got to know them, they were just like everyone else.'

'They can't have been *just* like everyone else, when they lived in caravans.'

'At the end of the war,' Henry said, 'I had the chance to go into quite a decent publishing firm. The only trouble was that they wanted me to put some money into it and of course father wouldn't produce any.'

'But other people's fathers put money into businesses for them.'

'Can you imagine father doing that?' Henry said. And quite frankly I couldn't.

It was a pity that Henry and father hadn't got on better together. If only father had tried to help Henry instead of just being angry with him, Henry might not have drifted quite so aimlessly through life, or wouldn't it have made any difference? The fault is in ourselves, dear Brutus—dear Henry, for 'There's a divinity that shapes our ends rough-hew them how we will.'

One didn't know yet what Henry's end would be. He might, against all probability, put a stop to the charming and ineffectual drifting. Somehow, in some way that one could not foresee, he might yet make a success of life. But what was success? The same as comedy, the triumph of man over his circumstances, and the alternative was tragedy where man is overwhelmed by forces outside himself. Where had I read that? I couldn't remember; perhaps it was part of the education which I had acquired without knowing it in the library.

But the trouble with Henry was that he couldn't concentrate. I looked across at him; what was going to happen to him? Would he, when he left the army, really go and live at Trelynt, which he couldn't afford? Perhaps, as he had suggested to mother, he would remarry and then his wife could concentrate for him. But one did so hope that he wasn't going to marry that horrible woman. Only, one knew, she was very determined; probably he would find that he couldn't get away from her.

'Mind you,' Henry said, 'I'm not fussy. I don't really notice where I live, as long as I've got a bed, you know.'

I said that was lucky, and Henry said, yes it was, and that he was quite happy having his dinner off the floor.

It made an unconvincing picture of home life, but he had probably never actually done it and I reflected on his charming inconsistency. He didn't mind where he lived; but he *must* live at Trelynt.

The train arrived at Paddington. Henry and I parted, without making any plans for meeting again. After waiting a long time in the queue, I got a taxi and drove to Chalk Farm. It would have been quicker to have taken the underground.

I arrived. Stephanie and Lawrence were both in the sitting room; neither of them asked me about the funeral.

Stephanie had started a new picture. It was mostly streaks, but the colours were pretty, blues and green and a very little dark red.

'How is Henry?' Stephanie asked. She asked it in the same voice in which she would enquire for the latest Lady Merton.

I said that he was all right; but I thought that he had gone mad because he was determined to live at home.

'Why is that mad?' Stephanie asked.

'Because he can't afford it, and he's always hated it.'

Lawrence said it was interesting the difference that possession made to people's points of view.

Stephanie said, 'What about Pamela?'

That didn't seem to fit into the conversation so I didn't say anything.

Lawrence said, didn't I know about Pamela and Henry, and I said no. I thought that Lawrence was probably mistaken. There could be nothing to know about Henry and Pamela, taken together, that is. Naturally there must be a great deal to know about each of them individually.

Lawrence said that he had understood that Pamela and Henry were having dinner together this evening.

I was startled. Why on earth should Henry want to have dinner with Pamela? I imagined them leaning confidentially towards each other across a restaurant table. In the distance was Henry's mistress. She sat alone on the floor of her flat. She had just finished her dinner and beside her was an empty plate.

I wondered what Henry and Pamela were saying to each other? Was he telling her that he was going to live at Trelynt? Was he asking her to live there with him? The whole idea was preposterous, and, besides, that horrible woman would never let him; she had held her own against Lady Merton. She would have no trouble with Pamela.

But actually that is exactly what she did have.

During the next few weeks I puzzled a good deal as to why Henry, who was attractive to a great many women, and was therefore in a position to choose, should have chosen Pamela. If he *had* chosen Pamela, that is.

Lawrence had said that he had; but perhaps Lawrence was mistaken.

'Though I don't see why Lawrence should know particularly, do you?' I said to Gerald.

'He might,' Gerald said. 'He has to be on the look-out for things to put into his books.'

It was one of the evenings when Gerald had dropped in at Stephanie's and we were talking together in a corner of the sitting room.

'I don't think those are the kind of books Lawrence writes.'

'Don't be silly, even Lawrence's kind of novels have got to be about something.'

'Well, I hope Henry doesn't marry Pamela,' I said. 'I hope he gets disentangled from "that woman," and not entangled with anyone else.'

'You're going a little fast, aren't you?' Gerald asked. 'And anyhow, why don't you want him to?'

'Because if Henry wasn't married mother might stay on at Trelynt and keep house for him.' I was being selfish again, sacrificing Henry to mother, or mother to Henry, I wasn't sure which. But it would be so wonderful if something should happen to make mother change her mind about taking the flat near Westminster Cathedral.

It would be so suitable, a widowed mother living in the country with her only son who was unmarried; and, if mother remained at Trelynt, Henry might be able to afford to live there. After all, mother must have *some* money; it stood to reason.

From my point of view it would be lovely if mother remained in Devonshire, and I would write to her. If only she didn't come and live in London I would write to her *every* week. I would be quite different, and very dutiful, if only it was granted to me to be it from a distance.

'So you do see, don't you,' I said to Gerald, 'what an awful lot depends on Henry?'

Gerald said he saw, and that mothers, fond as one was of them, were better kept in the country. His own mother never *moved* out of Northamptonshire.

* * * * *

I continued to wonder what it was that Henry could see in Pamela. Granted that he was tired of 'that woman,' and that Lady Merton hadn't come up to his expectations, there were still a great many other women in the world. Then *why* Pamela? It was Stephanie who suggested an answer: she said that Pamela had a great deal of vitality. 'You don't happen to like her; but as it happens she is quite attractive.'

'I don't *dis*like her,' I said hurriedly.

'Well, obviously you aren't in sympathy with her or you wouldn't be so surprised at Henry's taking a fancy to her. I don't know him terribly well, but I should think he is the sort of man that is attracted to a stronger character than his own. Besides,' Stephanie finished decisively, 'Pamela isn't at all bad-looking.'

'When she doesn't wear pink,' I said, and thought of the ostrich feathers.

'You see what I mean,' Stephanie said. 'You aren't in sympathy with her.'

So it had turned into a battle between Pamela and 'that woman.' Lady Merton was out. Her brief interest in Henry was now at an end. She would still occasionally ask, somewhat ironically, about 'my brother'; but most of her conversation, when it was not confined to business, was now concerned with various Wing-Co's and A.V.M.s and also, and somewhat surprisingly, with Professor Stooks.

For Professor Stooks had taken Lady Merton's suggestion about the hockey seriously. His strained arm was now better; and he spent nearly every Saturday afternoon on Hampstead Heath playing hockey against Lady Merton and her team of lady canteen workers. Professor Stooks's team was usually made up of scientists and philosophers together with some young ladies who, when they were not playing hockey, wrote for the papers. Sometimes I would go and watch them, but it was never as funny as I hoped it would be, and I used to get very cold. My offer to blow the whistle had been refused. Apparently one could only do that if one knew the rules of the game.

I did not think that Henry's mistress would let Henry go without a struggle; for one thing, she had been cited as the intervening woman in his divorce case, so it was her right to marry him.

When she and Henry had first known each other there had been a lot of talk about freedom. One was given to understand that they believed in it. Not freedom for everybody, of course, but freedom for themselves not to get married. They had both been much troubled with people wanting to marry them.

I supposed that at the beginning both their intentions had been strictly honourable and that neither wished to bind the other with conventional ties, only perhaps neither of them had considered the possibility of the other becoming tired of them.

Pamela's ideas on freedom were more objective. She felt strongly about the political freedom of people in other countries. She was determined that the people of this country should be free to walk across grouse moors. But she did not see that there was any particular advantage in the person she was fond of being free to leave her. It was a point of view, and behind Pamela's point of view one felt that there lurked all the austere authority of the Birmingham Municipal Council.

I first knew definitely that Pamela was making headway when I got a letter from mother in which she demanded to be told *who* this Doctor Merritt was. Was she really a doctor? She must be years older than Henry, and why did none of us ever *tell* mother anything? It was a great pity that I had ever gone to Stephanie's. I should have remained with Aunt Mary, who would have been only too glad to have kept me.

From every point of view it was a difficult letter. For some days I did not answer it. When I did write, I said that Pamela was very nice and quite young. I suggested that if mother wanted to know *who* Pamela was she should look her up in a book. The library in Exeter would be able to tell her which book, and would probably have a copy of it.

The next piece of information I had was from Henry himself. He came round to Chalk Farm one evening towards the end of March. I was alone, as the others were all out somewhere. Henry mooned about the sitting room, looking at Stephanie's pictures.

The picture of the streaks was still on the easel. Henry stood for a long time in front of it without saying anything. I began to be afraid that he was going to ask what it was a picture of. Finally, he said that he liked it. I said that I did, too, and Henry seemed to take courage. It reminded him, he said, of some poems that he had been reading. I asked him what poems, but Henry said that he couldn't remember. Then he said that one couldn't spend all one's time taking people to the cinema and to race meetings. There were, Henry gave me to understand, other things, things of the mind. Besides what was the use of somebody who wasn't interested in going to race meetings?

Henry stopped walking about and stood glaring at me from the middle of the room.

One knew that 'that woman' was not interested in racing. She only went to the meetings to please Henry. Once I had gone with them and she had spent the whole of the time in a sort of glass cage at the top of the stand. She had only emerged after the last race. It must have been very dull for her and I had thought at the time how unselfish it was of her to have come at all; she had explained to me that Henry liked to have her there. One wondered why, as he had not spoken to her or even seen her during the whole of the afternoon. Perhaps he thought she was lucky and kept her in the glass cage, as actors are supposed to keep hare's feet in their dressing rooms. That would have reduced 'that woman' to the level of a broken horseshoe or a medallion of St Christopher. It didn't seem very dignified.

Henry went and sat down on the sofa. He said that things were very difficult and I nodded sympathetically.

Then he looked shy and said he was really very fond of Pamela.

I said, yes, she was awfully nice.

Then he said that it would be awkward if anyone was to sue him for breach of promise.

I said not to be silly.

Henry said it wasn't as silly as all that, and that, anyhow, one didn't want to behave too badly. 'Trouble is, she's got too fond of me.' He stopped and frowned. Unused to thinking, he was evidently having trouble in arranging his thoughts.

'I mean'—Henry still frowned—'neither of us ever meant it to be so desperately permanent, and it suited her quite well, *too*, you know. I mean I paid the rent and all that sort of thing.'

Again I nodded, and wondered if there was anything I could do to help.

'The thing is she can make a lot of trouble,' Henry said, 'and she keeps saying that she has given up her life to me.'

'And has she?'

'How should I know?' Henry said crossly.

It was awkward, I saw that, and even if 'that woman' didn't sue him for breach of promise, she would almost certainly slander him to his friends and to his family. Looked at from Henry's point of view it was all very unfair.

He was quite ready to forget his past, and naturally he expected everyone else to do the same. But how could he do that if people were going to go around slandering him?

In April mother arrived in London. She had come to make the final arrangements for taking over the flat near Westminster Cathedral. Walking round it with mother I felt defeated.

The flat had been already denuded of most of the previous owner's furniture. Our feet sounded on the bare boards. Mother said that it could be made very nice. I looked at the heavy cornices and picture rails and hoped that something would happen to prevent me living here. But I couldn't live here. I should never have to have a bath in the dark bathroom with the green cracked linoleum. I should never have to say, 'I left it in my bedroom,' and mean that small room at the end of the passage. I should never have to live here, so there was no point in becoming hysterical over the possibility.

Mother turned to me as we stood in the drawing room. She was almost exactly in the middle of the room, under the large plaster rose which disfigured the ceiling. Electric wires hung from the rose, so Aunt Emily's friend had taken the chandelier to the country. I wondered if it had been an inverted plastic bowl or a large brass affair with imitation candles. I wondered what mother would put in its place; almost certainly brass and imitation candles.

'I have had a letter from "that woman,"' mother said.

'Oh, yes.' I smiled politely, wondering what was to come next, perhaps nothing. Perhaps the information was complete in itself.

'It's about the washing. She seems to think that she has some of my best sheets.'

'Then why doesn't she send them back?'

'It's not as simple as that, dear.' Mother frowned and went to the window. She opened her bag and took out a letter. I recognised the large mannered handwriting.

'It's most extraordinary,' I said, 'writing to you about sheets.'

'Yes,' mother agreed, 'and I can't make out from this letter whether she and Henry have parted or not.'

I remained silent, for I didn't know either whether Henry had succeeded in getting free.

'I suppose I ought to answer the woman,' mother said.

'You might send her a postcard,' I said cautiously.

'It's all very disagreeable.' Mother put the letter back in her bag and snapped the thick clasp. She was obviously worried, not about the sheets, but about Henry. She looked round the drawing room of Aunt Emily's friend's flat, and I imagined that for a moment she also saw it as an impossible place to live. But only for a moment, for mother, once she had decided upon a plan, was not easily to be deterred.

It was about three weeks later that I came in to find Pamela brooding in front of the fire. She sat hunched up on the sofa, her knees nearly touching her chin. She was wearing trousers and a blue jersey. If one had not known that these were Pamela's brooding clothes, one might have thought that she was going sailing. Beside her was the inevitable black coffee.

I sat down beside one of the bookcases. I was worrying again about improving my mind; but where to start? Motley's *Dutch Republic*, *Tudor Cornwall*, *The History of Greece*? It would take ages to read any of them and even then my knowledge would be specialised. I didn't want to be a specialist, I wanted to know everything.

I wanted to know everything and I didn't even know arithmetic. There hadn't, after all, been time to learn it in the evenings, or even during office hours.

'An intelligent child could learn more in a well-stocked library than in all the schools in England.' But I hadn't been an intelligent child, I had wasted my time in the library reading the *Gentleman's Magazine.* And I had read the beginnings of most of Dickens's novels; when the characters had grown up I had lost interest in them. And I had looked at the engravings of Royal Residences, and at the photograph albums which had belonged to grandmother. I had lain on my stomach, with a drawing book in front of me, and drawn pictures out of my head. An intelligent child would have studied perspective. 'Let O be the observer, let D be the point of distance, let S be . . .' something I had forgotten.

Pamela said if I fetched a cup I could have some of the coffee.

I went down to the kitchen; when I came back Pamela roused herself and said that she was going to marry Henry. Her extremely gloomy manner seemed to make the ordinary forms of congratulation somehow unsuitable.

'You find that difficult to understand?'

'Oh, no,' I said hurriedly. 'I think it's a terribly good idea.' I wondered what had possessed Pamela. Henry couldn't possibly be the sort of husband that she could ever have had in mind. Somebody like Lawrence would have been much more suitable.

'There have, of course, been philosophical difficulties.'

I smiled encouragingly. 'I think you'll be most awfully good for Henry.'

Pamela sighed and said that there we would be entering the realm of ends and means.

I nodded sympathetically to show that I was quite willing to discuss ends and means with her if she wanted to. I thought that it meant that we would make a list beginning: 'Telephone, say, twenty pounds,' and then go on through wages and rent, and end with 'Sundries,' say, a hundred pounds or perhaps eighty. When I had been in the W.R.N.S. I had helped quite a lot of my friends with that sort of list. The object of it was to prove that you could perfectly well afford to get married.

Pamela muttered a little and finally said that, of course, it would be easy to think of a lot of apposite arguments out of Aristotle's *Ethics*.

This was confusing.

I made a great effort to try to understand what Pamela was talking about. By concentrating terribly hard I made out that, in an oblique or philosophical way, she was discussing Henry's character and perhaps her own. But it came back really to Pamela being good for Henry, which is what I'd said at the beginning.

We continued to sit in front of the fire; and I wondered how 'that woman' had been got rid of. I didn't exactly like to ask; but obviously 'that woman' had been a difficulty, and not only a philosophical one.

It wasn't until much later that Pamela told me what had happened. At the time I only knew that 'that woman' had disappeared out of everyone's lives and that she had ceased to be a problem.

It would have been better, I suppose, if Henry had managed to get rid of her himself. It would have been more manly, more honourable, but also infinitely more difficult, and it would have taken time. As it was, it was Pamela who, in the most business-like way, finally settled the matter, and it took her exactly half an hour.

Pamela and 'that woman' had met by appointment at a teashop in Holborn. Pamela had telephoned and arranged the meeting and 'that woman' had put on her fox furs and gone to Holborn.

I could imagine Henry's mistress searching amongst the marble-topped tables for Pamela whom she had never seen before. The queue standing with their tin trays beside the cafeteria would have turned round to stare, and Pamela would have stood up and waved, for Pamela would have known who 'that woman' was from the moment she came in.

They had sat together at a table, which I could only hope
they had had to themselves, and Pamela would have offered tea
and 'that woman' would have ordered rather a lot of cakes. And
then quite suddenly and ruthlessly Pamela was offering to pay
her off. It was a simple solution; but it must have taken courage
to put it into effect. Pamela had offered the two hundred pounds
which had lately been left her by a cousin of her mother's. (For
Pamela had the kind of relations who prefer to leave their sav-
ings to distant cousins whom they have never seen, rather than
to their friends who have loved them.)

'That woman' must have been very surprised, but she agreed
to take the two hundred pounds. She had taken the two hundred pounds and then she had gone home and told Henry that
she was tired of having him live in her flat. Then she sailed for
America in the company of a very rich financier, which is what
she had been going to do in any case. Pamela's two hundred
pounds had been sacrificed unnecessarily; but I'm not sure that
she ever realised it. (And it is, of course, quite possible that they
did hurry things up a little.)

Henry was delighted and surprised to find that the whole
affair had settled itself so easily. I don't think that Pamela ever
told him exactly what had happened, probably he preferred not
to know.

I didn't hear of 'that woman' again until the following winter.
Then she was in Switzerland with a winter-sports enthusiast.
She did not ski herself, but I was told that she never failed to
watch his departures in the mornings, and that she was always
there, ensconced behind the plate-glass of the hotel, when he
returned in the evening.

One way and another 'that woman' seemed to spend so
much of her time behind glass that it would probably have been
a relief to her if she could have lived in an aquarium and had
done with it.

Pamela and Henry announced their engagement in *The
Times*. They received letters of congratulation. Some people
even wrote and congratulated mother, which was a mistake, for

mother was not pleased. A film extra and now a lady doctor. Mother did not feel that she had been fortunate in her daughters-in-law.

FIVE

There were very few people who really thought that the engagement was a good idea. On the morning it was announced, Lady Merton was reading *The Times* in the office; she burst into loud and rude laughter.

'Well, he's certainly bought it *this* time, Pallisser.'

I tried to look offended. I tried to look as if I did not know what she meant. I said that Pamela was very nice.

'Oh, come off it, Pallisser. But I suppose it will be handy to have a doctor in the family, for sleeping pills and that kind of thing.'

So it was going to be handy to have a doctor in the family. I wondered if I might suggest this view to mother. Mother, who disapproved strongly of *all* drugs, except veganin, which for some reason didn't count and had been placed in the same category as hot milk and redcurrant tea.

To celebrate the engagement Henry was going to take Pamela to the Thousand Guineas. It would have been nice to have gone to the whole meeting, but it seemed that Pamela's clinics could only spare her on Friday, and she told Henry that she could not neglect her work. I don't suppose any woman had ever told Henry that before.

At the last moment it was arranged that Gerald Ross and I would go with them; we would share the cost of the car which would take us to Newmarket. Lady Merton had given me the day off. She was nice about that sort of thing.

The car arrived to fetch me and Pamela just before eleven o'clock. It was driven by a chauffeur, so I imagined that Henry's licence was still suspended. Henry was looking very smart in a bowler hat and was a good deal surrounded by umbrellas and race glasses.

Gerald didn't look smart at all; he looked as if he were going to the pictures. He had brought a packet of sandwiches, for, as he explained, one never knew.

Henry, absorbed in the paper, said that one could always get luncheon on the course.

'Well, I may get hungry on the way down,' Gerald said, 'and I always say that one can't be too careful.' He smiled at Pamela and me.

Henry went on reading the papers and comparing them with a book called *Raceform*.

Pamela was fairly silent during the drive. Whenever one looked in her direction she seemed always to be looking at Henry. 'The patient,' one felt, was being kept under observation.

Pamela was wearing the outfit well known to us at Chalk Farm as her conference clothes: dark blue with touches of white; but not too many touches, so she looked quite nice.

Stephanie had waved to us from the bathroom window as we drove off. Lawrence had stood at the front door while we were getting into the car. This was an outing and everything was going to be lovely. It was an excellent thing that Pamela and Henry were engaged.

Gerald opened his sandwiches and offered them to us. Henry told us what was going to win the second race. He had still not made up his mind about the Guineas. About seven miles from the course we were stopped by a level crossing and after that the traffic became congested and we were continually stopping and starting. Henry kept fussing and looking at his watch. If things went on like this we should miss the first race.

'And there will be no time to have luncheon,' Gerald said triumphantly, and produced another packet of sandwiches out of his overcoat which lay on the floor.

Henry said, rather unsympathetically, that it would be all right in the enclosure, of course. That was unkind, because Gerald and I weren't going to be in the enclosure. We hadn't got the necessary vouchers for it, so we would be in Tattersall's. Nobody had to sign for you to get into Tattersall's, you just paid. Henry assured us that we would be perfectly happy there.

'It was pretty crowded on Wednesday, though'—and he returned to the papers.

I noticed that Gerald didn't offer him any more sandwiches.

Henry said that if he ran into old George he might possibly be able to get him to sign a Ladies' Voucher. He would meet me in the paddock after the first race and let me know. He took a long time explaining exactly where in the paddock I was to wait for him. In the end he drew a map.

We arrived; Pamela and Henry disappeared into the members' enclosure. There was some confusion before Gerald and I finally got into Tattersall's. First Gerald found that he had left his overcoat in the car and we had to go to the car park to look for it; and then a man rushed up to Gerald, called him 'Captain' and tried to sell him a race card. The man said that he had marked off all the winners, and that it was nice to see Gerald again. Gerald said that it was nice to see the man and had almost bought the card before I had time to stop him.

'But you know, I think I *did* know him.' Gerald was still arguing as we went through the turnstiles.

I explained that the only genuine cards were sold inside.

Gerald stood on the asphalt looking bewildered while people pushed past us. Then Gerald pulled himself together and said that we were here to make money and must be serious about it.

I said yes and that anyway we knew what was going to win the second race. We went under the stand and came out on the other side and stood looking at the course and at the book-makers. We were a good deal jostled.

It seemed that Henry had been unnecessarily despondent about the time as there were still twenty minutes before the first race. I suggested to Gerald that we might go and look at the horses in the paddock.

'Are we allowed to do that?' Gerald asked. 'You're sure they're not keeping it especially cleared for your brother?'

We went to the paddock; it was fairly crowded but we managed to push our way into a reasonably good position and watched the two-year-olds being walked round by their stable boys. At first we watched in respectful silence. Then I nudged Gerald and suggested that the horse which was now immediately in front of us was a good mover. Good moving is a question of opinion: nobody can do more than disagree with you; but Gerald agreed enthusiastically.

'It looks,' he said, 'like a dear little ladies' maid.'

The extraordinary thing was that it *did*, and we read in *The Times* the next day that most of the runners in this race were of a shape not fitted to racing.

The jockeys began to come into the ring. They stood about in the middle talking to the owners and trainers; as usual they looked incredibly tiny; they made the owners' wives look gross and over life-size. One jockey had no one to talk to him. He stood alone tapping his leg with his switch and I felt sorry for him; by carefully studying the numbers and colours, as set out in the race card, I made out that he was going to ride the ladies' maid and I toyed with the idea of backing them.

On the way back to the stand Gerald was stopped by a man who called him Captain and was extremely pleased to see him. I looked to see if the man was selling anything; but it turned out that he and Gerald had been in the war together.

The man said that nothing could beat Anarkali. As it happened he was right, and we were sorry afterwards that we had only put ten shillings on her.

The race over, we went and waited for Henry in the paddock. Gerald was worrying because he couldn't remember the name of the man who had given him Anarkali.

'And I used to see quite a lot of him one way and another. He was always being had up for pinching things; there was rather a scandal about it in the end.'

We were joined by Henry and Pamela. Henry said that he had managed to get a voucher for me. I could get it changed at the members' entrance and they would give me a rebate on my Tattersall's ticket.

We asked him if he had backed Anarkali and he said, 'Lord, no,' in a rather preoccupied way, and we were left with the impression that it had been a silly race on which to have a bet.

Pamela, determined to take an intelligent interest in all that was going on, asked what was happening in the small ring in which Anarkali was being auctioned. And I explained the principles of a selling race.

'It seems such a shame,' Gerald said, 'when the poor thing has won and everything.'

Then we explained about the Daily Double, and Gerald started fussing about finding the man who had been in the war with him.

'He probably knows what's going to win all the races. Do you think his name could have been Mathews?'

'It doesn't matter what his name is if you can find him,' Gerald said, hadn't I better go and see about the enclosure, and I said it wouldn't be any fun if Gerald was to remain outside.

Gerald said, 'Nonsense!' and that it was silly to come all this way to see the Thousand Guineas and then perhaps not see it after all. 'It's overcrowded where we are, and one of those very fat men is bound to come and stand in front of you.'

We started towards the enclosure.

'Besides,' Gerald said, 'I shouldn't be surprised if I managed to get a voucher myself before the third race. I've been seeing quite a lot of people I know one way and another. The next one will probably turn out to be a number of the Jockey Club. Anyhow, we can meet in the paddock after each race, so we won't be losing touch altogether.'

He left me and I went up the steps to the members' stand. There, they knew all about exchanging the Tattersall's badge. I had been afraid that I would have to explain it to them. I went on through the hall. In front of the stand was a beautiful empty space.

I fingered my pale blue badge (Ladies or Youths) and regretted that I had no race glasses to which to attach it. Soon I would go to the cloakroom. I was almost certain that my hair needed brushing, and here everyone was very tidy.

In the cloakroom I saw that I had been right about my hair. I decided that my hat was more funny than smart. That was the trouble with hats; they looked perfectly all right in the shop and then you got them home and they were funny. It didn't seem to happen to other people, but it was *always* happening to me, and my friends were inclined to say that they liked me better with no hat at all.

On the way downstairs I met a girl who had been in the W.R.N.S. with me. She was wearing a mink coat and asked me what I was doing here.

Back in front of the stand I marked off my card and put a question mark against the horse which Henry had said was going to win the second race. I decided not to back anything until I had seen them coming down.

I sat on one of the benches and presently I was joined by Pamela. Pamela's hat didn't look a bit funny. Her conference clothes seemed to be exactly right for Newmarket.

'This is very interesting,' Pamela said.

I nodded my agreement.

Pamela waited a second before she spoke again, then she said that this was the first time, since the night of Stephanie's party, that she had seen Henry really enjoying himself. Usually he was detached, as though nothing were worth bothering about.

The first of the horses was going down to the start. I stood up to get a better view. I was glad that Henry was happy, but, just now, nothing was important but the racing. I had to decide whether the horse which Henry had given us could beat the favourite, and there was Cloudless May ridden by Harry Wragg. Some of the papers had tipped Cloudless May, which was now second favourite, and the papers couldn't always be wrong; in fact, quite often they were right. Henry's horse was practically an outsider. If it won one would get a lot more money. Suddenly I decided to back Cloudless May.

After Cloudless May won I began to fancy myself tremendously. I began to fancy that I had a flair for these things. I thought that I would ask Henry to introduce me to his book-maker so that I could stop putting on small sums in cash on the tote and start placing much larger bets through a credit account. Besides it was grander to have a book-maker.

When we all met in the paddock Henry was rather moody. When one spoke to him he behaved as people do when you have interrupted them in the middle of adding up a column of figures.

The next race was the Thousand Guineas. Already the tension was greater than it had been before the first two races and there were ten extra minutes to be got through before the start. Ten extra minutes during which we could change our minds and remain doubtful and undecided.

The crowd milled about the paddock. People clustered round the stables; they pressed against the wooden rails of the ring and waited for the horses.

A child belonging to a family party ran past us shouting for its mother.

Henry asked why the hell people had to bring children to race meetings.

Gerald said, why indeed? It was a nasty dirty habit.

Henry moved away. Pamela whispered that he had an enormous bet on this race.

I nodded. I was thinking of having a large bet myself.

Pamela said that Henry had gone to listen to the prices.

'They won't have started yet,' I said.

This race was the first leg of the Tote Double. So it was terribly important that one should find the winner.

Henry thought he knew what was going to win; but as he had not told us, I knew better than to ask him, for Henry was superstitious; and anyhow his tip for the second race had been most misleading.

Suddenly Gerald's old army friend was beside us. Without preliminary he said that nothing could beat Cama. Gerald said that that settled it then, and how about a drink. The friend said that he didn't mind if he did.

Pamela and I started to walk back to the stand.

'Henry says that if this bet comes off we shall be able to afford to live at Trelynt.'

I was startled. I knew that Henry gambled very heavily; but a bet which, if it came off, would enable him to live at Trelynt!

I caught sight of Henry standing by the railings which divided the members from the bookmakers, waiting for the betting to open, waiting for the exact moment to place a bet. 'Six to four,' 'Thirteen to eight,' would they go any further? Or should he place his bet now, before the prices began to go back? It required a nice feeling for probabilities. But at least he knew what he was going to back. I had not yet decided even that.

As Henry listened to the odds his face was serious and intent. I saw a man go up and speak to him and he hardly answered. I reminded myself that Henry always behaved like this at race meetings; there was nothing to indicate that this time was more important than any of the others. But looking at him again, I knew that it was terribly important. It didn't matter any more what I was going to back myself. In any case I could only win or lose a few pounds. If I won I would buy a leather despatch case to carry to the office and if I lost I would pawn my grandmother's brooch. Either way it didn't matter.

'And how's that brother of yours getting on?'

I tried hard to remember the name of the man who was speaking to me. He was quite old, he was probably a friend of Aunt Emily's, probably I had met him before the war.

I said that Henry was getting on splendidly. I resented the half-patronising, half-jocular tone in which the question had been asked. I hated this old man, safe and smug in his security. As I smiled at him, I thought it would be rather nice if all his shares were to slump at the same time. 'The bottom simply fell out of the market, everything just disappeared overnight.' That would learn him.

Now the horses were coming down. I went to the tote and put two pounds on Cama; but all the time I was only interested in Henry.

The nervous tension which I had felt in the paddock was intensified. The faces around me were serious. The day had ceased to be an outing. I wandered down to the rails. From where I stood I could see Henry. He looked terribly worried.

I wanted to walk over to him and tell him that it was all right. That his horse would win. But that would have been silly.

I didn't know what was going to win. I didn't know what Henry had backed.

The minutes dragged on interminably. One expected every movement or shout from the crowd to grow into that roar which you hear as the flag goes down. A roar and then silence and then further roars as the horses approach the stands. Those are the noises of a big race.

But now the minutes dragged on and nothing happened. This was the year when the King's horse Hypericum won The Guineas, after breaking away at the starting post, throwing her jockey, and galloping freely about the countryside for about a quarter of an hour.

While we waited, the tension which had been growing steadily, gradually relaxed. There were conflicting rumours.

It was Hypericum, it was not Hypericum. She would be scratched, she would remain in the race. The whole thing was unfair. There were murmurs of dissatisfaction. The crowd was no longer corporate. It was breaking up into its separate entities.

Suddenly Gerald appeared beside me; he was smiling happily.

'You managed to get a voucher?' I said.

'Oh, no,' Gerald said. 'I just walked in.'

'But you aren't allowed to do that.'

Gerald shrugged his shoulders and said that he couldn't see that he was spoiling anybody's fun. 'All this business about Hypericum seems to have upset those terrible officials who guard the gates. They are no longer up to their work. They didn't take any notice of me at all.'

I was glad to have Gerald's company, but I rather hoped that Henry would not notice he was here. Henry might not approve of people who slipped under the arms of officials, in order to enjoy privileges to which they were not entitled.

But Henry was looking away from us. His face was quite expressionless.

'Let's go and get a drink,' Gerald said. 'Nothing can happen now for hours and hours, or anyhow until they have caught that dreary horse, and I want to enjoy this place before I get thrown out of it.'

The best bar was at the top of the stand. Gerald and I started towards it. On the way I saw Pamela, who was looking rather derelict, so I asked her to come with us. We threaded our way between the people who stood on the steps. We walked in single file, not pushing anyone. Behind me I heard the shocked tones of a woman speaking to her escort. 'What a *time* to go and have a drink!' Did she consider us to be lacking in proper feeling, or to be guilty of *lèse-majesté*? I would never know.

As a matter of fact it was a very *good* time to have a drink. The long room was almost completely empty.

Gerald looked at the rows of bottles. 'Chablis,' he said. 'We will drink a bottle of Chablis.'

'You can't,' I said. 'It's too expensive.'

'It couldn't possibly be,' and Gerald took a crumpled handful of pound notes out of his pocket. He was behaving very oddly.

The room was built on the glass-cage principle, and we sat at a table and looked down on the course and on the people below us. I thought that I could still distinguish Henry. Pamela sat silent, no longer asking her eager questions.

'It's most irregular,' Gerald said. 'I mean, horses aren't supposed to run away like this are they?'

I didn't answer. I felt certain now that Henry had put everything he had on this damned race. Perhaps if he lost he wouldn't be able to pay. That was dishonest; or alternatively, it was a magnificent gesture. Undoubtedly Henry would see it as a gesture, for he liked any situation in which he was involved to be dramatic.

He had been dramatic when, as a very small child on his first visit to London, he and mother had lost sight of each other for a few moments in Harrod's Stores. Henry had rushed screaming up to the nearest saleswoman and told her that his mother had been kidnapped.

When he had joined the circus (which he did almost entirely to annoy father) he had written home after the first week to say that he had been forced into taking this step. It was either the circus or death from starvation. Which was silly, when you remembered that father was willing to pay for him to stay at Harrow and afterwards to go to Oxford or Sandhurst.

Henry was being dramatic now; he was risking everything on one game of pitch and toss. It seemed silly and rather pathetic; but it was great fun.

If he lost he would be ruined and in a position to die from starvation. If he won he would live at Trelynt with Pamela. (One wouldn't have thought that that would have been very amusing; but maybe it was what he wanted.)

But the real point was that he was risking everything on this one race; what happened in the next few minutes would perhaps affect the whole of the rest of his life.

Now, I was urgently on Henry's side. More than anything else in the world I wanted him to win.

Surely the race must start soon.

'Please, God, let it win.' But I didn't know which horse I was praying for; it was maddening. Besides, even religious people didn't believe that it did any good to pray for the result of a horse race. But it would be so wonderful if Henry won.

'Please, it isn't necessary to alter the result of the race. Just let him have backed the winner.'

I crossed my fingers and wished. It couldn't do any harm to do that, and it just *might* make all the difference. With my other hand I felt in my pocket for my amethyst. Two years ago I had decided that amethysts were lucky and I had bought one set in a hideous little brooch. The brooch was so hideous that you couldn't possibly wear it, but you could carry it in your pocket for luck. I felt slightly guilty about it, for officially I was not superstitious.

'They're running!' Further along the room the waiters were bending down and peering out of the cage. Gerald, Pamela and I peered, too. We could see very little.

I turned to Pamela. 'Do you know what he's backed?'

She nodded. She looked, as the Victorians would have said, very much agitated.

'I can't see Cama *anywhere*.' Gerald's voice ended almost in a wail.

The field was very close now.

'One never can,' I said. 'All the colours look exactly the same when one gets excited.'

But there was no mistaking the King's colours. Hypericum was in the lead now and a moment later she was past the winning post. There was no doubt about the result. Cama wasn't even placed.

Pamela stood quite still staring in front of her and I thought that her eyes were filled with tears.

'That blasted Mathews,' Gerald said angrily. 'You never *could* trust him for long.'

Now our cage was invaded by vast hordes of people. Pamela had rushed away the moment the race was over. People who wanted their tea were sitting down at our table. Gerald and I moved across to the bar. We didn't want a drink; but we felt that we wanted to move about. What with one thing and another and comforting Gerald it was some time before I found out whether Henry had won or lost.

Pamela's sudden emotional flight might have meant anything.

When I next saw her, she and Henry were drinking cups of tea.

'Not a bad race,' Henry said. His manner was so markedly offhand that I knew at once that he had won.

'Did you make much?' I asked.

'A few thousand,' Henry said.

Gerald said that he wished Henry had *told* us that Hypericum was going to win. 'As it was, we went and believed Mathews, and look what's happened.'

'It might have lost,' Henry said, not unreasonably.

As far as we were concerned the rest of the meeting was uneventful. By the end of the day Gerald had made about fifteen pounds, I had lost three, and Henry had added a little to his thousands. He was mysterious about the exact amount; but anyhow it was a great deal and I was surprised that Pamela wasn't more excited about it.

Personally, I was exultant. Henry could now afford to live at Trelynt. Surely that would confound the people who had disapproved of him? 'And how's that brother of yours getting on?'—'Splendidly, thank you. He's living in our old home in Devonshire; he's very rich now, you know, he has been most fortunate in his investments.' They wouldn't find an answer to that one so quickly.

I forgot altogether how immoral it was to live on unearned income. Besides, the money that you made racing wasn't really unearned, you went through an awful lot to get it.

Henry had confounded Aunt Emily and her horrible rich friends. 'Poor Millicent, always so unlucky, and the son—gone entirely to the bad I'm afraid. He lives in a Pimlico slum.' At the moment Aunt Emily represented everything that I hated. It was wonderful that Henry had won those thousands of pounds. But perhaps it was as well that he hadn't won a few million. He might have turned into an Aunt Emily.

'Gerald, isn't it wonderful about Henry?' It was after the last race and we sat on a bench and waited for Pamela and Henry.

'Not bad at all,' Gerald said, 'but I do think he might have *told* us about Hypericum.'

'Why isn't Pamela more pleased about it?'

Gerald said that he had no idea, and did I think that a murder on a race course would be nice.

'Wouldn't it depend on who was murdered?'

Gerald said that that didn't matter. 'The important thing is to have a really sympathetic murderer, and the background, the background's most horribly important; they're always wanting the winter sports and the opening of the Monte Carlo Casino. That sort of thing.'

'Just to make it more difficult?'

'It makes it more difficult for *me*,' Gerald said, 'because I haven't been to those places; but they're what people like reading about.'

'*I* don't,' I said. 'I like reading about nice quiet people who don't *do* anything very much.'

'A psychologist would say that that was because your own life was so exciting.'

'Then the psychologist would be wrong. I do think it's funny that Pamela is looking so worried.'

'Perhaps she's afraid that Henry will spend the money on the wrong things,' Gerald said. 'Though, speaking for myself, I think it's nice to spend money on anything.'

I said, yes, wasn't it, and wished I hadn't lost my three pounds.

On the drive back to London Henry was very gay. He said that he and Pamela could quite easily afford to live at Trelynt for two years—or three, if they were careful.

'What happens after that?' Gerald asked.

'With any luck we shall be dead. Anyhow three years is a long time.' Henry settled himself more comfortably into his corner.

I looked at Pamela; she was frowning a little. Obviously her Birmingham relations wouldn't have approved of this irresponsible attitude. I thought of those advertisements which are headed, 'Will *you* have a pension at sixty-five?' or, 'What will happen to *them* if you are run over by a bus?' The answer, of course, is insurance.

Henry wasn't a bit like the people who go in for insurance. The only time he had ever considered it was when somebody told him that you could borrow money on a Life Insurance Policy; then he found out that you couldn't until you had paid some premiums, so he lost interest.

'Oughtn't you to think of the future?' I said. I felt I was being rather interfering; but I was sorry for Pamela.

'I'm not keen on the future,' Henry said. 'I leave that to the fortune-tellers. Which reminds me'—he turned to Pamela—'we ought to go to one.'

'Now you're being silly.' Pamela sounded terribly disapproving.

'There's no need to look so worried,' Henry said. 'It will all work out all right in the end. We can talk it over at the weekend.'

'There's nothing to talk over,' Pamela said.

'Oh, but surely,' Henry said. 'We've got a lot of things to arrange, and it doesn't do any good to *worry* about money, you know, and we've got *heaps* for the time being.'

Pamela didn't say anything. Perhaps she was regretting the two hundred pounds she had given to 'that woman.'

'Besides,' Henry went on, 'I can always reckon to make quite a bit racing, and then there's backgammon. Backgammon can be terribly paying if you go the right way about it.'

'You can't play backgammon in Devonshire,' Pamela said.

'There may be a special club for it in Torquay,' Gerald said helpfully. 'I've never been there actually, but I understand that Torquay is simply *seething* with vice. I'm thinking of putting it into my next book.'

'It wouldn't be very true to life,' Henry said. 'What would you call it, Hells I have known on the South Coast?'

'It's better if you can bring in the word "murder,"' Gerald said seriously.

Pamela returned to the main theme and said you couldn't live by gambling.

'*I* can,' Henry said magnificently. 'Anyway, if we wanted any more money we could run a market garden. A chap I was talking to the other day said that market gardens can be most frightfully paying.'

'How very interesting. I've never heard *that* about them.' Gerald turned round.

'Fact,' Henry said. 'Of course, you've got to take a personal interest. It's no good leaving the whole thing to gardeners, they steal the bulbs, this chap was telling me. Anyhow, we can talk the whole thing over at the weekend.'

Henry was taking Pamela to spend Saturday and Sunday with some friends of his who lived in Hertfordshire. He had described them to her as a frightfully nice couple if you knew how to take them. He had said that Bob was one of the funniest men he knew and that Jean was terribly nice and that Pamela would be sure to like her. 'There's a very good pub almost next door to their house and they spend practically all their time there and they're not fussy about meals or anything.'

One had felt some sympathy with Pamela's attempts to avoid going to stay with these people; but Henry had been insistent. He said they'd probably have to meet each other's friends in the end and it was just as well to get it over.

So on Saturday he and Pamela went to Hertfordshire, and that evening Henry developed appendicitis and was taken to the local hospital.

SIX

A WEEK LATER, in response to an appeal sent through Pamela, I went to see Henry in the hospital. He was very depressed.

'They tell me that it hurts to laugh; but I just wouldn't know.'

I looked round the room. It had the general ill-kept appearance common to most nursing homes and the private wards of hospitals. Some flowers were arranged in a sputum mug.

'You have a nice view,' I said, going over to the window.

'It depends,' Henry said, 'if you like a flat field and a hedge. Terrible people come there in the early morning and play football.'

I said that sounded beastly and sat down on a chair which had looked as if it were soft.

'And that isn't *all*. They have sing-songs in the public ward, which one can hear *quite* distinctly. The woman next door to me screams all night because they never will give her her morphia, and they wake me up at six o'clock with a cup of stone-cold tea. The whole thing's absolutely *bloody*.'

I sympathised as well as I could and told Henry some jokes I had thought up in the train, but he didn't think them very funny. I began to regret that I had wasted my Saturday in coming to see him.

'Pamela said to say that she would be down this afternoon.'

'Nice girl, Pamela.' Henry stared out of the window at the field. 'You know what's the trouble with me? I'm manic-depressive.'

'That means sometimes you're depressed and sometimes you aren't?'

'That's right,' Henry said. 'But what's so maddening is that there's a perfectly good cure for it, only the doctor here won't believe that I've got it.'

'Couldn't Pamela do something about it?'

'Pamela agrees with the doctor. She doesn't think that I've got it either. But I don't care what they say, I *am* manic-depressive,' and Henry drummed with his fingers on the hospital table which straddled his bed.

'I'm sure you are,' I said soothingly.

'It's what makes people take to drink,' Henry said presently. 'Pamela doesn't understand that. I don't believe doctors do, you know.'

'I suppose not.'

'Some people might think that I drink too much as it is?'

'Surely not.'

'I'm not being funny,' Henry said rather irritably, 'and if you've never had them, you can't understand what absolute hell those sort of moods can be. I can't stop them. Hamlet knew about it, I should think; but what's the use of that? You can't go to a doctor and say, "My trouble is exactly the same as Hamlet's, what are you going to do about it?"'

'Perhaps you could say it to a really good doctor?'

'Oh, what's the use,' Henry said, 'what's the use of anything if it comes to that?'

I felt terribly sorry for him and wished that the bedclothes had been less crumpled, and that the pillows had not looked so hard and uncomfortable; for then perhaps one wouldn't have minded so much.

'The only good thing about it,' Henry said, 'is that one *knows* that it can't last for ever'—now he was talking aloud, trying to convince himself.

'And does that make it any better?'

'No,' Henry said, 'no, as a matter of fact it doesn't.'

The door was thrown open; a nurse carrying an ominous black medicine bottle said, 'Sorry, wrong room,' and rushed out again slamming the door behind her.

She was ludicrous; but she had been a relief.

'I suppose she's got the job of putting the hopeless cases out of their misery,' Henry said. 'George tells me that when they can't cure people here, they put them down. I haven't told you about George, have I?'

I said he hadn't, and Henry said that George was a sort of orderly.

'He does all the things that the nurses don't care about. As a matter of fact, he's the only reasonable person in the whole place and he's always able to put his hand on a bottle of whisky. Never known him to fail.'

I said that that was nice, and at that moment a burly man with an enormous broom opened the door.

'Hullo,' he said, 'didn't know you'd got visitors. Still, the sweeping's got to be done or I'll have Sister after me.' He winked ponderously and then, in case we hadn't noticed, he winked again.

This must be George. He had a bald forehead and a missing front tooth and he appeared to be dressed for the tropics.

Henry introduced us and George said that he was pleased to meet me. Then he leant his broom against his chest and began feeling in the pockets of his tropical suit. Eventually he produced a piece of crumpled paper which he laid on the sheet under Henry's nose.

'The stop press,' George said. 'I've been around the ward and those are the three that most of them are backing.'

'Thank you.' Henry picked up the paper. George listened anxiously and clicked his tongue in a confirmative way while Henry read out the names of the horses. He was so interested that one forgot that he had written the paper himself.

There were quick steps outside and George began pushing his broom about the room, banging the bed several times as he did so. The steps passed on down the corridor and George and his brush came to a standstill.

'Have a cigarette?' Henry said.

George glanced hastily round in case he had overlooked the presence of Sister, then he accepted the cigarette in a quick furtive manner. He began to put it behind his ear, then he looked round the room again and finally put the cigarette in his mouth and lit it.

'Gets you down sometimes, this job.' George nodded in my direction.

'When I get out of here,' Henry said, 'George and I are going to run our own hospital.'

'That's right,' George nodded. 'Be able to have it all our own way then.'

'I think Trelynt would make a good hospital, don't you?' Henry said. 'And if anybody got ill or anything we'd have Pamela.'

'I should have thought there were too many stairs,' I said.

'Oh, we'd lug 'em up and down them fast enough,' George said. 'We'd only be going in for inebriates.'

'I thought it would be a good way of getting my friends to come and stay,' Henry said. 'All the pleasure of their company, and one would be making money at the same time.'

'Tell you what'—George turned to me again—'you can be the matron, that would make a nice surprise for the patients, and they'd be bound to need cheering up if we weren't going to allow them anything to drink, which reminds me'—and he looked at the cupboard.

'Go ahead,' Henry said.

'Never touch a thing on duty,' George said virtuously. 'I was thinking that your sister might be tired after her journey.'

There were further quick steps in the corridor and George went into action with the broom. A middle-aged nurse came in without knocking.

'Have you got the penicillin in here?' She looked severely at Henry.

'Not that I know of,' Henry said. 'Have a drink.'

The nurse leered at him flirtatiously and said that she couldn't stop now. She frisked round the room, presumably looking for her penicillin.

'There should be a big pot of it somewhere,' she complained. 'Never mind. I expect it will turn up sometime or other.'

'And in the meantime everyone dies of blood poisoning?' Henry suggested.

'Oh, they won't *die*,' the nurse said, and hurried out of the room leaving the door open.

George made a few more ineffective swipes with his broom, remarked that that was the housework done for today, and withdrew. He did not shut the door. I began to understand why it is that people so often catch pneumonia when they are in hospital.

'Do you think Pamela will like the idea of turning Trelynt into a nursing home?' Henry asked. He was looking quite cheerful again now and I wondered if I had imagined his despair of a little while ago.

'You don't *seriously* mean that that you're going to run a nursing home?'

'Why not?' Henry asked. 'It would probably pay just as well as a market garden. And what's the good of marrying a doctor if you aren't going to make some use of her?'

That was true, and I supposed that one doctor was as good as another when it came to drink cures.

'You only have to wash them all over in whisky,' Henry said. 'I should think George and I would probably be able to manage on our own. There are the injections, of course; but George tells me that he's pretty nippy at those. Pamela could do the psychological part, not that she understands it, of course, but then who does?'

'I see what you mean.'

'So Pamela would be good enough,' Henry said. 'You only have to tell them that they'd be happier without it, and going to the pictures is more fun, and why don't they pull themselves together and write a book, or go into the Navy. Money for old rope. Only trouble is when they give up whisky and take to drugs instead. Still you've cured them of drink and that's what they came to you for.'

I said it all sounded quite a good idea, and Henry said, 'Oh, hell, you don't think I'm going to do it, do you?'

Another nurse came in and asked Henry why he hadn't had his temperature taken this morning.

Henry said he really didn't know.

The nurse said, Sister was ever so wild about it, and went away again leaving the door open.

'You'd hardly believe it,' Henry said, 'but they tell me that people queue up to get into this place. Every time I see the Sister she tells me how lucky I was to get a bed.'

I told Henry that mother had at last signed the lease of her flat and was expecting me to live in it with her. 'Isn't it *awful*?'

Henry said that he didn't expect I'd mind it too much, and that he had a headache.

I said I wasn't surprised with all those nurses popping in and out.

'There are other days,' Henry said, 'when they leave one alone for hours and hours, and if anyone does answer the bell, they say it's their dinner-time and go away again.'

'I thought that nurses were always supposed to fall in love with their male patients.'

'So did I,' Henry said, and was aggrieved.

Late that evening when I was passing the door of Pamela's room she called me in. She was sitting cross-legged on her bed and was wearing her brooding clothes.

Downstairs Stephanie and Lawrence were coping with the tail-end of an intellectual party. The last bus had long since gone, so either the guests would be leaving on bicycles or they would be spending the night on camp-beds in the dining room.

Pamela offered me some black coffee. Lately she had bought a little machine which burnt methylated spirits, so now she was able to make coffee without going down to the kitchen.

Pamela began by telling me that she had spent the afternoon with Henry at his hospital. I had known that already, but

I nodded and asked her how she thought he was getting on? I asked her in her professional character, as a doctor, much as you ask the skipper of a yacht what sort of a morning it is, although you can see for yourself that it is quite fine.

Pamela said that Henry was getting on well. Then she told me that they were going to turn Trelynt into a nursing home. She was evidently very excited about the idea.

I looked at her in amazement.

'I think it's so wonderful that he should want to do it.' Pamela's eyes were shining. She was really looking very pretty. I remembered that that was what love was supposed to do to people; but I had never seen it actually happen before. Generally when my friends had become engaged they had looked about the same, only a bit more harassed.

This morning, Henry had talked about turning Trelynt into a nursing home. But he hadn't meant to do it. The plan hadn't been serious. Henry had used it to pass the time. It had taken the place of a jigsaw puzzle and had had the same importance.

Pamela talked on eagerly. It seemed that Trelynt wasn't going to be an Inebriates' Home after all. Pamela was going to run it as a combined Maternity and Convalescent Home.

'That won't be awfully restful for the convalescents, will it?' I asked. 'Having a lot of babies around.'

Pamela said that the babies would be in a separate department. Immediately I had a vision of one of those hut hospitals one had got used to during the war. Then I remembered that all these convalescents and people were going to be spread about Trelynt. Nurses would rustle up and down the stairs; the front hall would smell of Jeyes' fluid. It seemed very strange and anyhow Trelynt had the wrong sort of bathrooms for a nursing home.

'And the sister who's in charge of my Tuesday clinic,' Pamela was saying, 'would make a perfectly splendid matron. I shall talk to her about it next week, or perhaps I could get her on the telephone tomorrow.'

I nodded, humouring her. We had now reached the realms of fantasy. If Pamela had suggested that she should keep performing midgets in Sophia's disused hen houses and run up a glass factory in the attics, I would have agreed that it was a good idea, and been prepared to go into the probable costs of the undertaking.

But, she was asking me about the house. As soon as Henry was well enough, they were going down there to see what would need doing to it.

'It will need a lot,' I said; but I still didn't believe in the plan. I told Pamela about the neat plain eighteenth-century part of the house and about the bit which grandfather had added on. I told her about the sprawling back premises. About the long front drive which needed to be repaired, and which would be so unsuitable for ambulances. About the back drive which was so bad that it could not be used at all except by farm carts or persons on foot. Nothing put Pamela off. Her eyes continued to shine. She had seen a vision which she mistook for reality.

'Anne, telephone!'

It was Lawrence calling from the bottom of the stairs.

I jumped up feeling guilty. Mother had always objected to people telephoning to us after nine o'clock. It showed, she said, a lack of consideration and she had held us directly responsible whenever any of our friends had broken across this rule.

At Stephanie's it didn't matter how late people telephoned; but she got annoyed when they rang up too early in the morning and woke her up. This made it rather awkward for me, because Lady Merton was inclined to telephone at horrible hours to tell me that she would be late at the office and what I was to do there until she arrived.

I picked my way across the legs of Stephanie's friends. They were having quite a cosy argument about the Pavilion at Brighton. I should have liked to join in; but the telephone waited for me in the corner of the room.

'How about a murder in a liner?'

It was Gerald.

'As well as on the race course?'

The corpse in Gerald's book was beginning to resemble those sacks stuffed with straw, and used for bayonet practice. The same sack does day after day for soldier after soldier. Eventually they must wear out, and so, if he wasn't careful, would Gerald's corpse. It was becoming altogether too mangled.

'But this is the governess.' Gerald's voice was reproachful. 'It was her employer who was murdered at the races.'

'In that case I think a liner would be lovely.'

I wanted to sound eager and intelligent, worthy of being consulted about the plot of a book.

'You don't think it's too obvious?'

'Oh, no, no, not at all, and you can have a wonderful time describing what they all had for breakfast.'

'I beg your pardon?'

'But that's the point of a liner, they always have about six courses and hundreds of different things to choose from, at least, that's what I've always been told.'

'So have I,' Gerald said, 'and I could have a lot of false clues about poisoning. I think it's excellent; I shall get on with it at once.'

'You aren't working now?' I hoped that he wasn't, for I had read somewhere that writers who did their writing at night let themselves in for a short expectation of life.

'Of course I'm working now,' Gerald said virtuously. 'It's the only time of day one can get complete quiet, besides I've got behind on my last schedule; this book ought to have been finished last month.'

'Oh, dear, then I suppose I shouldn't keep you.' I wished I could do something to help. In offices when people fell behind with their work you could do the post or the filing for them and then they caught up again. In the W.R.N.S. people had sometimes washed one's lorry for one; but all that had been rather different.

'How about luncheon on Monday?' Gerald said. 'We might go to that rather nasty teashop opposite your office?'

I said that would be lovely.

'And I could bring chapter eight with me,' Gerald rang off.

I turned and was quite surprised to find the room still filled with people who were discussing the Brighton Pavilion, or perhaps it wasn't the Pavilion any longer. I stepped carefully over their legs again and went slowly upstairs. I had made a very surprising discovery. I was very fond of Gerald. I walked very quietly past Pamela's door. I didn't want to be talked to any more this evening. I wanted to have time to think.

In my own room, I shut the door. I sat down on the bed. I wasn't fond of Gerald, I loved him. How extremely odd. I felt myself blushing as if I was telling this to somebody else. I wished I had a diary to which I could confide all this. Perhaps I would start one in an exercise book. 'Anne P. loves Gerald R.' Amongst other ruder remarks you sometimes saw things like that chalked on brick walls. Until now, in my ignorance, I had always thought that the writer on the wall must be some interfering third party. Now I knew differently. People wrote those things about themselves. It was so obvious if you came to consider it.

The luncheon with Gerald was only partly successful. The teashop was much too crowded. We had first to share a table with two typists wearing spectacles, and then when the typists went away their places were taken by two enormous men who kept on their overcoats and took up more than their fair share of room. These people talked rather a lot, which made it difficult to concentrate when Gerald began reading chapter eight aloud between mouthfuls of food. I went back to the office feeling vaguely depressed. That afternoon even the card index wasn't any fun.

Sister Andrews was bright and bustling and unsympathetic. It was bad enough meeting her at tea, it would have been a horror to have been her patient. Sister Andrews was going to be the matron of Pamela's nursing home.

It was Saturday and I had come into the sitting room at Chalk Farm to find this going on. A tea-party with Pamela as the hostess and Sister Andrews as the only guest. I had tried to back out of the door; but Pamela had been too quick for me, she had introduced us.

'My fiancé's sister.'

I had smiled sheepishly and not known what to say. A fiancé's sister is a difficult character to know what to do with. She is a future sister-in-law and therefore a potential source of trouble. At the same time she is the representative, anyhow, for the time being, of the fiancé's family. It is up to her to welcome friends and relations from the opposing camp.

I smiled again and told Sister Andrews that it was a beautiful afternoon. That ought to do. It was quite friendly anyway.

Sister Andrews nodded and went on eating the utility cakes with pink squiggles on the top. She lay back on Stephanie's sofa as if to demonstrate that she was as much at home here as in a hospital ward or a birth-control clinic. What interesting secrets Pamela and this woman must share.

'It will mean plenty of hard work, of course.' Sister was addressing herself to Pamela, and I imagined her running about Trelynt carrying some thermometers in one hand and a bucket of coals in the other.

'But very interesting,' Pamela said. 'And you know you've always wanted something like this.'

Sister Andrews, but from now on she must be Matron, looked at Pamela with a trace of resentment. She was not going to concede that she wanted to go to Trelynt. If favours were going to be handed around, it was Matron who was going to do the handing. One began to wonder if Pamela had been altogether wise in her choice. One regretted George's dream of the nursing home staffed only by himself and Henry, with me as a possible candidate for Matron.

'I suppose it will be quite easy to get patients,' I said, still trying to be pleasant.

Matron sipped her tea complacently, 'Oh, there should be no difficulty about *that*. Why, I've already had a letter from Miss Hannafore promising me the overflow from the Dawn. Miss Hannafore and I did our training together, you know.'

'Did you *really*?' I said and thought how strange it all sounded. I myself had been born at Trelynt, but not because my mother couldn't get into some other hospital.

'I'm not so sure about the convalescents,' Matron went on. 'Once patients get walking about they're often more trouble than they're worth.'

'They'll want fresh eggs,' I said, remembering advertisements in the *New Statesman*, 'and farm produce and running water in their bedrooms.' I stopped short; Trelynt had very little running water. It had no gas-fires or warm lounges. I saw Matron's point. Patients who could walk about and complain might easily be more trouble than they were worth.

'How long do you think it will take you to get it all going?' I asked.

'About three or four months,' Pamela said. 'It depends on the licences. From what Henry tells me, there is a good deal that will need doing. We're going down there next week to make our preliminary plans. Matron is coming with us.'

'Does mother know?' I didn't think mother would like Matron. Mother had never cared for hospital nurses.

'She has invited us to stay,' Pamela said. 'I had a most charming letter from her. I do hope that she won't be too upset at the thought of her old home being altered. One wouldn't want to cause her any unnecessary pain.'

This was a false note; one could detect it quite easily without any reference to Aristotle's *Ethics*.

'You needn't worry about that,' I said. 'Mother simply hates Trelynt. I think if you really wanted to please her you'd pull it down.'

I saw a smile of sympathy pass between Matron and Pamela.

'Your mother is going to live in London?' Matron asked.

'Oh, yes,' I said, anxious to co-operate with her and realising that I had been rude. 'She's taken a flat near Westminster Cathedral. Handy for the Army and Navy Stores.' Matron nodded quite kindly and Pamela began pouring us out extra cups of what was by now rather cold tea.

A few days later Henry was released from the Hertfordshire hospital. He arrived back in London. Pamela engaged a room for him at a hotel, and there he was to rest for two days, until he was strong enough to travel down to Devonshire. There was rather a fuss about it all. For a doctor Pamela was making a great deal of a simple operation for appendicitis; but perhaps she knew best and anyhow there are always adhesions. Adhesions don't seem to happen until rather a long time after an operation, but they can be guarded against from the first.

Pamela and Matron and Henry were to travel down to Trelynt by an afternoon train on Friday. Henry must not be rushed, so it was better not to travel in the morning.

On Tuesday I had a letter from mother. I always feel a certain misgiving whenever I see mother's neat, not very legible, Edwardian writing on an envelope. There is a French poem which begins, 'One doesn't tear up one's mother's letters.' Actually I very seldom tear up anybody's letters, but I have often wished that I was brave enough to put mother's straight in the fire without reading them. This particular one I took to the office. Perhaps I would read it while I drank my mid-morning cup of tea, or perhaps I would be particularly lucky and forget all about it.

Once, when I was in the W.R.N.S., I had forgotten one of mother's letters for a whole week and a letter which is out of date has lost its sting. Its reproaches don't matter any more. The whole thing is over.

On Tuesday morning I wasn't lucky. I opened my bag and mother's letter shot up at me. It was impossible to forget it; I would read it and get it over.

There were two pages. Mother was sorry I hadn't written. There had been several important questions in her last letter and she would like to have them answered. I was not to be surprised if the moth had got into all my clothes. Mother had done her best, but if I didn't answer letters it made it extremely difficult. Did I know that there were fourteen hats at the top of my cupboard, and was there really any point in keeping my Wren uniforms? Surely I ought to try to sell them. I turned over the page. Mother had decided that I must come down and sort out my things myself. She and Sophia had enough to do. In a fortnight they would be arriving in London, and it wasn't only clothes, it was books, and the books were all over the house. That sounded pleasant, perhaps I had the beginnings of a library; but perhaps it was only *The Girl's Own Annual* and *Mamma's Bible Stories*. That wouldn't be so nice. I had nearly reached the end of the letter before I realised where it was all leading us. I was to go to Trelynt for the weekend and support mother against the first onslaughts of Pamela and Matron. That wasn't exactly the way mother put it; but it was what she meant. She hoped that I would be a help and not a hindrance. She and Sophia were both too busy to be able to give up their entire time to entertaining a lot of nurses.

I wouldn't go, I definitely wouldn't go.

The letter ended with a postscript. Mother had decided that I needn't move to the Westminster flat for another month or so. The painters would be in, only I wasn't to tell anybody. Mother said that she was being quite legal about the painters, only there were so many informers about that one couldn't be too careful. I saw mother as a fugitive from justice running across Dartmoor and crouching behind stone walls.

'When you have quite finished with your correspondence, Pallisser, we might get on with those lists.' It was Lady Merton; she was in a bad temper this morning.

I put mother's letter away and reached for the lists. I reflected that mother had offered me a bribe. If I would go and help with Pamela and Matron, mother wouldn't insist upon my immediate removal from Chalk Farm to Westminster.

I asked Lady Merton if I could have Friday afternoon off. I counted upon her refusal. I counted upon her saying that she particularly wanted me to work on Saturday morning; that would have made it impossible for me to go down to Devonshire. But Lady Merton's bad temper had unfortunately vanished. I could have all the time off I wanted. We had a second assistant in the office now, a small fat woman called Miss Napier-Smith, who looked even sillier in her uniform than I did; but she adored Lady Merton.

The weekend at Trelynt began on the platform at Paddington. Pamela, or perhaps Matron, had arranged that we were all to travel together. There was to be a reserved seat on the train for Henry, who, as an invalid, moved about only under cover of doctor's certificates and special permits. I suggested to Pamela that she might write a certificate for me; she was very shocked by the idea.

Henry, for whom a car had been ordered to take him to the station, very nearly missed the train. When he did arrive he was accompanied by Ambrose, one of the men who had dined with us at the black-market club, and by a very pretty girl called Daphne. One could only hope that she belonged to Ambrose. Pamela immediately took possession of Henry and hustled him into his corner seat. She was introduced to Ambrose and Daphne, but did not appear to notice them. Matron, on the other hand, noticed a good deal. In the short time at her disposal she was very gracious indeed to Ambrose. Probably she already saw him as an escort for her afternoon out. Matron was evidently a quick worker. It was interesting.

Daphne continued to talk to Henry through and over the barrage which Pamela was creating. She commiserated with him loudly on having to go to Devonshire. Windsor Races to-morrow would be no fun without him.

Henry said, Oh, well, Windsor was never much good anyhow. But surely he would rather have been there than in this train having his knees covered with Pamela's travelling rug. Or would he? I wasn't certain. Perhaps he would rather have been doing both at the same time.

'You and Ambrose might come down to Torquay; we could do something on Sunday.' I don't think that Henry meant Daphne to take the suggestion seriously.

Doors were being slammed. Ambrose seized Daphne's arm and dragged her off the train. Even without Ambrose and Daphne the carriage was very crowded. I noticed to my horror that in the far corner there was a small child. I couldn't think how it was that I hadn't noticed it before. Usually I can see children coming for miles and I had never yet shared a railway carriage with one. I glared resentfully at Pamela who had let us in for this. Now I would have to take my suitcase and sit in the corridor. Henry in his corner was sunk in gloom; Matron was glancing round brightly on the look-out for new friends. It wasn't a nice journey at all; but then they never are.

'I think it is a great pity,' mother was saying. We were sitting round the dining-room table at Trelynt pretending to be a dinner party. The effect was a little spoilt by Sophia having to keep on getting up to dodge in and out of the room with the bread-and-butter pudding or whatever it was we were eating. If one offered to help, Sophia said one was getting in the way.

'I think it's a very great pity,' mother repeated, waving away the bread-and-butter pudding. 'There are too many hospitals as it is.'

'But this will be a nursing home.' Pamela was being maddeningly reasonable.

'The house isn't suitable,' mother said. 'You won't get any servants and before you know where you are you'll be nationalised.'

Pamela started to answer. I knew what was coming. In a moment we would be having an exposé of the National Health Bill. How lucky Sophia was to be able to escape to the kitchen. There she would be able to have a pleasant gossip with Mrs Corwell who, out of the goodness of her heart, had come in to help with the washing-up. Mrs Corwell didn't believe in nurses, not trained ones anyway. Mrs Corwell disapproved of Henry's marrying a lady doctor. There had to be doctors, one knew that; but she couldn't feel it was right that Henry should marry one, not when you thought what a dear little boy he had been.

Yes, the kitchen at this moment must be much gayer than the dining room. Mrs Corwell and Sophia would end by having a nice strong cup of tea together. For us there would be nothing but the weak coffee tasting faintly of ammonia.

The front-door bell pealed. It was very startling. No one had been invited to the house that evening. There was no one who had the right to disturb mother at this hour.

Henry, who had been sitting silent at the top of the table, got up. 'I suppose there's nobody to answer it?' The question was redundant. Did he expect mother to tell him that the answering of bells must be left to the footman?

The bell sounded again.

'Really!' Mother was outraged.

Henry went into the hall, shutting the door of the dining room behind him.

There were confused noises in the hall, the sound of several voices and the yapping of at least one dog. In the dining room nobody spoke, we were straining our ears to hear what was going on. Above the other noises I could hear Henry's laugh. It sounded very gay. Then the front door slammed and there was silence. Very faintly we could hear a car driving away from the house.

Mother got up. 'If everyone has finished?'

Matron folded up her napkin. Mother opened the door, and stood aside to allow her guests to precede her. She remarked on the chilliness of the evening; perhaps Pamela would like the fire to be lit in the drawing room? Of course, it was nearly the beginning of July, but then this house was so inclined to be damp, what did Pamela think?

Mother was behaving perfectly conventionally. The look of triumph on her face was hardly perceptible.

'What do you think has happened to Henry?' Pamela blurted it out as soon as we were in the drawing room.

Mother drew her *petit-point* towards her. 'He probably won't be long.' Mother had made it clear that she considered the question not quite becoming. Pamela was no longer a clever lady doctor, she was an awkward girl who must be prevented from making a fool of herself. Mother began to talk to Matron, who played up beautifully. Matron was quite at her best this evening.

At half-past ten mother announced that it was bedtime. She reminded Sophia not to lock the front door. She hoped that Henry would not make too much noise when he came in; she did not want anyone to be disturbed.

On the way upstairs Pamela reminded mother that Henry was still an invalid.

'Oh, surely not.' Mother did not even pause in her progress. 'I thought they managed those operations so well nowadays.

'All the same he ought to be careful.'

Mother had reached the top of the stairs. She told Pamela that Henry was extremely healthy and had thrown off the measles remarkably quickly.

Henry eventually came in at three in the morning. I didn't hear him myself, but Sophia told me about it when she woke me up at eight.

'Was he drunk?'

'Oh, I don't think so,' Sophia said. 'He didn't fall over anything; in fact, he hardly made any noise at all. The only thing was he put his shoes out to be cleaned.'

'Perhaps he thought Mrs Corwell would do them.'

'Perhaps he did'—and Sophia's face cleared of its momentary anxiety.

The rest of the day, and indeed the whole weekend, was rather confusing.

Mrs Corwell rushed into the drawing room just after breakfast and breathlessly announced to mother that she had found a young lady in the coal hole.

Mother, who was sitting at her writing table making out a list of things that she must do in Exeter that morning, looked up abstractedly, and asked Mrs Corwell to repeat herself.

'In the *coal* hole.' Mrs Corwell looked round the room for a more appreciative audience; but there was only me doing the dusting for Sophia.

'Dead?' mother asked briskly.

'No, she isn't *dead*.' Mrs Corwell was aware that the dramatic quality of her announcement had been largely spoiled.

'Then *that's* all right.' Mother smiled reassuringly. It seemed that she had only wanted to know if she was to add 'Call at undertaker's,' to the bottom of her list.

'But something ought to be done about her surely.' Mrs Corwell's voice rose indignantly. 'I mean it isn't *right* for people to be in other people's coal holes.'

'You must tell her to go away,' mother said.

'But supposing she turns obstinate; it's my belief that she's been there half the night.'

'All the more reason why she should go away now.'

Mother turned her back on Mrs Corwell who, after a moment's indecision, withdrew.

As soon as I could, without arousing comment, I left the drawing room. I found Mrs Corwell in the kitchen in conference with Sophia. They were in a high state of excitement. The young lady had told both of them that she would not leave the house until she had seen Henry. She was sitting now on the grass outside the kitchen window. Urged by Sophia and Mrs Corwell to use the utmost caution I peeped at her. It was Daphne. She was somewhat dishevelled but still looking very pretty.

'The nerve of her,' Mrs Corwell hissed in a delighted stage whisper. 'And he'll have a terrible time of it with those hospital nurses if they so much as catch sight of her.'

'Have you told Henry?' I turned to Sophia.

'He refuses to do anything about it. As a matter of fact, he climbed out of the library window and he's gone down to the village by the back drive.'

'Climbed out of the window!' Mrs Corwell had nothing but admiration for this bold action in the face of danger.

'Hadn't you better tell Daphne that?' I said to Sophia. 'She'd probably go and look for him and then we'd get rid of her.'

Sophia agreed that that was probably the best thing to do and sent me to do it.

I approached Daphne warily. I said good morning and reminded her that we had met on the train the day before. I don't think she remembered me particularly; but she was quite friendly and invited me to sit on the grass beside her. I told her that we thought Henry had gone down to the village.

'But I *must* see him,' Daphne said urgently. 'He's so terribly sweet.'

I nodded sympathetically and repeated that Henry had left the house. At first Daphne was disinclined to believe me; but eventually I persuaded her that I was speaking the truth so far as I knew it.

'You will help me, won't you?' she said impulsively. To emphasise her point she thumped the ground beside her with her closed fist.

'Of course, I'll help you,' I said, 'but what is it exactly that you want?'

'Only to see him,' Daphne repeated. 'He wants to see me too, only he's terrified of that woman.'

'If you went down to the village,' I said, 'you'd probably find him. They always let him into the pub even when it isn't opening hours.'

'Are you sure?' Daphne asked.

'Fairly sure,' I said. 'And you'll be able to get something to eat. I'm sorry I can't ask you to luncheon or anything; but I don't think my mother would like it, and anyhow there wouldn't be enough cutlets, you know what it is with rationing.'

Daphne got up off the ground and said she would go to the village. She looked cautiously round and asked if that woman was anywhere about.

'Not at the moment,' I said and hoped that Pamela would not choose this moment to appear.

'It isn't far, is it?'

'Oh, no,' I said inaccurately, 'only about ten minutes' walk; you keep straight on down the drive and then you turn to your left and the Pallisser Arms is almost the first house on your left.'

'Does it belong to you?'

'Not now,' I said. 'It used to.'

Reluctantly Daphne started down the drive. I stood and watched her, afraid that she might change her mind and come back, but she didn't.

Returning to the kitchen I gave an account of the interview to Sophia and Mrs Corwell.

'I never thought she'd go that quiet.' Mrs Corwell's voice held an infinite regret.

I think that Daphne probably did find Henry in the village. I am not sure and, as I said, the rest of the weekend was confusing. Daphne carried out a series of sallies against the house. Sometimes she was alone and sometimes she was accompanied by a somewhat reluctant Ambrose. On Monday morning Mrs Corwell found her in the coal hole again, but by that time I was safely back in London. In the meantime Matron and Pamela tramped over the house a good deal, and their conversation was inclined, even at meal-times, to turn to sewage; on which Matron, it seemed, was an expert.

Pamela took no apparent notice of what was going on about Daphne. Only on Sunday afternoon she announced that she and Henry were to be married in a fortnight's time.

Henry looked up in surprise. 'As soon as that?'

'I thought so,' Pamela said. 'Is there really any point in waiting until the house is ready?'

'Oh, none at all,' Henry said hurriedly. 'In fact I think it would be best if we were married as soon as possible,' and he looked uneasily out of the window as if he were afraid that Daphne might appear on the path outside, as indeed she was only too likely to do.

So it was settled, and the rooms for the patients were agreed upon and also the rooms which were to be set aside for the occupation of Henry and Pamela.

This time there was no discussion about what furniture mother would be taking to London, for, before we had arrived, she had taken the precaution of tying large labels on everything she intended to remove. The labels flapped at you when you walked quickly through the rooms. There seemed to be rather a lot of them; but, as mother pointed out to Henry, she was taking nothing which could not strictly be considered to be her own. Henry didn't seem to be particularly interested and Pamela remarked to Matron, when mother was in the room, that they were lucky in not having to find storage space for a lot of Victorian furniture which would be quite useless in a nursing home.

Pamela and Henry were married in a London registry office, in the presence of mother and Sophia and me, and on the other side Matron and a small contingent from Chalk Farm. Between us we wore too many sprays of white flowers. Ambrose was best man, in so far as there *is* one at a registry-office wedding. There was, perhaps fortunately, no sign of Daphne.

The honeymoon, as far as one could make out, was spent at race meetings and at various shops specialising in the sale of hospital furnishings and supplies. I think Henry was relieved to be married again. He found it safer. He was grateful to Pamela for the security she provided.

Mother and Sophia moved to London and settled down to sharing the flat in Pemberthy Mansions with two very charming painters who carried up the coals for them. As long as the painters remained there was no room for me, as they had turned the room which was to be my bedroom into a combined paint store and sitting room for themselves. I prayed that they would never leave.

Lady Merton started on a prolonged tour of her canteens in Occupied Europe; she took Miss Napier-Smith with her. Miss Napier-Smith was going to spend her time pretending to be Lady Merton's batman, a role which had first been suggested to Lady Merton when Miss Napier-Smith had arrived at the office with a clothes-brush and a bottle of thawpit with which to dab at Lady Merton before she went out to luncheon.

Before she left on her tour, Lady Merton impressed upon me what a great honour she was doing me in leaving me alone in charge of the office. I was to send her almost daily bulletins and I was to use as little of the petty cash as possible. Lady Merton supposed that I wouldn't mind waiting for my summer holiday until the end of September.

As a matter of fact I didn't mind, for Gerald was still in London.

SEVEN

A CAR drew up at the front door, a cumbersome figure was propelled out of it; there was a moment of confusion while other slimmer figures paid the taxi-driver and dealt with a suitcase and various cardboard boxes. Then the cumbersome figure was seen to be flanked by a small elderly woman and by a weakly smiling young man. Matron was bustling forward fully starched and smiling professionally. The first patient had arrived at Trelynt.

In the months that followed, that scene was re-enacted quite a number of times. Always there was the cumbersome figure and its various supporters. But it was Mrs Green who turned Trelynt into a nursing home, for a nursing home without a patient is still only a house.

'Our First Mother,' as Matron strangely continued to call the young woman from the Exeter suburbs, arrived at Trelynt at the beginning of October and caused a tremendous amount of excitement (although not by anything that she did personally, for the birth itself was disappointingly 'easy'). But the house wasn't really ready for her, painters and plumbers still lurked about the place, the domestic and nursing staff not fully assembled.

Pamela had been doubtful about taking the case, but Matron had promised Miss Hannafore (with whom she had done her training) and the promise must be kept.

I was spending my holidays at Trelynt and with Henry I watched Mrs Green's arrival from behind some laurel bushes. George, who had himself arrived only the day before, hung about the hall the whole morning so as to be sure and not miss the great moment. Matron, who for reasons of dignity had had to pretend that the event was of no very great importance, had gone so far as to have her elevenses put forward to half-past ten. Pamela had found that she must be busy in the office with its good view of the front door.

Henry and I waited patiently behind the bushes. It was as if we were still playing hide-and-seek. Once or twice, when I was a child, children had been brought over to tea at Trelynt and we had played hide-and-seek in the garden. Never in the house, that would have made too much noise.

'It's fantastic,' Henry said.

'You mean Trelynt being a nursing home?'

'In a way,' Henry said. 'I mean, isn't it?'

'It was your own idea,' I said.

'I know'—Henry looked perplexed—'and don't think for a moment that I've anything against it, and I see Pamela's point about babies being easier really than drunks, and I'm sure we'll make heaps of money . . .' His voice trailed off.

One knew what he meant. One has ideas, one even makes a few plans to carry them into effect, and then suddenly one is confronted with a *fait accompli*. It is very surprising. It was like that when I went into the W.R.N.S. and when I went to work for Lady Merton in London. I had not expected either of these things to happen.

'Mind you, I think I'm going to like this life,' Henry said. He spoke as if this were a point to be considered now, after most of the bathrooms had been put in, and the beds and the pota-to-peeling machines and all the other gadgets had been bought.

'You won't miss the racing?' I asked.

'But I haven't given it up.' Henry was horrified. 'I just haven't been going so much lately; but as soon as we get thoroughly settled I'll be able to get away whenever I want to.'

I wondered whether Pamela would ever approve that arrangement.

'You know the extraordinary thing *is*,' Henry went on, 'I'm getting quite fond of this place now it doesn't belong to father.'

'It makes a difference if things belong to you,' I said. 'I remember noticing that with pencil boxes.'

Mrs Green's car arrived, and, after a suitable interval, Henry and I left our cover and went into the house.

The house, although all the alterations were not yet finished, had changed a great deal since last July. Only the hall and library seemed to have remained exactly the same, and, as had always been the case, nobody went into the library. There was a vague idea that later on it might be turned into a recreation room for the convalescents, or expectant fathers might be put in there to read the county history. It might take their minds off the terrible things that were happening to their wives.

Upstairs had changed the most. Some of the bedrooms had been divided into two by means of unsound-proof partitions.

The room which had been mother's was now a small ward containing four beds. It didn't look right, somehow, and it still had its original wallpaper of green trellis work and you could see where mother's pictures had hung.

'I was born in this room,' I had said reminiscently to Matron who had been taking me on a tour of the improvements.

'Really? Well, nobody else will be,' Matron had said crisply. 'The patients from this room will all be using the labour ward.'

'Where are you going to put the convalescents?' I had asked.

'In the north wing. Most of them will be able to use the dining room, so it won't matter about the stairs.'

'The north wing!' At one stroke Matron had turned Trelynt into a stately home. One forgot that the north wing could only mean that huddle of rooms which had once been the nurseries and the servants' bedrooms.

They had taken Mrs Green upstairs. Henry went into the drawing room and I retired to the kitchen. A young trainee cook was mincing about amongst a lot of machinery. Another even younger trainee was taking something out of the oven. Mrs Corwell was stacking china. George was leaning against the table drinking a cup of tea.

'Well, we never thought we'd see this.' Mrs Corwell's face was flushed; she was somewhat distraught.

'It looks nice,' I said.

'Steamers and everything,' Mrs Corwell said. 'A lot of old kickshaws if you ask me.'

We had had this conversation before. It was restful talking to Mrs Corwell, one didn't have to keep thinking of new things to say.

'Miss Sophia wouldn't know herself if she was to walk into the place.'

Mrs Corwell evidently thought of Sophia as someone in-finitely remote who would be astounded at the trends of modern life and the discoveries of science.

'You wait until a few more patients start arriving,' George said. 'It will be nothing but junkets and jellies and heating up milk all day long.'

'The milk will be heated in the ward kitchen.' It was the young cook. She spoke authoritatively out of the deep experience of her governmental training. Her name was Miss Maitland.

'The ward kitchen. That used to be the housemaids' cupboard,' Mrs Corwell said to me in an aside. 'It's wonderful what they think of, isn't it?'

The door opened and Nurse Brawn, the newly-engaged assistant midwife, came in.

'Well, how are things going?' With his thumb George pointed to the ceiling. We all knew that he referred to Mrs Green.

Nurse Brawn said that it would be some time yet and helped herself to a cup of tea.

'It's her first, isn't it?' Mrs Corwell asked, avid for horrid details.

Nurse Brawn said that it seemed funny having only one patient. In her last nursing home they'd been kept terribly busy, we wouldn't believe.

George said that you had to make a start somewhere.

Miss Maitland said nothing. I don't think she quite liked Nurse Brawn helping herself to tea. Perhaps she would have liked to tell Nurse Brawn that the nurses' dining room was along the passage and sixth door on the left. That was the room which had been the servants' hall. It was enormous and almost pitch-black. One couldn't imagine there had ever been enough servants to fill it, even in grandmother's time.

Next door to it was the old lamp room where the present domestic staff were supposed to have their meals.

Miss Maitland, *en route* for a cupboard, bumped into me unnecessarily; I took that to mean that she wished to have her kitchen to herself. I went upstairs again. Tomorrow was the last day of my holidays. I must think about packing.

I wished that I didn't have to leave. Nothing waited for me in London but the threat of mother and Sophia and the unorderly routine of Lady Merton's office.

It had been kind of Pamela to have me to stay; but then the great point about Pamela *was* her kindness. She had written to say that she hoped I would continue to regard Trelynt as my home and come there whenever possible. When Trelynt had really been my home I had always been trying to get away from it. But now that we were only going to pretend that it was my home it was different. I had enjoyed this visit. When I had arrived I had been tired and depressed. I had spent August and September in London, and I had hated it. Lady Merton and Miss Napier-Smith had been away from the office nearly the whole time. Chalk Farm, too, had been deserted, for Stephanie and Lawrence had been in Suffolk; and the charwoman had had extensive holidays. Gerald, on whom I had counted for companionship, had gone off to visit his mother for the weekend and had remained with her for nearly two months, only coming back to London just before I left. It had, in fact, been a perfectly horrible and very lonely summer.

I started on my packing and then the gong rang for luncheon. In the passage outside my room an electrician knelt amidst lengths of wire. As I came into the hall, I heard the end of an argument between Pamela and a plumber who had thought it would be a good idea if he turned all the water off for twenty-four hours.

After luncheon Henry and I sat on the grass outside the drawing-room windows. The drawing room was now Pamela's and Henry's sitting room; the Edwardianism created by mother had disappeared. The silver photograph, frames had gone and mostly the room was furnished with things which Pamela had had in store; they dated, I think, from the days when she had had the basement flat and the Hungarian had fallen madly in love with her. The woven-string motif was fairly strong.

'Do you remember Clarissa?' Henry asked.

I did. Clarissa had been a hideous spaniel which he had owned when he was still at school. She had been named to annoy father, Henry having a theory that father had once been engaged to a lady who was called that.

'She was a nice dog,' Henry said. 'She used to sleep on the end of my bed.'

I remembered that, all right. Dogs belonging to me or Sophia always had to sleep in the yard. Mother had been very firm about that.

Pamela stepped out of the french windows. She was wearing a white overall over her grey flannel suit. It was unfortunate that it made her look like a kennel-maid.

'How are we doing?' Henry asked. 'Mrs Green getting on with it all right?'

Pamela's eyes rested on him lovingly. She said that Mrs Green was a splendid patient and that her baby ought to be born about tea-time.

'Wonderful how you know,' Henry said admiringly.

Pamela pulled an iron chair away from the wall and sat beside us. 'The night nurse is arriving by the five-o'clock train. I suppose somebody will have to go into Exeter and meet her.'

Henry said that all those kind of arrangements could be left to him.

Pamela smiled at him and said that the night nurse was to lodge in the village, 'at Mrs Corwell's.'

Henry said that he supposed that would be a good arrangement.

I said I must go and pack. I picked my way among the electricians and went up to my bedroom. The bedroom which had always been mine and which Pamela had said should never, except in the last necessity, be given to a convalescent. I looked round the room. My suitcase lay open on the floor, most of my clothes were spread over the bed. This was the result of starting my packing before luncheon. I went over to the window, a fine north view of the backyard and some ailing macracapa.

This had been the night nursery. The iron-and-brass bedstead had once belonged to my nurse; but she had been only a bird of passage. I could hardly remember her. In the corner was the pitch-pine bookcase which had been in the day nursery. In the bottom shelf there were still some old exercise books which had been there for years. They mostly contained French and Latin exercises, and at the back of one or two of them there were the beginnings of several plays and novels. These seldom went beyond a page or two. We had not been literary children.

I picked up one of the note-books. It opened at a picture of men with clubs and hairy legs chasing each other about the Gobi desert. In the bottom right-hand corner was written, 'H. Pallisser (aged 9¼).' I wished, as I had often done before, that Henry had been nearer my age. 'A. Pallisser (aged 1¼)' must have been a dreary little object at the time when Henry was drawing that picture, and what had Henry been like? Charming and, from father's point of view, probably already unsatisfactory. Gayer than anyone else in this gloomy house, and yet a prey to sudden moods of wild despair.

I put the Gobi desert back in the bookcase. The trouble was that you never *could* tell what anybody was like, not even when you knew them quite well. And perhaps they weren't *really* like anything. Perhaps Lawrence was right and there were no absolute values, not anywhere in the world, and everything, including people's characters, was relative. It was rather frightening. I hoped it wasn't true.

Putting the Gobi desert back in the bookcase, I resisted a strong temptation to settle down and read *Stumps* and resolutely got on with my packing.

At five o'clock Mrs Green, as predicted by Pamela, produced her baby. In the evening Pamela received a telegram asking her if she would accept another emergency case. There was no doubt now that Trelynt was a nursing home. I thought about it in the train next morning as I travelled up to London.

The house which had always smelt comfortably mouldy, now smelled of ether and floor polish and sometimes, just a little, of flowers. Matron and Pamela bustled where mother had walked slowly. Miss Maitland was efficient in the kitchen where Sophia had pottered. The change was complete; but to arrive at the house you still had to use the long dank drive, and, as you turned into it, you still felt it was unlikely that anyone lived at the end of it.

I arrived in London. Stephanie's house looked shabby, rather battered. It was losing its enchantment. There should have been bills waiting for me on the shelf in the hall; but I was not rich enough for bills.

Stephanie was back from the country, but she was not in.

She had left a message scrawled on the back of an old envelope. 'Your mother has rung up four times in the last two days, please tell her not to.' One of the advantages of the flat in Pemberthy Mansions was that it already had a telephone installed. It was a purely personal advantage: it benefited no one but mother.

The only way to prevent mother ringing up again was to ring her. I dialled the number and hoped there would be no answer. I was afraid my reprieve was at an end. Mother would answer the telephone and tell me that the room in Pemberthy Mansions was now ready for my occupation. I despised myself for the craven way in which I had behaved over the whole business of living with her and Sophia. I should have taken a firm line from the very beginning and I should have stuck to it. But hadn't I been firm? It was difficult to remember after so many months. I had an idea that perhaps I *had*, only mother had not listened, and how could *anyone* be firm if people didn't listen to what they said?

'Hullo!' It was mother doing her telephone voice. Speaking in an assumed voice and not announcing her identity was one of her precautions against burglars.

'Stephanie says you've been trying to get hold of me.'

'Oh, yes.' There was a pause, mother was collecting her thoughts and probably her spectacles. I could imagine her pushing her thick hairpins more firmly into place.

'I want you to come to dinner this evening.'

I made a confused sort of answer, bringing in something about the difficulties of rationing.

'You aren't doing anything else?'

I had to admit that I wasn't. Gerald knew that I was coming back today. Gerald might possibly ring up and invite me out to dinner, or he mightn't, but I would like to have kept the evening free in case.

'At half-past seven then,' mother said firmly. 'Don't be late because we like to get the washing-up done as soon as possible.' She rang off. She hadn't said anything about my going to live with her, but perhaps she was keeping that until we met. Or perhaps she was making me go and see her in order to get from me a full report on Henry. That wouldn't be so bad.

I didn't have to go to the office until tomorrow. I carried my suitcases upstairs and began to unpack. It would have been nice if there had been a letter from Gerald. I had only had one from him while I was at Trelynt. I had allowed myself to answer it after two days' delay. Then I hadn't written again. There had been no reason to.

The Victorians and the *Daily Mirror* had been right. 'Never fall in love with a man until he has fallen in love with you.' But I wasn't even sure that I *was* in love, and it was just possible that Gerald *had* fallen in love with me and hadn't liked to mention it. It would have saved a lot of trouble if only I could have asked him. But I couldn't do that. Mother's conventional upbringing was too strong for me. Mother was on the side of the *Daily Mirror*.

Stephanie and her friends weren't. I wondered if Stephanie had waited demurely for Lawrence to say the word, and what words Lawrence had said. Presumably not: 'Will you marry me?' because they weren't married. Although, presumably, one day they would be. Had Lawrence said, 'Will you marry me later on?' That didn't sound very impassioned or even very likely.

I finished my unpacking, up to a point. Tomorrow I would really tidy up my room. I would take everything out of the drawers and put them back in a different order. I would throw away old letters and things I no longer needed. I would never allow things to get into a muddle again. I would be a pattern of orderliness and efficiency. In the meantime I would go down to the sitting room and read the paper. On the way downstairs I met a strange young man, who said, 'Hullo,' and disappeared into the room which had been Pamela's. This must be the new lodger. I wondered if we knew him at all, or if he had come to us via the advertisement columns of the *New Statesman*.

* * * * *

At twenty-five past seven I arrived at mother's flat. The door was opened to me by mother herself. Somehow she was looking younger than I had expected. Then I remembered how well it usually suits people to be widows. Mother took me into the drawing room and offered me a glass of sherry. That wasn't in character. The silver photograph frames were in place on the mantelpiece, and most of the furniture was recognisable as having come from Trelynt. Under the windows there was a grand piano, that had *not* come from Trelynt, and it looked brand-new.

Sophia came into the room and helped herself to sherry. She was wearing a dainty plastic cooking apron over her black dress.

'Mother is writing an opera.' Sophia waved her hand in the direction of the piano.

'All of it?' I asked. I looked at mother with some surprise. 'I didn't know you were musical.'

'I used to be when I was a girl.' Mother's face had turned quite pink.

'She thought she ought to have something to do,' Sophia explained. 'And now that the war is over there doesn't seem to be very much.'

Mother glanced at her watch. 'Sophia, it's after half-past seven.'

Sophia looked guilty and scuttled out of the room.

'She will insist upon doing everything herself,' mother complained. 'I offer to help, but she will never let me. Of course, I do the washing-up.'

'Well, that's *something*,' I said.

Sophia called to say that dinner was ready.

Dinner was served not in the dining room, but in the kitchen. Here was another thing I had not expected. It was not a very peaceful meal. As soon as we had finished the soup (bovril and hot water), mother jumped up and began to wash the plates. She called my attention to the excellent qualities of the water-softener. It stood on the draining board, looking alien to this domestic scene. With its shining chromium and its rubber tubes, it should surely have formed part of the equipment of a hospital laboratory. The bovril was followed by a fairly elaborate mixed grill; and the plates and knives and forks which had been used for this had to be washed before we were allowed to go on to the sweet. The same performance happened over the coffee. Mother called it 'clearing as you go,' and it had its advantages, but it wasn't peaceful.

'The painters have left.' Mother announced it with some regret as soon as we were back in the drawing room.

'They'd both been in the Navy, you know, and they used to make our tea for us when they arrived in the mornings.'

The painters had left. Now was my moment to be firm. I stood up. It is easier to be firm standing up. At least I hoped it was going to be.

'But you won't be able to move in yet,' mother was saying. 'There is still the electrician.'

'You ought to have had him *first*,' I said, proud that I should know even this much about house decorating.

'I know that perfectly well,' and mother jabbed at her hairpins. 'But as he isn't exactly official we had to have him in his own time and he couldn't come before, because he was in the hospital. As it is he usually works in the evenings, and he keeps all his wires and things in your bedroom. I'm afraid he'll be here for some time, as the whole installation has to be renewed. He says we might catch on fire at any moment,' and mother looked round the room to make sure that no fire had started.

'He has promised to be out by the fifteenth of November.' I imagined that Sophia looked at me threateningly.

That would be nearly another month. I wavered in my intention of firmness. Anything might happen in a month. Other workmen might come to my rescue. Why had there as yet been no talk of a plumber?

'I have had your bedroom painted blue,' mother said. 'Don't you want to go and look at it?'

I went to look at my bedroom. I determined that I would write mother a letter. Not at once perhaps, but in a week or two. It was better to have these things in writing. 'Dearest Mother,

All things considered I think it would be better if I did not come to live with you. I really think you'd be happier without me and I'd only make more washing-up and more work for Sophia . . . .' It didn't sound very good; but perhaps if I thought hard for a week I should be able to find something better. Perhaps I could get Gerald to help me. He was, after all, a writer.

The following morning I went to the office. Nothing had changed very much. Miss Napier-Smith had got the applicants' file out of order. There had been a scandal at one of the smaller canteens. It had to do with stealing money out of the till, which made a change from the eternal sex scandals.

Lady Merton was in good form, rather boisterous. It was one of her back-slapping days. She snubbed Miss Napier-Smith twice between half-past eleven and twelve o'clock. Miss Napier-Smith retired to the lavatory in tears. Lady Merton took no notice of her, and asked me how that brother of mine was getting on with the lady M.O.

'He's taking it all very seriously.'

'Settling down, what?'

I said that I supposed he must be.

'Well, it will be interesting to see how long it lasts,' and Lady Merton crossed her legs, lit a cigarette and applied herself to the petrol returns which called for all her concentration. Later on I would have to type them out and check her additions.

After luncheon Gerald rang up.

'Did you have a nice time in Devonshire at all? I've only got fifteen thousand more words to go.'

'Then you've nearly finished?'

Gerald said that he wouldn't say that exactly. 'The end is always very tricky and I've run out of plot.'

'Oh, dear!'

'Are you doing anything this evening, because I'd like to read you the last few chapters? Where had I got to when you went away?'

I panicked. I couldn't remember. 'The governess was being thrown off the liner?'

'That was right at the beginning.' Gerald was offended.

'Of course, how stupid of me. The detective had just arrived at the girls' school.'

'Yes, I think that's right. I had a very nice time with it, the head-mistress came off beautifully.'

'I am glad.'

'How about meeting around seven o'clock, then we could have something to eat, and afterwards we could come back here and I'll read to you.'

A whole evening with Gerald. It was delightful.

He gave me complicated directions for finding his latest dis-covery in eating houses. 'Bacon and tomatoes and very often they have eggs as well, and if you want a drink there's a pub opposite.'

It wasn't exactly a lavish invitation. Gerald must be short of money again.

Now that I had something to look forward to, the rest of the afternoon passed very happily. Lady Merton went out and I lis-tened while Miss Napier-Smith gave me a full account of their tour in Germany and of how sweet Lady Merton had been to her. I had had it all before, but that didn't matter.

Gerald's eating house turned out to be one of those places with a marble counter and a tea-urn. It smelt of very old frying fat. We sat at a table in the corner and it was relatively pleasant until we were joined by a woman with a loud sniff and a carpet bag. She ordered a cup of tea and asked us to pass her the salt. I began to be afraid that she was not quite right in the head; or else that she was liable to fits. How awful it would be if she were to have one now before we had finished our bacon and toma-toes. Gerald seemed to be happily oblivious of her. He went on talking about his book and asking my advice about girls' schools.

'I've done a certain amount of research at the British Museum among the Angela Brazils; but I can't be sure they're authentic.'

As I had never been to school at all, I couldn't in any case have been very helpful. The presence of the mad woman had made it impossible for me to concentrate and I found that I was answering Gerald's questions completely at random. After a while he noticed this and called to the waitress to bring us the date pudding and the stewed whatever it was. Gerald's answer to any *malaise*, whether physical or mental, was more food. It didn't matter what it was if only there was enough. At last he had finished. When we got outside it was raining. We walked the length of the street and then stood in a doorway waiting for the bus which would take us within distant walking distance of Gerald's flat.

Gerald's flat was a new acquisition. All the summer he had lived in a furnished bed-sitting room in Paddington. Suddenly he had said that he could no longer afford it and had moved into a flat in Pimlico.

'It's rather large,' Gerald had explained. 'That's why it's so cheap.'

The flat was in a basement and was approached in the first instance by area steps. Gerald had some difficulty in opening what must have originally been the back-door of the house. Once inside he switched on the light. The flat abounded in wide passages and very tiny butlers' pantries. There didn't seem exactly to be any rooms.

'But there is one,' Gerald said, and opened a door into wet darkness. 'We just have to go across this courtyard. Some people might call it a backyard. Mind where you walk, there's a lot of rubble about.' Gerald plunged ahead and I was left to follow him. The room on the other side of the backyard was rather nice. Anyhow, it was quite clean. In one corner was a narrow bed. Not a divan, but a bed.

'I brought that from home,' Gerald said. 'It used to travel round my bed-sitting rooms with me.'

'What a good idea.'

'Won't you sit down?' Gerald made a hospitable movement in the direction of a sofa and two armchairs which were drawn up in an open square in front of the fireplace. I sat down on the sofa. It was covered in brown leatherette.

'Government surplus,' Gerald said. 'Practically unused and very cheap.' He switched on a minute electric fire which stood in the grate.

There were two deal tables in the room. One which stood under the window was in use as a desk. It was piled with manuscripts and papers and there was a typewriter, minus its cover. Lady Merton wouldn't have approved of that, putting the cover back on the typewriter was one of her fetishes.

'Let's see now.' Gerald picked up a folder which was neatly labelled, 'Beautiful Murder, Part Two.' Here Lady Merton would have approved. She was fond of labels.

Gerald settled himself in one of the armchairs (buttoned red leather and mahogany feet); one had seen its prototype in billiard rooms when one had played those awful games at children's parties.

'An offering from my mother.' Gerald lit a cigarette.

'Why don't you try the other one, they're so much more comfortable than the government surplus.'

It didn't bother me any more being read to by Gerald. At first I had found it a tremendous strain. I had sat, not daring to breathe, an agonised appreciative smile spread over my face. When any of the characters had said anything remotely funny, I had forced myself to laugh aloud. If at any point Gerald had paused and asked my advice I was in a turmoil of indecision. The responsibility was too great. It was as bad as being asked to decide whether England should go to war or not. Worse, in a way, because I hadn't been asked about the war and I was being about Gerald's book. Supposing I was to say something and it wasn't quite right and it got printed? But now, after nearly six months, I was used to being consulted. I had realised that for Gerald it was merely another form of thinking aloud. Also, the printed word, now that I actually knew two authors fairly well, had somehow become a little less sacred.

Lawrence had never, of course, read me the manuscript of *his* book. He didn't consider me sufficiently intelligent even to be thought aloud at, and anyhow he had Stephanie. Also, he was usually stuck, so there probably wasn't very much to read anyway. I thought this viciously for I much resented his superior attitude to Gerald.

Gerald read on and on. His detective and his school-teachers were becoming hopelessly entangled. The murderer was in hiding in the laboratory; but one moment, was that the murderer, or merely one of the suspects?

In the distance I could hear a bell ringing insistently. Probably it had something to do with the people who lived on the floors above. It went on and on. It was followed by a considerable banging. Gerald laid down his manuscript and listened.

'What on earth's that?'

'I don't know.'

The banging started again.

'Oh, hell!' Gerald got out of his chair. 'It sounds as if it's someone trying to get in here. Why on earth can't people leave one alone at this hour of night?'

I looked at the alarm clock on the mantelpiece. It was ten o'clock.

Gerald went to the door. He didn't completely shut it after him and I could hear his footsteps as he crossed the yard. He reached the other part of the house and I could hear nothing further.

The alarm clock ticked loudly. It was painted a bright Cambridge blue. The room, with its stone floor, only partly covered with matting, began to seem depressing.

I waited. I realised that I was very cold. The tiny electric fire was no more than a token. I waited for what seemed a very long time. Then I heard Gerald coming back across the yard. He was not alone. There was another set of footsteps and Gerald was saying to be careful as there was a lot of rubble about. The door was pushed open. With something very like dismay I saw that the visitor was Henry.

Henry came in laughing. 'I've run away from Pamela.'

'Don't be silly.'

From under his arm he produced a bottle of whisky and a bottle of sherry. 'I say, it's absolutely icy in here, why don't you have a fire?'

'Trouble with filling in a form,' Gerald said. 'So I haven't been allowed any coal.'

Henry looked round the room. 'I say, it's a bit austere, isn't it? Still, nice to be living by yourself. How about getting some glasses, or shall we all go out somewhere?'

Gerald went to a cupboard which hung on the wall and got out cut-glass tumblers, possibly another offering from his mother, and a mug.

'Will you be wanting some water?'

'Might as well,' Henry said.

Gerald went out into the night. The water supply was evidently attached to the front of the house. There must be a bathroom there, too. Gerald would never have taken a flat which didn't have a bathroom.

'Henry, what are you doing here?'

'I've told you,' Henry said. 'I've run away from Pamela. I just suddenly couldn't stand it any longer. It was having all those patients arriving; it unsettled me.'

'How many have you got now?'

'Three,' Henry said, 'and it's too many.'

'How did you know I was here?'

Henry shrugged his shoulders and opened his hands. The gesture indicated that wherever Gerald was, there I was to be found. It was annoying.

Later, I discovered that Henry had had no idea of finding me at Gerald's. He had merely gone straight from the station to his club, been disappointed that none of his friends were there, ordered a taxi and started on a tour of his acquaintances until he should find one of them who was in. Gerald had been about fourth or fifth on the list.

'Those blasted babies,' Henry said. 'They don't seem able to stop being born, and Matron being so sprightly at meals. Well, here's to them.' And he drained nearly half a tumblerful of neat whisky.

'Most disagreeable for you,' Gerald said soothingly.

'It wasn't what I meant when I suggested having a nursing home,' Henry complained. 'All those blasted women, most undignified.'

'You seemed quite happy about it two days ago,' I said.

'How do *you* know I was happy?' Henry scowled. 'Anyhow I've left them flat, I've suffered enough.'

'Had you thought what you're going to do next?'

Henry poured himself out another drink. 'They've made it frightfully inconvenient for me. There isn't any room at the club. Then in the taxi I had the idea I might stay with you.' He turned to Gerald. 'But I don't know now'—and he looked rather bleakly round the bare room.

This was *too* much. Gerald was *my* friend. There was no reason why he should be inconvenienced by Henry.

'You can go to an hotel,' I said.

'Try,' Henry said. 'Just try, that's all.'

'Very well, I will. Where's the telephone?' I asked Gerald.

'Unfortunately there isn't one.'

'We can go to Victoria,' I said to Henry. 'Or to mother's flat. If it comes to that you could sleep among the wires in the spare bedroom, they're not connected to anything so it would be quite safe.'

'It sounds delightful,' Henry said. He was not taking any responsibility for his own disposal.

Eventually I went out and made arrangements with a private hotel a few doors from Gerald's house. It didn't look somehow as if it would be terribly comfortable, but Henry had so often said he didn't mind what sort of a place he slept in that I hoped that perhaps it wouldn't matter. The night-porter who was also the receptionist wasn't particularly respectful. Perhaps he didn't believe that I really wanted the room for my brother. I promised that Henry would be along quite shortly. The night-porter winked and said that he simply couldn't wait to see him.

Back at the flat I found Henry sitting on the sofa advising Gerald against marriage. I told him about the hotel and he seemed quite pleased, but not wildly interested.

After nearly another hour I said that I must go. I had provided a room for Henry. If Gerald let him stay now it was his own fault. But Henry, still surprisingly sober, said that he must leave also. We said goodbye to Gerald, who came with us as far as the bottom of the area steps. When we were in the street, I showed Henry the outside of his hotel.

He said that it looked splendid, and I immediately felt mean. He said he would walk with me as far as the Buckingham Palace Road and try to find me a taxi.

I had made a resolution when I came back from my holidays that I would *never* take a taxi again. I couldn't afford them and it was silly, but tonight was an exception.

Henry put his arm through mine. 'Beautiful night.'

'It's stopped raining, anyhow.'

'So it has.' Henry seemed surprised. 'It's Cheltenham tomorrow.'

'I couldn't get the time off.'

'Oh, hell!' Henry kicked a non-existent stone out of his way. 'Well, don't come if you don't want to; but I think I shall go anyhow and there'll probably be a through train to Exeter after the meeting.'

'To Exeter!'

'Why not? It's all on the Great Western, or as near as makes no difference, and if I was too late to get a cab, George could meet me in the van.'

'But I thought you'd run away from Pamela for ever?'

'Oh, don't be *silly*,' Henry said. 'How could I possibly do that when she's living in my house, and all my capital's sunk in the bloody nursing home. Do you think that taxi's free?'

It was. Henry yelled at it and it stopped.

'Besides,' he went on, as he handed me into it, 'I'm really very fond of her.'

EIGHT

'THERE IS something horrid,' Henry had said in one of his more enlightened moments, 'about things which do not catch the dust.'

It was a reaction against austerity and woven string. A rococo palace would catch the dust tremendously; perhaps that was why one felt it was exactly what one wanted.

Mrs Isaacs might have been designed especially for dust-catching. There was a great deal of her and she had added more in the way of ostrich-feathered hats and pearl necklaces. She was not composed of smooth planes, her contours were complicated in the manner of a Grinling Gibbons carving.

I found her at Trelynt when I went there for Christmas. Her position in the establishment was a little obscure. She had arrived there as a convalescent, but she seemed now to be perfectly well. She had known Pamela in what she described as 'the old days in Birmingham.' She sat in the drawing room and her presence made the woven string look simply silly. She went for long walks wearing her pearls and her feathered hats. Matron drew away from her; but then Matron could not be expected to appreciate the East. Not that Mrs Isaacs was *very* Eastern. One, in fact, imagined her family as having originally been resident even a little to the left of Suez; but she was too Eastern for Matron. I could imagine Matron travelling to the East with her eyes tight shut, only opening them when she came to Australia, where thankfully she would compare Melbourne, perhaps even favourably, with Beckenham.

'If we go on like this, the place will be nothing more than a hotel.' That was Matron's refrain, which rose to a crescendo every morning when Mrs Isaacs's breakfast had to be carried upstairs to her by Nurse Brawn.

An hotel was anathema to Matron. She gave everyone to understand on every possible occasion that she would never have anything to do with one. She wanted Pamela to give Mrs Isaacs notice. That was all very well for Matron, who didn't have to try to make Trelynt 'pay.'

During the first two months things had gone extremely well. Immediately following Mrs Green, 'our first mother,' there had been a baronet's wife, and then a rather dubious case of premature twins who both died, which was annoying for Matron, who had wanted to be able to boast that she had never lost a patient.

After the twins, expectant mothers had begun to come in fairly regularly, and soon all the beds and most of the cradles were full. Matron and Pamela and Nurse Brawn were kept extremely busy. The elderly night nurse, Mrs Onslow, complained that she was kept *too* busy. Mrs Corwell didn't know where to turn. Two V.A.D.s came up from the village every day to help. George swept the passages by his own method of leaning on the broom.

But at Christmas, as it happened, there was rather a lull in mothers and babies. Only one Noel and a very belated Ivy came into the world over the holidays.

Pamela was harassed and spent more time than was necessary going over the books. The week before, a chartered accountant had come out from Exeter. He had proved to her that Trelynt was not, so far, a paying proposition. Pamela found that very worrying. Henry, it seemed, didn't care. He had only said, 'Oh, good, we can get it off the income tax,' which he apparently regarded as a source of revenue.

If it hadn't been for Mrs Isaacs, Christmas would have been rather drab. George was in a bad temper. He considered that he should have been given time off to go and visit his aunt at Brighton. He revenged himself on the household generally by doing no work at all. Half the time he didn't even bother to lean on his broom. He exchanged ribald comments with the V.A.D.s. I think that the real trouble was that he was disappointed in Henry and with the form which the nursing-home had taken. He regretted the inebriates who had never materialized. Once I heard him tell Nurse Brawn that anyhow he wasn't married to *this* job. Nurse Brawn, who was in a hurry, clicked her tongue, said that it was all in a lifetime and continued her pursuit of some errant mackintosh sheets.

The house was sparsely decorated with holly, which had failed to form any berries. One could only suppose that the branches had been especially selected by the gardener, who was a friend of George.

Miss Maitland and her fellow trainee produced a kind of plum duff which went under the name of Christmas pudding. One was glad for the patients, when their husbands arrived bringing iced cakes and tangerines. One husband brought a bottle of near-champagne in which he and his wife toasted their fairly new-born and quite horrible-looking baby. Matron did her best to discourage any enthusiasm they might be feeling by telling them that champagne was 'bad for the milk'; but then it seemed that anything which hadn't passed through the de-vitalising atmosphere of Miss Maitland's kitchen was 'bad for the milk.'

After supper on Christmas Eve, Matron suddenly suggested that we should get up a charade and act it for the patients. There were only five of them, two in mother's bedroom and three in private wards. It seemed that in all Matron's other hospitals it had been the custom to torture patients in this way at Christmas. As if it wasn't bad enough for them to see the nurses in their ordinary clothes, let alone tricked out as Little Red Riding Hood or Fairy Clutterbuck.

'I should think it would do very well if you and Nurse Brawn were to sing duets to them,' Henry said.

Matron looked doubtful and remarked that there was no ward piano.

Henry said what were the V.A.D.s for, anyhow, and Matron was offended.

'Do you sing?' Mrs Isaacs asked Matron. It was the first direct remark that I had heard either of them address to the other since my arrival the previous evening.

Matron admitted that she had sung in her time, but only for a lark. 'Not *like* a lark,' she added after a pause and giggled, for she had made a joke.

Pamela smiled politely, for lately she had been afraid that Matron might be going to decide to leave.

'This is absolutely frightful,' Henry said, not very politely. 'We ought to have had a party.' And he glared at Pamela who pretended not to have heard.

I had gathered earlier that they had quarrelled over whom they should invite and had consequently invited no one.

'*My* friends wouldn't have minded hospital beds and I should think that *yours* would be used to them.'

Henry was determined that Pamela should listen.

Matron said that rationing made everything very difficult, and Henry left the room.

Certainly Christmas without Mrs Isaacs would have been drab; but Mrs Isaacs appeared as a warm tower of strength. On Christmas Day she produced presents for all of us and six bottles of very good champagne.

She silenced any attempts at thanking her by saying that it was years since she had been so comfortable. Alone with me she confided that what she liked about Trelynt was its 'hominess.'

'I've lived in hotels a lot and I've learned to hate them. Nursing homes aren't so good as a rule either, too many rules and regulations,' and Mrs Isaacs laughed, giving one to understand that in the absence of rules and regulations she could be a perfect devil.

'Rest,' she said. 'Perfectly all right, so long as I have rest and complete absence from worry.'

It sounded an almost ideal prescription. I began to feel envious of Mrs Isaacs.

'I had a terrible war,' she went on. 'Sometimes I think it'll take me years to get over it.'

I imagined Mrs Isaacs as having spent the war in the lounge of a Bournemouth hotel. It came as a shock when she mentioned quite casually that she had worked with the French Intelligence Service and been a prisoner of war in Germany.

'Does Matron know that?'

Mrs Isaacs said that she hoped *not*. 'I don't mind Pamela. She's a doctor and I've known her for years anyhow; but I don't want a lot of chat from a hospital nurse. They're always too nosey anyhow; either that or they don't take any interest in you at all. I don't know which is the worst. The fact is'—and Mrs Isaacs paused as if to give the matter full thought—'I don't *like* trained nurses.'

'I expect you've seen too many of them.'

'Far too many. In theory they may be ministering angels and all that, but, in real life'—and Mrs Isaacs shivered and added the word—'sadists. And most nursing homes are nothing but second-rate boarding houses with a slaughter department on the top floor. It's different here, of course; here it's beautifully homey.'

'It wasn't when we really lived here,' I said.

Mrs Isaacs laughed and said, oh, well, she could imagine that. She said that Henry was a bit of a lad, wasn't he?

I didn't make any particular answer. I wasn't going to be drawn about Henry.

'Pamela's making a mistake in trying to keep him on such a tight rein, though.'

I remained silent. I wasn't going to discuss either Pamela *or* Henry. I wondered what Mrs Isaacs knew about tight reins; but I had been so wrong about her up till now that I was quite prepared to hear that she had worked for years in a re-mount stables or had been a lady jockey.

'Her mother made exactly the same mistake.'

Mrs Isaacs was seemingly oblivious of my disapproval and lack of co-operation.

'She led poor old George Merritt a hell of a life until she finally decided to hop it.' This was casting a doubt upon the respectability of provincial town councillors. I was disturbed. Was nothing the way one had supposed it? I was glad when Pamela came into the room and interrupted our *tête-à-tête*.

On Boxing Day Mrs Isaacs took us to the pantomime.

Without her I don't think we should have had the initiative to have gone. You had to engage seats, for one thing, and you had to make arrangements to get there.

When we arrived the orchestra was already playing a selection of fairly contemporary tunes. We sat in the front row. Me and Mrs Isaacs, Henry and Pamela and Nurse Brawn. At the last moment Matron had been prevented, by professional reasons, from coming. Her place was taken by George, who was still inclined to be sulky. He drew loud attention to the fact that the Torness theatre compared unfavourably with the theatres at Brighton.

'Unhealthy!' George said. 'There's nothing like all this red velveteen for collecting germs.'

Henry told him to shut up because really he was as boring as Matron.

Nurse Brawn giggled disloyally and we settled down to read our threepenny programmes.

Mrs Isaacs said she had a surprise for us. The principal boy was a friend of hers and we would all go round and see her after the show.

Nurse Brawn said, 'Ooh, why didn't you tell us and I wouldn't have worn my mac.'

This was nonsense. Nurse Brawn never went even so far as the village without her mackintosh.

'You can take it off, surely?' George said kindly.

Nurse Brawn still looked unhappy and George said he would carry it for her.

The curtain went up. The young ladies of the chorus were discovered walking about the stage and remarking, more or less in unison, that they were going hunting with the prince. In front of them about twelve little girls with flea-bitten legs were jumping up and down in time to the music. They wore red sateen coats and white ballet skirts, so obviously they were going hunting, too. The Post Horn Gallop came to an abrupt end. There was a pause. One of the young ladies stepped forward and said, 'But here he comes,' in a refined and audible voice. Everyone on the stage turned half-right. The little girls took this opportunity to scratch their legs. There was a fanfare of trumpets (or perhaps of only one trumpet), and after another pause Mrs Isaacs friend, resplendent in tights and a brocaded coat and surrounded by members of her court, stepped out of the wings. She was greeted by a cheer.

('You must give him a cheer, The Prince himself is here.')

The prince was splendid, a good old-fashioned type with a large bust and large thighs. There was no nonsense about her, no kill-joy refinement. She stepped towards the footlights and as she did so she winked at the gallery.

'Bit awkwardly shaped, isn't she?' I heard George whisper to Nurse Brawn. But his expression belied the words. He was obviously very well satisfied with the prince.

The audience as a whole was very well satisfied. We settled back in our seats, prepared for hours of uncritical enjoyment. *Cinderella*, that only possible pantomime, had begun and could be relied upon to stick slavishly to tradition until the curtain came down on the transformation scene.

I sat between Henry and Nurse Brawn and I remembered the first time I had been in the Torness theatre. We had driven over from Trelynt: a family party with the governess in attendance. The play had been *Cinderella* and we had had a box, for mother, like George, had believed in the germs which lurked in the red-velveteen stalls. There was quite a lot of velveteen about the box, too; but, as soon as we arrived, the governess was instructed to spray it with the flit gun, which we had brought with us for the purpose.

I remembered Henry, a sulky boy of sixteen. He had not wanted to come with us; he had said many times that he had not wanted to come, but father had insisted that he should.

'All this palaver,' Henry had said crossly. 'If I've got to see the blasted pantomime, I'd sooner take the kitchen maid and go in the pit.' Inevitably father had been angry. Mother had merely pointed out, quite mildly, that we hadn't got a kitchenmaid.

At the time, a boring child of eight, I had not much concerned myself with their wrangling. This was my first pantomime and I was almost sick with excitement.

* * * * *

Now, glancing sideways at Henry, I saw that his face wore the same sulky expression that it had done all those years ago. He had not wanted to come with us; but Mrs Isaacs, or more likely Pamela, had insisted.

I turned my attention back to the stage. Buttons and the Ugly Sisters in the Baron's kitchen. Soon they would sing a song and the audience would be invited to join in; or was it too soon for that?

Back over the years to that other pantomime. I would have worn white socks and bronze dancing slippers and a blue silk dress which I had hated.

I had been aware of very little that went on outside myself. Henry's discontent and the frustration that had settled upon Sophia.

I had recorded sights and sounds, but I had made little sense of them. I had undergone experiences but they hadn't done anything for me. Henry was sulky; but it had never occurred to me to wonder why, and now I realised that I was not thinking of myself as I had been at eight years old but as I was now at twenty-seven.

It was an appalling revelation. I had played for all these years at being a child. 'The innocence of a child.' 'The idiocy of a child.' I heard Lawrence's voice: 'The only thing I cannot forgive is unawareness.'

I had been unforgivable. I had been unforgivable for twenty-seven years.

I drew a long breath and again I glanced at Henry. I had no interest for what was happening on the stage. I was prepared to look at Henry with understanding and sympathy. The veils had been lifted from my eyes. Pamela had told Lawrence that he was one of the few truly adult people she had known. Well, so was I now, very adult indeed and very aware of other people's moods and of the reasons behind them. I glanced at Henry. It was something of a shock when I saw that he was laughing, quite loudly, as if he had not a care in the world.

* * * * *

Mrs Isaacs spent the interval in sending notes round to her friend whose name was Gloria. This was more difficult than it sounds, for the Theatre Royal, Torness, is not constructed for the passing of notes between audience and players.

Henry and George went off to the bar. Nurse Brawn tried to explain to me which of the tiny flea-bitten tots she had liked best. Pamela regretted aloud that Matron had had to miss this treat. Nurse Brawn nudged me in the ribs and whispered that it was a jolly good thing; she wouldn't have felt a bit free if Matron had been there listening to everything that was said.

'Don't you like Matron?'

Nurse Brawn said, ooh, yes, she liked her all right, but it didn't seem natural somehow being friendly with someone in a blue dress. I imagine that that is the point of view which tends to narrow hospital life.

Mrs Isaacs was talking to Pamela. There was a bright gleam in Mrs Isaacs's eye, a high colour in her cheek. They might be due to excitement or the heat of the theatre. They might mean that Mrs Isaacs was 'up to no good.' Why should Mrs Isaacs be 'up to no good'? It was all very well to be adult and to understand other people's moods. It was another thing altogether to invent the moods for them. I was reminded of over-understanding women whom I had met in the past. They were a menace; there was something vaguely obscene about them.

All the same, I found myself watching Mrs Isaacs carefully. She wasn't trustworthy. Anybody could see that; I hoped that Pamela could.

Mrs Isaacs had known Pamela's father and mother. In the end the much-tried George Merritt had hopped it. But where to, and with whom? I hadn't allowed Mrs Isaacs to tell me.

Pamela hardly ever spoke of her childhood, but why should she? One's childhood is the least interesting time of one's life. She spoke sometimes of her training at St Gregory's Medical School. Later she had been an interne at St Gregory's. Then she had come to London and held appointments in various clinics and been assistant to that doctor in Fulham. There had been the unsatisfactory affair with the Hungarian.

I wondered what it would have been like to have been brought up in a provincial city. It might have been cosy. You would have next-door neighbours, like the people who wrote letters to the *Daily Mirror*. 'My neighbour says . . .' At Trelynt we had no neighbours. There had been us and there had been the village.

Pamela was in love with Henry. When he came into a room her whole face changed. When he snubbed her she was bitterly hurt. But she tried to possess him. I thought of her as one of those over-understanding women. They tried to possess one, even for the space of a conversation.

Henry had wanted to live for a few years at Trelynt on the money he had won at Newmarket. Pamela had objected, so Henry had said that he would turn it into a market garden or a reform home for drunkards. Pamela had seemed to agree, but now Trelynt was a Maternity Home. Pamela had got her own way, but she had not got what she wanted.

The orchestra was striking up for the second half of the pantomime. People were coming back to their seats. George arrived and plonked himself down next to Nurse Brawn. There was no sign of Henry. As the lights dimmed, I saw that Pamela was looking worried. When the curtain rose and our faces were illuminated by the bright lights from the stage I looked at her again. She was wearing a set smile of anticipated enjoyment.

Pamela would never admit that there was anything wrong. The show must go grimly on whether the actors forgot their lines or the audience booed or went away.

'Until,' as Pamela would have said, 'her life lay around her in fragments,' she would continue to smile and pretend that all was as it should be.

But I was making histories again. Henry had probably only gone to the lavatory. He would be with us in a moment.

But it was a long time before Henry rejoined us. Cinderella had been to the ball and come back again. The Ugly Sisters had done their washing. There had been at least two of those duets between the Fairy Queen and the Demon King. I remembered the year when I had utterly lost my head and booed the Fairy Queen, and the lecture about kindness which I had received from mother as a result. The Fairy Queen was a hard-working elderly woman and was entitled to my consideration and respect. Ever since then I have endured Fairy Queens in silence, but I have never cared for them.

Henry whispered that it was quite gay round at the back.

'Dandini's a poppet when she's not actually on the stage.'

'But how did you get there?'

'I found a friend in the bar,' Henry said. 'You see that chorus girl right at the back? Well, she thinks she's going to have a baby. I've been trying to get her to come and have it at Trelynt.'

'What did she say?'

'She hasn't said anything yet. I've been doing it all through Dandini. She's going to ask her about it before the end of the show.'

Pamela leant over to hear what we were talking about. Henry started to tell her about the chorus girl. The people in the row behind were telling him to hush.

We reached the transformation scene. It is here that provincial pantomime is at its most provincial. The transformation scene is never grand enough. The tawdriness of most of the costumes is painfully apparent. The smallness of the company can no longer be concealed. It is made smaller by the non-appearance of the twelve dancing tots, who have been withdrawn from the stage in compliance with a by-law which occupies itself with the conditions of employment of young workers. (On the whole it is better in the provinces to leave before the transformation scene; but generally one doesn't.)

The curtain remained up during the playing of the National Anthem which we all sang together. We were quite used to singing together by now and the National Anthem went exceptionally well. Cinderella stepped forward and thanked us for being such a wonderful audience. We clapped enthusiastically. Prince Charming stepped forward and thanked us for the wonderful reception we had given them.

All this was very pleasant. There was no reason why we shouldn't have kept it up for ages. Them thanking us and us clapping. But the curtain went down and didn't go up again.

It seemed a pity. Now there was nothing to do but shuffle into our coats and mackintoshes and search for the umbrellas and parcels which, being a provincial audience, we had brought with us in great profusion and put under our seats.

Better wait a little while,' Mrs Isaacs said, and we stood in a huddle watching the rest of the audience file out of the theatre.

Fussily Nurse Brawn powdered her nose. Henry stood with his hands in his pockets. He was smiling, he was no longer sulky. Mrs Isaacs was smiling, too. The smug, self-satisfied smile of someone who is about to provide a treat. George stood a little apart, Nurse Brown's mackintosh draped over his arm. His expression was the exact corollary of Mrs Isaacs's, a vacant though grateful grin. When he was a little boy, George had been taken for school outings by charitable ladies. He was behaving as he had been taught to behave.

Mrs Isaacs moved towards the pass door.

'Don't let's go.'

Suddenly Pamela held back.

Mrs Isaacs moved on, taking no notice of her.

'We shall be late,' Pamela said. 'Matron is all alone.'

'All by herself in the moonlight,' George hummed. He was behaving like the child who would later be given an orange and a bag of sweets.

Pamela stood quite still. It was impossible for Mrs Isaacs any longer to ignore her.

'Don't be silly,' she said, 'Gloria is expecting us.'

'Yes, don't be silly,' Henry said, and we moved on and I through the pass door.

Backstage at the Theatre Royal had the glamour of back-stages everywhere. At least, I think so; but I have not seen very many.

To reach the dressing rooms we had to cross the stage. We passed stage hands in their shirt-sleeves. We were confused by the semi-darkness. The stage, which in reality is fairly small, seemed immense. There were shouts which came from high above our heads, there were answering shouts which seemed to come from nowhere at all. We were in a passage and it smelt of beer.

Pantomime, we are taught, is tradition. Behind every Prince Charming there stand a thousand Prince Charmings, with their large bosoms and their cotton tights. Some of them wear stays which give them minute waists; but they are all traditional, all dressed in a gayer version of Hamlet's doublet and hose. Sometimes, we may even confuse Hamlet with Prince Charming. In one respect Prince Charming has the advantage of Hamlet; no one was ever tempted to play it in modern dress.

We arrived at the door of a dressing room. From within there was the confused noise of many people talking at once. The smell of beer was very powerful. Mrs Isaacs knocked on the door and it was opened to us by an old crone. The smell of beer was overwhelming.

Mrs Isaacs pushed her way through the crowd. It wasn't really such a very large crowd, but the dressing room was tiny.

'Darling!' Mrs Isaacs was advancing towards the dressing table with arms outstretched.

'Lily!' A figure had risen up to meet Mrs Isaacs. The figure was arrayed in a peacock blue kimono. Its golden hair, swept up with combs, glinted metallically under the naked electric light bulbs. Mrs Isaacs and Prince Charming were clasped in each other's arms.

Prince Charming's performance had been wonderful, superb.

Prince Charming could hardly express the delight she felt at being united with her dearest Lily and, looking towards us, with dearest Lily's friends.

Mrs Isaacs and Prince Charming came out of their clinch and we were introduced. To Prince Charming, to Dandini and to the Demon King. Everyone was delighted with everyone else. We were given warm beer in murky tumblers.

Nurse Brawn anxiously repowdered her nose. Henry and Dandini greeted each other as old friends, and retired to a corner; perhaps they were discussing the chorus girl who thought that she was going to have a baby.

George wished everyone good luck and drank his beer with an expression of repugnance.

The old crone muttered to herself. She was the dresser who had been officially attached to the theatre for the last thirty years. She had been there creeping about behind the scenes when we had come to the Theatre Royal as a family party and sat in our disinfected box. In her own way she was as traditional as Hamlet, though not as nice.

Pamela and Prince Charming (Gloria), and Mrs Isaacs were talking together. They formed a group round the dressing table. Pamela was looking unhappy and ill at ease. I wished that one could have told her not to stand like that. Not to hold her bag tucked under her arm as if she was afraid it would be stolen. Then I remembered the terrible gaiety that she had displayed at Stephanie's party and decided that after all perhaps it was better that she should be like this. Shy and a little taciturn and unbending.

Again my attention was caught by the bright gleam in Mrs Isaacs's eye, by her over-animated manner, and I was sure that she was 'up to no good.'

Prince Charming was removing the make-up from her face and neck with lazy disinterested movements. Probably she would not succeed in removing quite all the grease paint, and there would be a tide mark which in the morning would be grey and there would be traces of grease paint on her pillow.

'Of course,' the Demon King was saying, 'King Rat is really my *favourite* part.'

King Rat! That must be a character in some other pantomime. One that I had not yet seen. I smiled politely and looked round for George to help me sustain a conversation in which soon I would be out of my depth.

The door of the dressing room was continually opening and shutting. It seemed that Gloria was very popular. Everyone had to come and wish her good luck and tell her that she had been wonderful. One of the Ugly Sisters was a tiny little woman with the skin drawn tightly over her nose and cheek-bones. That was the sort of face to have if you were going to get old. Large faces are inclined to flop, to fall into folds and loops. On the stage the little woman had worn ringed stockings and men's boots, and had been extremely funny. One had wondered why she was not in a better pantomime somewhere else.

The door opened again and a young, or fairly young, woman came into the room. She was dressed in black. Her hair shone with the same metallic precision as Prince Charming's. At first, I did not recognise her; but there was something mincing about her which was drearily reminiscent.

Of course. Cinderella.

She stood in the doorway watching us and the effect was malevolent. In a moment she would speak and we would hear the flat-sounding Midland vowels which had been noticeable when she sang.

'Darling, you were wonderful.' Mrs Isaacs stood with arms outstretched.

Cinderella hesitated a moment. Her response was not as immediate as Prince Charming's.

'Lily!' Cinderella and Mrs Isaacs were in each other's arms. They broke away almost at once.

Mrs Isaacs started on introductions, but Cinderella took no notice. She and Pamela were staring at each other. The long unbelieving stare of old friends, or old enemies, who have not met for many years.

'It is.'

'The Church High School.'

'You were Rose Denton.'

'Pretty name, "Rose,"' George said conversationally. 'Wonder she didn't keep it for her stage name.' And he began searching his pockets for the programme. *Cinderella— Rosalind Winstanley.*

'Hell of a long time ago,' Cinderella said lightly. She didn't intend that anyone should take that seriously.

Pamela smiled, an uncertain, an almost miserable smile.

'You were very good.'

Cinderella simpered. 'But you didn't recognise me?'

I thought, I wasn't sure.' Pamela floundered on. I was reminded of someone walking up a steep hill in their gum-boots.

'You always had a lovely voice.'

Rose Denton shrugged her shoulders. She knew that she had a lovely voice. A pity that it wasn't quite lovely enough to get her a lead in a London pantomime.

The talk started again.

Henry beckoned to Pamela. 'My wife will know all about that,' I heard him say to Dandini. So all this time they had been discussing the chorus girl.

George had found his programme, and now Nurse Brawn was looking for hers. She had struck on the original idea of getting all these people to sign it. Then it would be a memento. She could stick it in her photograph album, or she could keep it at the back of her handkerchief drawer, where it would become more and more crumpled, and eventually it would be lost.

I had managed to finish my beer. Spitefully, as I thought, the Demon King refilled my glass. He took no notice when I protested that really I had had enough.

Pamela and Rose Denton had been at school together in the suburbs of Birmingham. It was a coincidence, of course, and coincidences are usually rather pleasant. But somehow this one hadn't been pleasant, and now the atmosphere, which before had been quite ordinary, had changed. Behind the offers of beer, and the squeakings of Nurse Brawn, was something which threatened. Or was I inventing again? Sternly I pulled myself together and began to talk rather feverishly to the Demon King.

'So you two were at school together?' Mrs Isaacs's voice (not lovely) rose clearly above the general racket.

'But, Lily, you *knew* that.' Prince Charming, Gloria, was reproachful.

Rose Denton laughed, and I did not deceive myself when I thought that the laugh sounded malicious.

'School!' said the Demon King. 'Never more unhappy in my life.'

'Of course, in those days the Merritts were very high and mighty.' Cinderella shook her curls provocatively.

'Now, Rose, you're not to be naughty.' Mrs Isaacs smiled encouragement.

'Mind you,' the Demon King went on, 'I had a good education. Latin and Greek and all that.'

Again the door opened and shut. Two chorus girls came giggling into the room.

'Do you remember the Bradawl?' Cinderella called across to Pamela who did not hear her.

Gloria remarked that she'd die soon if she didn't get something to eat.

'Nobody'll get anything to eat ever if you don't start dressing fairly soon,' Dandini called from her side of the room.

Gloria retired behind a screen and was reluctantly attended by the dresser who still muttered to herself.

'Parsley,' said the Demon King unexpectedly. 'Best thing out for indigestion.'

'Don't be silly,' I heard Henry say to Pamela. 'What's the good of having a nursing home if we can't *help* people?'

Nurse Brawn, who for some time had seemed rather out of it all, perked up immediately at the mention of indigestion. Nurse Brawn had very definite views about 'indy.' So, it seemed, had one of the chorus girls, and they had a cosy time of it exchanging anecdotes about bismuth and duodenal ulcers. The chorus girl and the Demon King were both interested to have Nurse Brawn's professional opinion.

Rose Denton was explaining to Mrs Isaacs that the Bradawl had been the head-mistress of the Birmingham school. 'A regular terror if ever there was one—talk about *strict*!'

Again I was filled with envy for people who had been to school. 'The unhappiest time of their lives.' Few of them could have been as unhappy as I had been, doing lessons in the library with the governess and later with Sophia. 'Anne, what is a hexameter? What is long-short-short?' I had never known. I didn't know now.

'Purple hatbands,' Cinderella was saying. 'And those gymnasium tunics. Didn't we look a sight?'

Purple and silver hatbands and walking home through the streets carrying an attaché case and talking to your best friend.

'You remember Gran? We lived with Gran when Mother and Dad were on tour.'

Mrs Isaacs nodded, she remembered Cinderella's grandmother. She had been a wonderful old girl.

'Gran always said that the Merritts were riding for a fall.' Rose Denton lowered her voice as she paid this tribute to Gran, but I could still hear what she was saying.

'Hush!' Mrs Isaacs said so loudly that nearly everyone looked round.

Everyone, that is, but Henry. Henry was too busy talking himself to take any notice of anyone else.

'If you're going to keep on turning people down on ethical grounds,' Henry said, 'how are we ever going to make any money?'

He sounded as if he was being extremely reasonable. Only if you knew him fairly well would you recognise that he was slightly drunk.

'Money isn't everything,' Pamela said, primly, unwisely.

'Pity her Dad didn't think of that years ago."' Rose Denton's aside was of the kind that echoes through a room.

'Hush.' This time I got the impression that Mrs Isaacs really wanted Rose to keep quiet.

'Of course, it depends a lot on how they run at Cheltenham.' George had managed to detach the Demon King from the indigestion discussion.

'Saw him at Windsor,' the Demon King said gloomily. 'Didn't like the look of him at all.'

'Course, he may have come on since then.' George was thoughtful, prepared to consider every possibility.

'Thought they'd seen the worst of it when the old man ran off with the woman in his office; that happened when we were still at school.' Really, Cinderella was being very disagreeable.

But Mrs Isaacs had told me about that before. George Merritt had hopped it because Mrs Merritt led him such a hell of a life.

I imagined Pamela coming home from school. Tea was laid in the dining room. Mrs Merritt sat in front of the Britannia metal tea-pot. No, that was going too far. There was a china tea-pot.

'Your father is away on business. Your father has hopped it with a woman out of his office. Pass the bread-and-butter and stop kicking the leg of your chair. Don't slouch, do you want to have permanently round shoulders? What is a hexameter? What is long-short-short? We are hoping that she will fine down. We are hoping that in a year or so she will be quite different. Sophia is so interested in her hens. Father doesn't want to be disturbed.' 'Why not, is he writing a book?' 'Don't be pert.'

Would one never grow up? Would one never be able to do as one wanted? Would the blue silk dress last for ever and would one always have to wear dancing slippers and shoes with low heels?

'Your father has run away from your mother.' But father hadn't, he had stayed at home and been very eccentric. It would have been more interesting if he had run away.

'You are being extremely childish. I suppose one day you will grow up. Then you will be able to come down to dinner. You will no longer have fried fish sent up to you in the schoolroom.'

Had Pamela been glad when her father had run away? I didn't think so. There was something disgraceful in a father who ran away, and that was only the beginning of it; but the beginning of what?

I looked across at Pamela. She stood with Henry and Dandini. One of the chorus girls was with them; perhaps it was the one who was going to have a baby.

Rose Denton still talked to Mrs Isaacs. Rose must have been a nasty child. I could imagine her with crimped hair and white socks, wearing the purple tunic, and she would have worn jewellery, rings perhaps. Only common children wore jewellery. A coral necklace didn't count; it was a necklace.

Gloria called that she was nearly ready. There was a cafe opposite the theatre where they were going to eat. It was run by a Swiss and it constituted the night life of Torness. We had not been allowed to go to it. Instead we had had tea at Goodbody's. The pantomime and tea at Goodbody's. It was all a long time ago.

Pamela repeated that we must go home. Matron would be expecting us. There was some cold food left out for us in the dining room.

'Dirty,' the Ugly Sister was saying. 'Never seen dirtier, and it made it all the worse him being a clergyman.'

'I don't believe in murder myself.' George looked truculently at the Demon King.

Gloria came round the side of the screen, she was wearing a very tightly-fitting coat and skirt.

'I shall die soon if I don't get something to eat.'

There was a general movement towards the door. The actor who had played Buttons appeared and took Cinderella by the arm.

'He's her husband, you know,' I heard one of the chorus girls say to Nurse Brawn.

'Really, we *must* get back.' Pamela was being very insistent.

Henry started to argue with her. He held one of Dandini's hands, but I do not think he noticed it.

Mrs Isaacs looked from Henry to Pamela. We had come here in her car, so really it was for her to decide when we were to go.

'Ooh, do let's stay, Dr Merritt. I'm sure Matron will be perfectly all right.' It was Nurse Brawn.

(Pamela, like Rose Denton, had a stage name. At Trelynt she was Dr Merritt.)

Dandini pulled her hand away from Henry. He still didn't notice.

We must go, Mrs Isaacs said. 'We mustn't keep the driver waiting any longer.' I think she was sorry now that she had brought us here.

The dresser switched off one of the lights. Probably she too wanted to go home.

'Well, Lily, are you coming or not?' Gloria stood impatiently beside Mrs Isaacs.

'We can't,' Mrs Isaacs said, 'but it has been lovely seeing you.'

'You must come again and we'll have a good old gossip.'

'When do I see you again?' Henry called urgently after Dandini.

'One of these days.'

'You promised you'd come out to Trelynt.'

'It's a bit difficult with all these matinees.'

It was then that Pamela was magnificent.

'Why don't you all come over on Sunday, any of you who would care to. We'll have a party.' She was the patroness of the arts. Queen Gertrude entertaining the strolling players.

She had invited them all; but she was looking directly at Rose Denton who stood in the doorway with Buttons.

There was a pause. Henry smiled a slow smile of satisfaction. Pamela no longer clasped her bag as if she was afraid of having it stolen. How right Pamela had been to wear that grey dress. I had not noticed before how elegant it was.

'That's very sweet of you.' But it was Gloria, not Rose Denton, who was speaking.

The crowd round the door shifted. Some of them would be going home on Sunday and some had other engagements; but most of them would come to Trelynt.

The little Ugly Sister came out of the shadows to thank Pamela. Her digs were all right, nothing to complain of, but it was a bit gloomy staying in them on a Sunday.

Torness on a Sunday was a bit grim, they told us. We had known that and we agreed.

Gloria would telephone to Pamela in the morning and let her know how many there would be.

Pamela hoped it would be all of them or as many as possible.

'Do you think they'll bring those children?' Nurse Brawn said to me. 'I'd love to see them running about in the garden.' She spoke as if a garden would be something completely new in the experience of the Tiny Tots.

'I shall die if I don't have something to eat.'

'We mustn't keep the driver waiting any longer.'

The party was breaking up. We must return to Trelynt and eat the cold food which had been left for us in the dining room. We had been to the pantomime; but we were not to go to the Swiss Restaurant. Perhaps if we had come to a matinee we might have had tea at Goodbody's.

At Goodbody's there had been a ladies' orchestra. I had thought it very good; but mother and the governess had derided it. When I grew up I would play in a ladies' orchestra. I would prove to mother that there was nothing funny about it. I had forgotten that to do that one would have to be musical.

'You do not really like the orchestra at all, you are only saying that you do in order to be annoying. And why haven't you finished your cake? It is affected to leave half of it.' I was very tiresome; it would have been better if I had never been born. But at other times I was sorry for mother. She hadn't got the sort of children she had wanted. 'Your father is very disappointed in Henry. Mr Wentworth's son has got a scholarship to Winchester. The daughter is playing at Wimbledon this year. They are such a united family and all so fond of each other.'

We squeezed into the car for the drive back to Trelynt. Nurse Brawn had put on her mackintosh again. She had tried to show us her programme signed by all the principal members of the cast; but it was too dark to see it.

'I hope Matron will be all right.'

'Why the hell shouldn't she be?'

The food was laid out in the dining room. It was less unappetising than one had imagined it. Pamela and Nurse Brawn went into the kitchen to heat up the soup.

Matron had had an uneventful evening. She did not think that Mrs Smith's baby would be born before tomorrow morning; but probably Pamela would just like to have a look at her.

It had been kind of Matron to stay at home.

Matron did not deny it.

We waited for Pamela in the dining room. Mrs Isaacs seemed depressed. Perhaps she was overtired. One must not forget that Mrs Isaacs was here as a convalescent. The place was not an hotel.

'I've always been fond of Gloria, but I had forgotten what a little bitch Rose Denton can be.'

I nodded. I was thinking of something else.

'It was sweet of Pamela to ask her over here after the way she behaved.' Mrs Isaacs looked unhappily at the pressed beef. 'I had no idea Rose would behave like that.'

'She didn't do anything,' I said. I wanted to be comforting.

'I had forgotten that the children had been to school together.' Mrs Isaacs was becoming immensely old. 'And of course Rose's family were always as jealous as hell of the Merritts. Pamela minded terribly about her father.' Mrs Isaacs's voice droned on in the empty dining room.

I was hardly listening.

'It was bad enough when he ran away with that woman, but later it was worse. Such a terrible scandal. A man in his position. If he had lived he would have gone to prison.'

I looked at Mrs Isaacs in horror; but I was powerless to stop her. The voice would drone on until it came to a stop of its own accord.

'Embezzlement,' Mrs Isaacs said, and, 'public funds. It had been going on for years. No one had the least idea.'

'Stop,' I said, 'please stop. I don't want to hear about it.

Mrs Isaacs leant across the table. 'I was at the trial; one of the men got ten years.' Her eyes narrowed. 'George Merritt wasn't there, he had committed suicide. He died by his own hand.'

Mrs Isaacs enjoyed telling this story.

'He had put a thousand pounds in Pamela's name. She paid for her training out of that, but it ought to have been given back. It was public money.'

NINE

NEXT DAY I had to go back to London. Lady Merton and the office; and at the end of the week I was moving to Victoria. Mother and Sophia and the photographs of the princess. Gerald's detective story had reached the point where the elusive clues were being neatly collected. 'But, don't you remember? He said in Chapter Three that he never smoked and then he took the cigarette.'

One had forgotten, but it was there, hidden away in Chapter Three.

I wrote to Pamela and thanked her for having me to stay. She wrote back. I had not expected her to. The Cinderella cast had spent Sunday afternoon at Trelynt. It had all been great fun; Matron had not disapproved, and now Matron had an admirer. A young man from the Torness bank, whose married sister had had her baby at Trelynt. Mrs Isaacs was still with them. She had had a relapse and was in bed. They had another convalescent now; but Pamela was afraid they would have to get rid of him. He was very old and he didn't seem to be quite right in the head. It was too bad of Dr Dennison to have recommended him.

Lady Merton had had a pleasant Christmas staying with titled friends in Norfolk. She was very jolly and described it all for Miss Napier-Smith and me.

Wonderful house. Everything practically pre-war. They wanted me to stay on, of course; but duty called. Awful rot us having to occupy Germany.'

This was not Lady Merton's usual opinion. Usually she told us that Germany ought to be occupied for a hundred years. That would mean a hundred years of canteens; so there was nothing at all temporary about our jobs.

It was very depressing moving to mother's. The small room at the end of the passage and do try to keep it tidy. If you leave everything on the floor it makes it so difficult for Irene. Irene was the plump young charwoman who had never known what it was to be in good service. We had never known what it was to have good servants. Sophia did most of the work of the flat in order to save Irene trouble, so Irene spent quite a restful three hours with us every morning. She was able to keep her strength for the people she worked for in the afternoons.

Mother was still writing her opera. When I came in from work the drawing room was usually littered with manuscripts, but mother tidied them up faithfully every evening before she went to bed. The people upstairs complained about mother playing the piano such a lot; so we complained about their children.

Sophia joined a society for investigating ghosts. She went to their meetings every Tuesday evening and she told us it was very interesting; so far she had not seen a ghost, but there was always a silver collection.

I was getting into a rut and I was not contented. I tried to look at mother and Sophia with understanding and sympathy. I tried to understand their moods. I tried to be adult about them. It was no good. Mother and Sophia irritated me. 'Try not to leave everything on the floor. What a pity you have not got more friends. What a pity you have not got nicer friends. Are you sure you can afford it? Somebody rang you up on the telephone; I can't remember who it was. You are so feckless, you have no idea of money. How many cigarettes do you smoke a day?'

Mother was at her most annoying when she took an interest and when she was sympathetic. It wasn't right that it should be like that. It was my fault. I wasn't adult, after all. Mother took an interest in Gerald. He was a nice young man. It would be nice perhaps if I married him. Did I think he would ask me to marry him? But perhaps he hadn't got any money.

I wouldn't get angry. I wouldn't *let* myself get angry. Mother hadn't got the sort of children she had wanted and it was bad luck for her. At times I felt a dreadful sense of responsibility. But there were Henry and Sophia. If only they had managed to be satisfactory to mother it wouldn't have mattered about me. Henry should have been a Colonel in the Grenadier Guards instead of a temporary Captain in the Royal Army Service Corps. Sophia should have made a brilliant marriage and there should have been grandchildren, lots of grandchildren, getting ready to go to Eton. Then Sophia would not have been here in her plastic apron cooking our supper for us; but what would that matter? A mother only wants her children to be happy. She does not consider her own convenience. If ever I had children of my own I would understand that. 'That young man rang up just before you came in; he seems to be very taken with you. Not at all, I am

only helping him with his book. How are you getting on with
your opera?'

One evening, just after the New Year, I had been sitting with
Gerald in his basement. He had finished reading and he was
boiling the water to make some coffee. I remembered Pamela
and her machine; but Gerald made coffee in a rather complicated way in a saucepan.

I had been telling him about the pantomime and about
the Demon King whose favourite part was really King Rat. He
said he was one of the best King Rats in the business. 'Did you
know that they specialise in particular parts in particular pan-
tomimes?'

Gerald said that he hadn't known and that it was very interesting.

I told him about Prince Charming and about Cinderella. I
hesitated before I told him that Rose Denton had been at school
with Pamela, and what Mrs Isaacs had said about Pamela's
father. But, after all, why not? Gerald was very discreet and he
was always sympathetic. But when mother was sympathetic one
didn't like it. Probably that was because you couldn't count on
her, 'Are you sure that you can afford it? He is a nice young man;
perhaps he will ask you to marry him.'

I told Gerald about Rose Denton and then about Mrs Isaacs.

Gerald said that she must be a beastly woman, and did I
mean to say they'd still got her staying there?

'There's no point in getting rid of her *now* after the damage
is done.'

'You mean Henry didn't know about the embezzlement.'

'I don't know whether he did or not. It's not the sort of thing
he'd mind about anyhow. It's Pamela who *minds*.'

'I've a sort of idea I remember the case,' Gerald said. 'It was
the sort of thing my Father was rather keen on, corruption of
local government. Rotten from top to bottom; you know the sort
of thing, it crops up every few years.'

I supposed it did; anyhow I was prepared to take Gerald's
word for it.

'I think Pamela was quite right to keep the money,' I said. 'She'd always wanted to be a doctor, and if she'd given it back she wouldn't have been able to.'

'I should have kept it myself,' Gerald said, 'but I'm sure that Pamela had terrible qualms about it.'

'Perhaps,' I said, 'but I don't believe she'd have allowed anything to stand in her way once she'd decided on becoming a doctor.'

'Then she ought to be a better one,' Gerald said. 'When we first knew her she was messing about with those birth-control clinics. That's no job for a *doctor*.'

'She may have thought they were important.'

'Well, so they are, of course.' Gerald took the coffee off the stove and strained it into the pot; some of it went on the floor and he fetched a cloth and mopped it up. There was really no advantage for him in having a slate floor.

'I mean'—Gerald rose from his knees—'she doesn't seem to be a serious kind of doctor.'

Not a research worker, not surrounded with the mumbo-jumbo of the specialist, not the highly valued second opinion. Would Pamela have liked to be any of those things? She had never said so.

'I suppose if it was a very bad scandal about the money, it might have been difficult for her to get an appointment in a hospital?'

'Possibly,' Gerald said. 'People are so narrow-minded.'

'Do you think one would mind if one had had a father who had committed suicide?'

'It's practically impossible to tell what people are going to mind.' Very carefully Gerald poured the coffee into earthenware cups. He looked troubled, but I don't know whether he was thinking about Pamela or about the coffee. I looked round this fantastic room and thought how much I loved him.

'Is he a nice young man? Do you think he will marry you?' It was really extraordinary to be as unaware of other people's feelings as mother was. It ought to have made her very happy. She had no troubles to consider but her own.

'Your mother had a very difficult time with your father. Your mother is a very remarkable woman. Your mother is hell.'

I was being absurd. At my age it didn't matter what one's mother was like; one had finished with that relationship.

'I must go,' I said to Gerald.

'So soon?' Gerald got up. He would see me to the bus; but first was I sure that I had liked the last chapter? Did it tie up all right with the rest of the book?

Of course. It was extremely clever. If I had not known beforehand I would never have suspected which one was the murderer. I did not say that I still wasn't quite sure. It would sound as if I hadn't listened properly while Gerald read aloud to me and that wasn't true. I had listened intently to every word. It was as if I had considered each of them separately on its own merits. Perhaps that was why the sense had sometimes eluded me. And it had been July when the body had been pushed through the porthole; September when the cigarette had been accepted; now it was January. There had been a lack of continuity. The clues straggled out across the months. The book when it was finished would not be the same book that Gerald had written. There would be nothing to show at which point he had had that shocking cold in the head or when he had gone to the country.

Gerald took my hand as we crossed the yard. The rubble had still not been removed and it was difficult to pick one's way.

We got into the front part of the house. Gerald held my elbow to guide me. Without his help I might have wandered into one of the cellars or butlers' pantries. He had trouble opening the back door. He always did; maybe one day he would have it fixed. Tonight it wasn't raining, but it was very cold and there was ice on the area steps.

We stood shivering at the bus-stop. I suggested that Gerald shouldn't wait, but he said he liked it.

When I got home, I tried to creep along to my bedroom, but it was no good. Mother had heard me. She called me into the drawing room. Reluctantly I went. Mother was alone.

'Did you have a nice evening?'

'It was all right,' I said, and realised that I was not being entertaining.

Mother put up a hand and pushed her thick hairpins into place. Her hands were really very beautiful. I was struck again by how young she looked.

'I am worried about Sophia.'

'Really!' I was enchanted. It was so much worse when mother was worried about me.

'She spends such a lot of time with those ghosts and I think they upset her.'

'I thought they only happened on Tuesdays.' Would mother notice that I had remembered the day? She was always complaining that I took an interest only in my own affairs.

'Try not to be flippant, I'm really worried.'

I sat down opposite to mother. It was the chair without the castor and I must remember to be careful.

'Sophia is too young for that sort of thing.'

I nodded. I was perfectly willing to agree.

'Such awful people,' mother complained. 'You've never seen anything like them.'

'Oh, well,' I said. I supposed that mother must be criticising the members of Sophia's Spiritualist Society.

How stupid of Sophia to let mother get anywhere near them.

'Very ordinary,' mother said. 'I only hope they don't get hold of her in any way.'

'That ought to be all right. Sophia hasn't got any money.'

'I meant, get hold of her mind.'

I wasn't quite certain that that *wasn't* what mother had meant when she started, but I didn't think it would do any good to argue it out with her.

'You haven't noticed anything strange about Sophia lately? But then you never notice anything.'

'I think she seems about the same as usual.'

'She's so irritable,' mother said, 'and difficult.'

This was really making a very pleasant change. So often it was me who was difficult. I leant back in my chair feeling, for once, rather self-satisfied.

I thought about Stephanie and Lawrence. I had hoped when I left Chalk Farm that they would ring me up and ask me to supper or something, but they hadn't. I had been the lodger and now I was no longer that; I had passed out of their lives.

'She ought to have a dog,' mother said suddenly. 'It would get her out into the air.'

I thought of Sophia trudging round the Green Park, throwing a ball for a broad-beamed spaniel. Or perhaps it would be a Sealyham, its coat grey and smudgy from the London grass.

'It would have to be let out,' I said, and imagined myself standing on the doorstep and calling into the cold night. 'He can't have gone far, he was here a minute ago.'

'Uncle George is getting out his yacht again this year.' Mother smiled a little wanly.

'Oh, good. Do you think he'll ask us to go boating with him?'

Mother said she didn't know. I suppose that she had given up the hope that Sophia and I would find husbands for ourselves on board Uncle George's yacht.

'It would do Sophia good,' I said. 'Lots of air.'

'She talks about spending the summer with those people,' mother said, 'in Czechoslovakia.'

I began to think that Sophia must be going a little crazy. It was mad to tell mother in January what one thought of doing in the summer. There would be months and months during which she would criticise and point out objections and during which she would be sympathetic and decide that after all a holiday in Czechoslovakia was a very good idea.

I told her it was ridiculous. 'They'll get themselves interned or something and they'll probably try to travel third-class.'

Whichever class they travelled it would be wrong, Sophia might be sure of that. First would be a ridiculous extravagance, in the third they would be murdered and 'pick things up,' and in the second . . . I couldn't think for the moment, but obviously there must be some very strong objection to the second.

Mother was impossible. I thought of the conversation I had had with her at Trelynt when I had told her that I was going to

London. 'I can't see why anyone should employ you. You are not being fair to Sophia.'

Then I had wanted Sophia to be unfair to mother. To leave her and come to London with me. To go anywhere, in fact, as long as it was *away* from mother.

I had gone away; but it hadn't done me very much good, for here I was living in mother's flat, sitting in the chair without the castor and trying to remember to be careful.

I had gone away but mother had followed me. If father had lived she wouldn't have been able to. It was the greatest pity that father had died.

For a moment I tried to be fair. Perhaps mother would really like to be rid of me and Sophia; but she considered us to be her duty. Family love, family feeling, they were conventions, they didn't mean anything. Mother was not a vampire, she was only trying to conform to convention. I hated her and I was sorry for her. She sat on the sofa looking rested and fairly young and, to escape from her, Sophia had to trail across half London and spend the evening with a lot of ghosts. Even when the ghosts didn't turn up it must be beastly. Fat women in lace jabots and men with Adam's apples and low collars. It wasn't fair. Usually I didn't notice Sophia at all, but now I boiled with rage on her behalf.

Mother *was* a vampire. A vampire with its head in the sand who refused to see anything it didn't want to. I stopped, the image wasn't very convincing. The vampire turned into a mouse digging a hole for itself in a sand dune. Fine white sand and the mouse was small and pathetic.

'It's inconsiderate,' mother was saying, 'and she's making a fool of herself.'

'Why can't you leave her alone?' I said. For now the sand dune had disappeared and I was looking at an ageing woman sitting on a chintz-covered sofa. The woman had beautiful hands and long elegant feet. Her hair was screwed into a bun and kept in place with thick hairpins.

'Anne!' Mother had turned pink with annoyance. 'How dare you speak to me like that!'

'I'm sorry,' I said. 'I wasn't thinking.'

'You are too old to behave in this way.'

'And Sophia is too young to spend the evening with a lot of dreary old women. You can never leave either of us alone, *ever*.'

I had jumped up, and in pushing back my chair I knocked over a little table which stood beside the fire.

'Really!' Mother jumped up too now and we stood facing each other across the hearth-rug. Two angry women with heightened colour and breathing a little too quickly. We must have looked very funny.

'You've got no right to behave like this. How dare you start breaking up the furniture!'

'It was an accident,' I said. 'And anyhow, what does it matter?'

'As you can't control yourself, you had better leave the room.'

'I won't,' I said hysterically. 'Why should I?'

'Then I shall leave *you*.' Mother walked towards the door. Immediately I felt sorry for her again.

'I hope that by the morning you will have come to your senses.' Mother had opened the door. She stood quite still, waiting for me to say something, waiting for me to apologise.

But I couldn't do it. I turned my back on her. I heard the door being firmly shut. If only she had banged it I could have forgiven her.

I turned back towards the room. The little table lay on its side. One of its feet was broken off. Tomorrow I would have to see about getting it mended. I collected the things which had been on the table. Little silver boxes, an ostrich egg or two. Fortunately nothing else was broken.

I sat down on the sofa and leant my head against the cushions. I was exhausted. I had only myself to blame. A little more firmness and I would still have been at Stephanie's instead of here, acting like an hysterical schoolgirl.

'Girls are difficult at that age, and inclined to be fat; in a year or two they will have become adjusted.' But Sophia and I were in our twenties and thirties and we were *still* difficult. It was rather degrading. The one comfort was that we were thin.

'Sophia ought to have married.' Lots of married women are difficult and disagreeable, of course, but the people who advise marriage never seem to take that into account.

'Sophia ought to have a lover.'

For sex, of course, was the answer to everything. Who had said that? It was rather funny; then I remembered it was one of the things I had thought before.

In the past one had been inclined to forget about sex. It had been going on all round one, of course (in the W.R.N.S. it had been going on a good deal), but one had not particularly noticed it.

You couldn't notice everything, there wasn't time. The photographs of mother's princess, for instance. They were always there on the mantelpiece, but sometimes for days together one didn't notice them.

Perhaps I was not being honest with myself, but why should I be? It was enough to be honest with other people.

I wished I was a man, then I should go out to my club and get drunk.

I heard the key turn in the lock of the front door. It must be Sophia. I had not known that she was still out. I called to her.

Sophia came into the drawing room. Her face had turned a pale mauve with the cold.

'Mother gone to bed?' Sophia started to take off her gloves.

'I've had a row with her.'

'How tiresome of you. Now she'll sulk for a week.'

'It wasn't my fault.'

'It never is,' Sophia said wearily and started to make up the fire which was almost out.

'Did you have a nice evening?'

'It was all right.' Sophia knelt on the hearth-rug. She noticed the table with its broken leg, but she didn't say anything. Years of repression had made Sophia very tactful.

'I'm not going to stay here a moment longer.'

'Neither am I.'

'You're not?' I was taken completely by surprise.

'Why should I?' Sophia said. 'It isn't very amusing.'

One knew that, one knew it only too well; but one had expected Sophia to go on putting up with it. After all, she wasn't used to being amused.

'I'm awfully glad,' I said, for in Sophia's case any change must be for the better.

'You think I'm right?' Sophia looked up suddenly.

'Oh, yes,' I said eagerly, but I still had no idea what she was proposing to do.

'Mother will be perfectly all right, you know. She's got her opera and Irene and there are always the aunts.'

Especially Aunt Emily, I agreed. 'Aunt Emily loves being a comfort. Aunt Mary isn't so good.'

'Aunt Mary's much nicer.'

'I know,' I said. 'That's why she won't come here and gloat with mother over her troubles.'

'Mother hasn't got any troubles.' Sophia held the poker and still fiddled with the fire.

'She'll think she has when we tell her that we're going.'

'It can't be helped.' Sophia was making a pattern in the soot which had gathered on the fireback.

'Sophia,' I said, 'please tell me what you are going to do.' But surely one didn't ask that sort of question. One should wait until one was told.

'I'm going abroad,' Sophia said. 'I've got a post as a governess.'

'Oh!' I was both relieved and disappointed. I had imagined the waters of the Thames closing over Sophia's head and I had imagined an elopement with a spiritualist.

'It's something,' Sophia went on. 'They live in Kenya; there will be plenty of sunshine.'

'And you'll be able to send us food parcels,' I said, and immediately regretted it.

'Do you never think of anyone but yourself?' Now Sophia was annoyed.

I apologised. I asked how she had got the job.

'Oh, privately, through a friend of mine who is a school-teacher in Capetown.'

Why should Sophia have a friend who was a school-teacher in Capetown? But then again, why not? She didn't know who most of my friends were.

'And you won't simply hate looking after the children?'

'There's only one child,' Sophia said. 'It's an invalid.'

'You mean mad.'

'Only very slightly. If it was sane its parents would expect me to have qualifications.'

'I think it's most terribly sporting of you.' I felt a real admiration for Sophia. Why couldn't I have done something like that? 'Won't it take a long time to get visas and a passage?'

'That's all arranged. I'm sailing on Wednesday.'

It was all very surprising.

'Mother thought you were going to Czechoslovakia in the summer.'

'I would have, if this hadn't come off.'

'Sophia, can you think of anywhere for me to go?'

'There are hundreds of places,' Sophia said. 'You only have to choose.' She got up from the floor. 'It's time we went to bed.'

'Are you going to tell mother you're going to Kenya?'

'It will do in the morning. Were you thinking of spending the night on the sofa?'

'No,' I said and got up.

I followed Sophia to the door and she switched off the lights. We crept down the passage to our rooms, and dodging each other we crept in and out of the bathroom. It would be a pity to disturb mother.

I lay on my back in bed and smoked. The furniture in this room must have come from Trelynt; out of one of the spare rooms perhaps, as I didn't remember it. The bedside lamp was small and squat. It threw a tiny circle of light on to the table on which it stood. The shade was not adjustable so it was lucky that I seldom wanted to read in bed.

Life was very surprising. It was also very difficult; but, perhaps other people didn't find it as difficult as I did.

'You are just the same as everyone else, there is no difference at all.' That had been one of the petty officers in the W.R.N.S., a horrible woman. Before the war she had taught dancing. When I knew her she was teaching me how to drill.

I had stopped concentrating and had walked into the railings. She had been very angry.

'It is no more difficult for you than for anybody else. You have no sense of discipline.'

I lit another cigarette.

Perhaps Petty Officer Morris had been right, after all. Perhaps if I had been very disciplined and very smart my life would have been quite different. Problems would not have arisen, or if they had, I should have been able to solve them quickly and easily.

Sophia had said there were hundreds of places I could go. I only had to choose; but Sophia hadn't always felt like that. It had taken her about thirty-six years to choose Kenya. But perhaps before she hadn't wanted to go anywhere. Perhaps she had been happy just living at Trelynt and bicycling to the village.

I had quarrelled with mother and I wouldn't live with her any more. Already I was beginning to forget what the quarrel had been about. Something to do with Sophia, and I had got very angry and had shouted. But Sophia had not needed my interference, she was going to Kenya.

It was getting cold. The partial central-heating did not extend as far as this room. I put out my cigarette and pulled the bedclothes over my shoulders.

Sophia and Henry and me. It seemed as though we floated round and round in a thin fog. We were like a solar system; but what was in the centre? Mother? But that didn't make sense. I tried Trelynt and I was left with Sophia and Henry circling round and round; but I had disappeared. No, the centre was intangible, an aggregate of emotions.

I sat up in bed. I mustn't fall asleep now, when I was beginning to understand things. But now I didn't understand. I was no longer on the verge of a discovery. The circle was the lamp and its centre was a 60-watt electric bulb. I switched off the light and lay there in the darkness.

One must be practical. Tomorrow I would ring up Stephanie and ask her if I could go back to Chalk Farm. Tomorrow I would get the leg of the table mended. The trouble was having so little money. But I had never had any so I ought to be used to that. I thought about Gerald. He would never ask me to marry him. He was a daydream. Thinking about him was about as practical as thinking about the solar system.

I would go right away and start all over again somewhere else. I imagined myself being a manicurist in New York. I would travel to work in the subway. And I would wear crisp little shirt-waists and be quite, quite different.

'And in the centre is jealousy'; but we are all envious of different things.

'You must not confuse jealousy with envy.' One is green and the other purple. Two colours that go rather well together.

Sophia is envious of Henry, and she is envious that he should have Trelynt.

'What an attractive little boy.' 'What a charming man.' Sophia had had too much of that. If she could not be as charming and attractive as Henry, she would wear black stockings and bicycle to the village.

Henry, so far as one knows, is not envious of anyone in particular. All the same he doesn't seem to be able to make a success of his life; and there are always the dark moods of despair which return again and again and which will one day perhaps annihilate him completely.

If only things were a little different, if only things were not so difficult.

'It is no more difficult for you than for anybody else.'

So I was to be haunted by Chief Petty Officer Morris?

If she taught dancing there is no reason why she should be so fat. I thought it was only fencing that developed the figure to that extent.

I turned over in bed. One thing was certain. I would never live with mother again. This was the last night I would spend under her roof. However difficult it was, I would leave tomorrow and I would never come back.

* * * * *

We always had breakfast early, because Irene liked us to have done the washing-up and be out of the kitchen before she arrived towards half-past nine.

Mother and Sophia and I sat round the kitchen table. This morning the meal was more formal than usual because mother and I were not on speaking terms.

Mother was waiting for me to apologise.

We finished the sausages and tomatoes which Sophia had cooked, then we had to wash the plates before going on to the toast and margarine.

'I really must change my library book this afternoon.' Mother was speaking exclusively to Sophia.

'What a good idea,' Sophia said brightly. I wondered when she was going to pluck up courage to tell mother about Kenya.

I heard the rattle of the letter-box and jumped up from the table.

Mother looked martyred and put her hand to her forehead. I was to understand that she had a headache and that it was my fault.

There was one letter for me and one for Sophia which had a South African stamp.

I went back to the kitchen, gave Sophia her letter and opened my own. It was from Pamela. I began to be afraid that Pamela was starting a correspondence.

'There's a book about the Transvaal,' mother was saying. 'I've had it on my list for a long time.' Hadn't she noticed that Sophia was reading a letter?

'Mother,' Sophia looked up, 'I've got something to tell you.'

She shouldn't have made it sound so portentous.

'I've got to put through a telephone call,' I said and moved away from the table. I was too late, Sophia was already 'telling' mother. Mother remarked, quite amiably, that Sophia must have gone out of her mind.

'You'll be all right, won't you?' Sophia seemed anxious. Perhaps if mother was to make a scene now Sophia would change her mind and not go to Kenya, after all.

'It won't agree with you, of course.' Mother began to collect the cups. 'Do you remember those awful spots you came up in during the heat wave?'

'They weren't spots, it was nettle rash.'

'Caused by the heat,' mother said triumphantly and moved across to the sink.

'I must put through a telephone call,' I repeated, but no one was listening to me.

'Wednesday,' Sophia was saying, 'and Kenya isn't particularly hot. It's like England.'

'I don't think so,' mother said and looked out on the snow.

I left them and went into the drawing room. The curtains had not yet been pulled back. The room was cold and depressing and somehow squalid. I switched on the lights, picked up the telephone receiver and dialled TRU.

Trunks thought that the snow might have brought some of the lines down; but even so they would try to connect me. They went on trying to connect me for about five minutes. Then I heard Pamela's voice. She was being brisk with Trunks. She admitted that she was speaking personally. I imagined her at Trelynt in the little office overlooking the front door.

'Pamela, it's me.'

'Yes?' Pamela waited, her voice was friendly but business-like. She was not imaginative. She had not got second-sight.

'Pamela, I've quarrelled with mother.'

'Oh, my dear, I'm so sorry.'

I felt that the reply was automatic. Soon I would hear the three pips and I would not have said anything.

'Can I come and stay with you for about ten days, until I make up my mind what to do?'

'But of course.' As soon as a direct appeal was made to her Pamela was helpful.

'Come for as long as you like; come today, we always love having you.' Now Pamela's voice was warm and sympathetic.

'There's Lady Merton,' I said, 'and the office.' I was being very silly. I had wanted to go to Trelynt today; but now that it was being suggested by someone else I found objections.

'Go and see her this morning and tell her that you must come down here on the afternoon train. I will send the car to meet you in Exeter. Is that perfectly clear?'

'But . . .' I began. I was interrupted by the sound of the three pips and I heard Pamela ring off. I was taken by surprise. Should I ring up again? But what was the use? Pamela had told me, ordered me, to do the very thing that I wanted to do. The sensible thing was to do it. Did Pamela think I was having a nervous breakdown? Possibly, possibly not. Either way it didn't matter very much. Although at the moment a nervous breakdown might be quite convenient. Tonsilitis would be better still; it was more definite. Hopefully I fingered my neck.

I would go to the office and see Lady Merton, then I would come back here and pack. I got up off the sofa. Pamela was really very kind. One saw exactly why Henry had married her. In the midst of uncertainties she was certain. She was perfectly sure of her opinion.

'I will send the car to meet you in Exeter,' and there was nothing further to discuss.

TEN

AGAIN THERE WAS the long damp drive, the two gates and the abrupt turn which came immediately before you reached the front door. This time I was driven by Mr Bethwick from the village. The Morris with the flapping side curtains. The car was large enough to take parties to the local dances, or over to Torquay to spend a day on the beach. But this evening there was only Mr Bethwick and me sitting in front, and at the back was my luggage—several cardboard leather suitcases and a haversack and a brown-paper parcel.

It was very dark.

I was coming home, but Trelynt was not my home. It was filled with hospital nurses and hygienic boilers and Pamela.

Before there had been mother and father and Sophia and sometimes Henry. But even then Trelynt had not been like the homes I had read about in the Victorian children's books, *Little White Violet* and *Ever Heavenwards*. The homes in the books had been safe and comforting, and, although children frequently died in them, they were usually happy.

I remembered coming back to Trelynt as a child and later on leave from the W.R.N.S. The anticipation one felt in the train, as one drove from the station, as one turned into the drive; and the disappointment which came almost as soon as the front door was opened. Sometimes the warmth would last until one had crossed the hall, but it had never been known to survive after one had opened the door into mother's Edwardian drawing room.

Once Henry, as an angry adolescent, had shouted at father, 'I didn't come home to be insulted!' It had been rude and silly and father had been very angry.

At the time I had been frightened that Henry should shout at father like that, at father who could be so coldly terrifying. I had remembered the words and the way Henry had looked, and afterwards I had thought that the angry words had really been a protest against Trelynt. You see, for us *Little White Violet* and the others had been escape literature, and not just records of grim Victorianism.

We turned into the drive. We were in front of the house and I must go in and thank Pamela for allowing me to come here. I jumped out of the car. Mr Bethwick got out slowly and began to fumble with the luggage. It was very dark; there were only the car lights and a line of orange light which came from the window of the office. I rang the bell and opened the door. Pamela came into the hall, switching on the lights as she did so.

'So here you are.'

Yes, here I was. It was fairly obvious. We kissed and our cheek-bones bumped painfully.

'You didn't have any trouble in getting away from Lady Merton's?' Pamela had put her arm through mine and was leading me towards the office.

But I had to pull away from her in order to pay Mr Bethwick. He gave a start of simulated surprise. Mr Bethwick liked it to be understood that he never expected to be paid for driving his taxi. He would murmur the fare, always rather a high one, under his breath and then be immensely surprised and grateful when one produced the money.

Pamela put her arm through mine again; this time it was less spontaneous. We went into the office.

'I was sitting in here. There's no fire in the drawing room.'

'What have you done with Mrs Isaacs then?'

'She's in bed; you must go up and see her later on, she's very excited about your coming.'

I tried to smile appreciatively. 'It's awfully kind of you to let me arrive just like this, Pamela.'

'Don't be silly. I told you it was your home.' Pamela sat down in the swivel chair behind her writing table. I sat opposite her. The machine for taking blood pressures loomed between us.

On a tray at Pamela's elbow was a coffee-pot and two thick white cups. I knew without looking that the coffee would be strong and black. Pamela hadn't changed since the days at Chalk Farm; but she wasn't wearing her brooding clothes. She had on a grey coat and skirt.

As she poured out the coffee: 'Supper won't be for another hour.' Pamela smiled and asked me for the latest Lady Merton.

It occurred to me that Pamela was going to treat me as a nerve case. I wondered if I should invite her (right away) to give me a sharp crack on the knee-cap with the ruler. Or we might have some fun with deep analysis, only that had to be done by a stranger, otherwise it would be too embarrassing or, alternatively, too easy.

'Lady Merton has given me special leave of absence for urgent private affairs.'

'Nice of her,' Pamela said.

'It was rather,' I said, 'because we were fairly busy, and Miss Napier-Smith isn't much use when we're busy, she gets flustered.'

'You only have to be firm with people,' Pamela said, 'and you get what you want.'

'I was most awfully firm with Lady Merton. I told her! I'd got to leave London immediately and if I couldn't she'd have to send for the Labour Exchange. She was very surprised.'

'Will you go back later on?' Pamela held an ivory ruler a between her fingers and allowed it to fall on the blotting pad.

'I might,' I said. 'It depends.'

'You know you can stay here as long as you want to. Later, if you'd like to do some of the secretarial part . . .' Pamela left the sentence unfinished.

'I'll do anything,' I said, 'as long as I don't have to be with mother.'

Pamela continued to tap the blotting pad with her ruler. 'Oedipus complex,' was that what she was thinking? But Oedipus hadn't hated his mother at all. He had liked her too much, that had been the trouble. But it was different for men. It almost always was.

'Lady Merton sent you a message,' I began tentatively. Lady Merton's message was going to be difficult to deliver. This morning one had thought it would be easy; now, sitting opposite to Pamela, it wasn't the same at all.

'Yes?' Pamela was starting on another cup of strong black coffee.

'She wants to know if you could cure somebody of being drunk?'

I hadn't put it well. I should have spoken first to Henry. Perhaps I shouldn't have spoken at all; but I was really very grateful to Lady Merton for letting me leave without giving her proper notice. Quite easily she might have made a fuss and she hadn't.

'There are plenty of places for that sort of thing.' Pamela was looking stubborn.

'But this friend of Lady Merton's,' I said, 'it isn't only drink, it's nerves as well, and it's terribly sad because he used to be terribly nice.'

There was a knock and a girl in V.A.D. uniform put her head round the door.

'Excuse me, but Matron says will you please come upstairs at once. Mrs Isaacs is in one of her tempers.'

Pamela, looking worried, went quickly out of the room and I was left alone.

Plainly Mrs Isaacs was suffering from nerves. It wasn't fair that Pamela should look after her and not after Lady Merton's friend.

Lady Merton's friend was remarkable for not being a Wing-Co or an A.V.M.

Miss Napier-Smith and I had known him for some time as 'the one who isn't in the Air Force.' He had started, as far as we were concerned, by being a voice on the telephone, rather a nice voice. Then later on we had met him when he called for Lady Merton at the office. He had seemed solid and reliable. Lady Merton had told us that he was an historian. When he had rung up or called he had always been quite sober. I would never have known that he drank, only Lady Merton had suddenly told me so when I told her that I wanted to leave.

'How awful for you,' I had said and, 'How dreadful,' but I hadn't been thinking about the historian. I had been thinking about getting away from London and from mother. 'It isn't his fault,' Lady Merton had said. 'The whole thing's due to nerves.' She had frowned. She was making an intense effort to put herself in the place of another person.

'He ought to go right away somewhere and rest. Couldn't your sister-in-law . . . ?' And a few seconds later I found myself promising that Pamela would take Mr Butler as a patient at Trelynt.

It had been a silly promise, I knew perfectly well that Pamela would never have anything to do with drunks. Now I would have to write and tell Lady Merton that her friend would have to go and rest and be cured somewhere else.

Henry came into the room. 'Hullo, I didn't know you'd arrived, I was looking for Pamela.'

'She's upstairs with Mrs Isaacs.'

'Oh, blast Mrs Isaacs,' Henry said. 'I suppose she's throwing one of her tantrums.'

'She's probably nervous.'

'That's what they say,' Henry agreed, 'but I don't know which I hate most, her or those terrifying babies; not that there've been so many of them lately, I'm thankful to say.'

'Isn't that rather a pity, from a money point of view?'

'I'm not interested in money,' Henry said grandly.

'It was kind of you to let me come down here.'

'That's all right,' Henry said. 'Anything human's a relief here.' He sat down by the fire and lit a cigarette. 'To tell you the truth, I'm getting fed up.'

'You said that when you were in London in October.'

'You *see*,' Henry said. 'I've been fed up for months and months. How's mother?' he asked presently. 'Perhaps now Sophia's going to Africa and you've bolted down here, she'd like to have me to stay.'

'I'm sure she'd love it.'

'Or then again she mightn't,' Henry said, but he knew perfectly well that mother would adore to have him stay with her.

'Do you know an artist called Stephen Craig?' Henry asked suddenly.

I said I didn't.

'Well, he's staying in the village. As a matter of fact he's going to paint my portrait.'

'I think it's a very good idea. There *ought* to be a portrait of you to go with the others.'

'Oh, the admirals!' Henry said. 'I hope it's going to be a bit better than most of *them*.'

I was rather fond of the admirals. They'd been our great-grandfathers and -uncles; and they'd all got a piece of sea and a ship in the background.

Henry said that he'd often thought how lucky it was that they'd all been painted by such terrible artists; because if any of the pictures had been valuable they'd have had to be sold.

'Aren't any of them worth anything?'

'Lord, no.' Henry shook his head. 'Not even that very very old one covered with bubbles.'

'I wonder if they had fun when they lived here?'

'More fun than I do, anyhow'—and Henry threw a log on the fire. 'But I don't expect they were here very much; they were always sailing about in their ships looking for the French fleet.'

'It was very difficult to get a ship in those days,' I said. 'I was reading about it the other day. Naval officers used to spend a great part of their time on shore. Even Nelson had trouble.'

'I think some of the admirals were really fishermen,' Henry said, 'so they'd have had their *own* boats.'

I hadn't thought of that, and I wondered what their boats had been called. What would be the eighteenth-century equivalents of *We Three* and *Our Daddy*?

'You must meet Stephen,' Henry said. 'He's an awfully nice chap. Paints well, too.'

'Are you going to have to pay an awful lot for the picture?'

'No, that's what is so splendid about it,' Henry said. 'He's doing it for practically nothing, because he says he likes my face.'

'Why's he living down here, anyhow?'

'He's got to live *somewhere* and apparently he was spending too much money in London. I think you'll like Stephen and I must say he's been a godsend to me.'

I wondered what the portrait would be like and whether it would have 'Mr Pallisser of Trelynt' painted in gold letters in the corner. That would be rather grand and old-fashioned like Mr Boswell of Auchinleck; but it wasn't the same when you could only afford to live in your house because your wife was a doctor and had turned it into a nursing home. Pamela should have been quite young and have driven out in a pony carriage, and been much occupied in having children of her own. Some of the children should have died, of course. It would have been too expensive if they had all lived to grow up.

There wasn't a modern equivalent to all that. It was better to live in a service flat and not to try. All the same people tried. They lived in thatched cottages and the sinks were always filled with the washing-up. If they had children it was more squalid than ever; but that was only to be expected.

I was being foolishly depressed. Things only got like that if people were inefficient. Most people weren't inefficient at all. Most people could look ahead and live if necessary in the future. I could live only for this afternoon, for the exact minute in time which is the present. Henry was like that too. If the present wasn't exactly the way he wanted it, then the world was without hope.

He wanted everything or he wanted nothing.

'Do you miss living in London?' I asked.

'Not particularly,' Henry said. 'As a matter of fact, I'd be very, very happy indeed if it didn't always seem to be so difficult to get to the races. But you see I do most of the driving now, because every time George takes the van out it has to have a new gear-box; it's away again at the moment.'

'The trouble with us is that we don't know *what* we want.'

'It may be the trouble with you,' Henry said crossly. 'Look here,' he lowered his voice, 'I want you to help me.'

'What with?'

'With Pamela mostly.'

He was interrupted by Pamela coming back into the room. She walked with quick steps and I imagined that she smelled very slightly of iodine.

'Quietened the old girl down?' Henry asked.

'I've given her a sedative.'

'We might all have one while we're at it.' Henry got up and took a bottle of gin out of the cupboard.

The telephone rang; Pamela answered it. 'It's for you.'

'Not mother?' I said and backed towards the door.

'Who is it speaking, please?'

It was Lady Merton, which was almost as bad. Unwillingly I picked up the receiver.

'Yes, thank you, I had a splendid journey. The carriage practically empty, most remarkable. Well, I haven't had a proper chance yet; but I don't think that she's keen.' I looked at Pamela. Her head was turned away. She was carefully not listening to my conversation. Very different from Henry who was leaning forward and urging me to give the old girl his love.

'I'll do the best I can,' I said to Lady Merton, 'but it isn't easy.'

'What isn't easy?' Henry asked.

'Shut up,' I said to Henry (in an aside). Meanwhile Lady Merton was demanding to speak to Pamela.

'You can't have explained it properly, Pallisser. Eric isn't an ordinary drunk, he's a nerve case. I told you this morning.'

I longed to say that Pamela was out, or engaged in the labour ward, but I didn't dare. I put my hand over the mouthpiece. 'Will you speak to Lady Merton?' I said to Pamela. 'It's about her drunk.'

'I told you,' Pamela said, 'I won't have anything to do with it.'

'Will you talk to her, though?'

'Oh, very well.' Pamela got up.

'Give the old girl my love,' Henry said. 'Perhaps we could have her down here and cure her of something.'

I remembered the brief friendship which had existed between Henry and Lady Merton. I wondered if it could be possible that Pamela was jealous of her.

We never knew what it was exactly that Lady Merton said to Pamela (George or Nurse Brawn may have, they often listened in to telephone conversations); but we knew what Pamela said to Lady Merton.

She began firmly enough, 'Certainly not'—'Quite impossible'—'No.' Then the pauses between Pamela's remarks got longer and longer and the remarks changed. 'So sorry'—'You realise you are placing me in a difficult position. His own doctor would have to be consulted'—'Very well, if he cares to ring me up'—'In any case I should have to think it over. We couldn't possibly accept him unless he had a Special.'

'Game to Lady Merton,' Henry said at this point and poured us all out a large double gin. Sympathetically he thrust Pamela's glass into her hand.

When Pamela was at last able to ring off she was looking rather shaken.

'The woman's a fiend.'

'What's the name of her boy-friend?' Henry asked.

'Eric Butler,' I said.

'Never heard of him.' Henry sounded disappointed. 'Still, he's probably all right. He isn't one of the ones who plays hockey with the professor, is he?'

'They've given up the hockey,' I said.

'Good.' Henry got up. 'Well, I'd better get down to the pub or I shall be late for supper.'

'Must you?' Pamela asked.

'Well, I don't actually *have* to, but I'm in the mood,' and Henry shut the door behind him.

Pamela passed the time which remained before supper in having a small nervous breakdown.

Matron appeared at supper wearing mufti. Her 'friend' was calling for her later and they were going out. I remembered that she had acquired the bank clerk from Torness.

Henry didn't appear until we had reached the sweet (marmalade pudding).

'I met Stephen at the pub,' Henry said. 'He knows Eric Butler and he says he's an awfully nice chap.'

This remark was received in silence by Pamela.

Matron looked at her gold wristwatch, the gift of a grateful patient.

'Counting the minutes, Matron?' Henry asked.

Matron bridled.

'I'll ring up the doctor myself this evening and tell him I can't take the case,' Pamela said decisively.

'Don't be silly,' Henry said. 'He's got pots of money; Stephen said so.' Henry sounded a little too assured; one was left with the impression that Stephen had not said anything of the kind.

'A new patient?' Matron asked and smiled benignly at no one in particular.

'A terrific charmer,' Henry said. 'Your young man will be frightfully jealous.'

Supper came to an end, and I said I would go and unpack.

'I expect George has taken up your luggage,' Pamela said.

'He hasn't,' Henry said. 'I fell over it in the hall just now.'

'George is really getting *impossible*; he will have to go.' But Pamela knew that Henry would never agree to the sacking of George.

'I'll carry the things myself,' Henry said good-naturedly and got up. He had forgotten to put his napkin in the napkin ring. Pamela did it for him.

Henry put the bags down in my room, leant against the mantelpiece and lit a cigarette.

'Can't you do something about cheering Pamela up?'

'I could make some jokes,' I said doubtfully.

'You see,' Henry went on, 'we could have a lot more fun than we do, but she's so sort of grim about everything.'

'Serious-minded,' I said.

'You can call it what you like, but take this evening, for instance. There was no need to make all that fuss about Eric Butler.'

I nodded.

'And then those pantomime people. Do you know she wouldn't even do an abortion for that wretched little chorus girl?'

'Why not?'

'Against her principles,' Henry said. 'But what I'm complaining about *is* that she makes everything so dreary.'

I didn't want to agree with him, but I saw exactly what Henry meant. Pamela was very earnest and very kind and she could be very dreary.

I started to unpack.

'I don't want you to think I'm complaining,' Henry said.

'No, of course you're not.' What an extraordinary amount of useless and rather sordid things I had collected. A leather powder-case which didn't shut any more and a little bit of looking glass with a view of Paris on it.

'It may be better now you're here,' Henry was saying. 'I think she worries about things too much and then she gets all wrought up about them.'

'Some people do,' I said, and put a terrible green evening dress, which had been a failure even when it was new, away in the wardrobe.

'I've done my best,' Henry said, 'but she's got to the stage where she doesn't believe what I say.'

I felt a good deal of sympathy for him. I knew from experience that Pamela could be very difficult when she brooded, when she worried, and when she became over-earnest.

Singleness of purpose is all very well, but it isn't much fun to live with.

I was sorry for Pamela, too. Henry wasn't making a satisfactory husband, and he was getting bored with respectability. But outside of that, Pamela had what she wanted, Henry and the nursing home.

Henry continued to smoke. I unpacked a paper folder which contained letters which I ought to have answered, some picture postcards and several theatre programmes. I always keep theatre programmes. There isn't very much point in it, because once out of the theatre I never look at them again.

I thought about Lady Merton and my first interview with her. I hadn't wanted the job and she had engaged me. Lady Merton was very strong-willed, or stubborn, or had a terrific personality; and it usually worked out that she got her own way. It wasn't fair really because Lady Merton was very stupid—but life wasn't fair. I couldn't remember that I had ever expected it to be.

Lady Merton was going to get her own way about Mr Butler. Perhaps that was rather a good thing. Mr Butler might quite possibly cheer us *all* up.

But had Lady Merton got her own way about Henry? Hadn't he been snatched from her and married out of hand by Pamela?

There was a bang on the door; it was George.

'You're wanted on the telephone and the doctor says you're to hurry because it's a trunk call.'

Again! This was too much. I had come to Trelynt to rest. I went to the door.

Henry was looking quite happy again. He enjoyed trunk calls, even when they were for other people.

'If you don't want to take it,' George said, 'I'll tell her that you're asleep.'

'They'd only ring up again,' I said, and went downstairs. Pamela was alone in the office.

'Who is it?' I asked.

'I've no idea; it's a personal call from Victoria.'

Mother, but it would be best to get it over. As I picked up the receiver, I remembered that Gerald, who had at last managed to get a telephone installed, was on the Victoria exchange. I had decided that for the sake of my peace of mind I would never see Gerald again, but it would be nice if he were to ring me up.

'Is that Miss Anne Palliser speaking personally?'

It was. The operator went away. I waited. Would it be mother or Gerald, or only Lady Merton all over again?

'Go ahead, London, Torness is waiting!'—the operator was reproachful and I was glad that I, at any rate, was not keeping anyone waiting.

'Is that you?' It was Gerald and he sounded cross. 'Why didn't you tell me that you were going away? I've had a frightful time finding you.'

One felt that he exaggerated. He had probably done no more than ring up mother and been told by her that I was at Trelynt.

'I'm dreadfully sorry.'

'It doesn't matter really, dear,' Gerald said, forgiving me for following my own plans. 'Only I wanted your advice about the beginning of the new book. When are you coming back?'

'I don't know.'

'But you *must* know.' Gerald spoke as if he were someone whose own plans were always in complete order.

'I've given up my job,' I said, 'and I've no idea at all what I'm going to do next. Couldn't you ask me my advice on the telephone?'

'Don't be silly, I'd have to read you the whole of the first chapter and tell you the plot.'

'You couldn't send it to me?'

'Not the plot, it isn't written down.'

'I'm dreadfully sorry,' I said again. I was feeling elated, I be-lieved that I was really free of Gerald. I was no longer foolishly in love with him. I hadn't offered to come straight back to London in order to listen to the beginning of his new detective story.

'It's too annoying,' Gerald said peevishly.

I suddenly noticed that Pamela was making faces at me from the other side of the room.

'Why don't you ask him to come down here?'

'What!' I was horrified, but Pamela was being kind and thought she was being tactful.

Gerald was still talking about his plot and the difficulties he was having with his heroine.

I shook my head at Pamela who smiled encouragingly and said, 'Yes, *do* ask him, we'd love to have him.'

'He can't leave London.' I was beginning to feel desperate.

'What?' Gerald asked.

'I was talking to Pamela,' I said.

Gerald said, 'Oh, dear, oh, dear, haven't you been listening to me at all?'

He sounded so desolate that I thought I was being mean in not giving him Pamela's message.

'Hold on a minute,' I said. I looked at Pamela. 'Shall I suggest he goes to the Pallisser Arms?'

'No, of course not, he must come here.' Now that she had determined on being kind, Pamela would have no half measures.

'Pamela says you can come and stay,' I said to Gerald. At least I could make the invitation as ungracious as possible.

But Gerald didn't notice anything; he was delighted. To get away to the country was exactly what he needed; he thanked me, he thanked Pamela. When would it be convenient for him to arrive?

The truthful answer to that one was 'never,' but I hadn't got the heart or more exactly the courage to say it.

'It's cold,' I said instead. 'I'm afraid you'll find it *very* cold.'

'You'd rather I didn't come?' Gerald asked.

So then I had to beg him to come as soon as possible; by tonight's train even, there was still time to catch it.

In the end it was decided that he should come in two days' time. I rang off. I was exhausted. Pamela was smiling. She expected me to be grateful to her. She had a right to expect me to be grateful.

The next afternoon Eric Butler arrived. He was accompanied by his doctor and by Lady Merton. We hadn't expected Lady Merton. The doctor was a small and obviously maladjusted psychiatrist. I never learnt his name. He immediately demanded an interview with Pamela.

We had been having tea in the drawing room when they arrived. Pamela led the psychiatrist away to the office. Henry and I were left alone with Lady Merton and Eric Butler. I offered them cups of tea.

'Or a drink,' Henry supplemented.

Lady Merton shook her head meaningly.

Eric said that he would rather have tea and Lady Merton looked self-complacent.

One was rather sorry for Eric. He sat in one of Pamela's orange armchairs and he looked solid and reliable. One supposed him to be getting on for fifty. He wore a dark blue suit, he was going a little bald, he was an historian. He didn't look at all the sort of man who had to travel about with a private psychiatrist.

'Jolly decent house,' Lady Merton said enthusiastically, looking out of the window at the laurels which since this morning had been whitened by a thin covering of snow.

'It's not bad,' Henry said. He was pleased.

Lady Merton turned to me. 'You didn't describe it at all well; it's perfectly lovely and much larger than I thought.'

I couldn't remember that I had ever described Trelynt to Lady Merton. I invited her to have another slice of the cake which had gone soggy in the middle.

Eric Butler never took his eyes off Lady Merton. He obviously adored her, or perhaps he was afraid that soon she would leave him alone with us.

'How's Miss Napier-Smith?' I asked. It was a silly question for I had last seen her only yesterday morning.

It seemed that Miss Napier-Smith was keeping the ball rolling until Lady Merton's return. 'I only hope she hasn't made a mess of things, but she ought to be all right for one afternoon.'

'How do you mean one afternoon?' Henry asked. 'You're surely not going to rush away the moment you've got here?'

'Got to,' Lady Merton said. 'Can't leave Smithy alone, no intelligence.'

'Oh, bosh,' Henry said.

'Now, if I still had Anne'—Lady Merton smiled at me quite kindly.

Henry scowled. 'Anyhow, you'll stay the night.'

Lady Merton shook her head. 'Got to be in the office at nine o'clock tomorrow morning.' She was absolutely determined and I found myself admiring her devotion to what she considered to be her duty. She enjoyed it, of course, and when she started playing at soldiers she was absurd; but she was completely conscientious.

'Perhaps you could come down for the weekend?' Eric said.

He put his cup down hurriedly and I noticed that his hands were shaking, so maybe he was a nerve case, after all.

'What you ought to do is to go straight to bed,' Lady Merton said decisively.

'I'm all right,' Eric said and felt for his cigarette-case. She was turning him into an invalid and perhaps he wasn't yet ready to be one.

'He doesn't want to go to bed,' Henry said. 'Though I must say it's the only place in this house where one gets reasonably warm. By the way'—he turned to Eric—'there's a friend of yours staying in the village,' and he told him about Stephen.

Eric was grateful, for now he wasn't an invalid any more. He and Henry talked about Stephen, and Henry repeated his offer of a drink. Again Eric refused. It was all very exemplary.

Pamela and the strange doctor came back. The doctor was still trying to explain *why* they hadn't brought a special nurse with them as he had promised on the telephone that they would. He said he must leave immediately, the taxi was waiting, he would just have time to catch the next train back to London. Lady Merton got up to go.

'You can't,' Henry said.

Mr Butler said nothing, he seemed utterly dejected.

Henry told Pamela that Lady Merton was coming back again on Saturday and Pamela was forced to look pleased and say how glad she was.

Lady Merton and the psychiatrist left. As we stood at the door to see them off, Pamela was telling the psychiatrist how very busy we were at the moment, practically every bed occupied. She didn't say it in front of him, but obviously the inference was that there wasn't enough staff to cope with Mr Butler properly, and that the psychiatrist had better look sharp and send the Special.

Eric was taken away and put to bed. Matron sent him up a tray and was, I believe, quite kind to him; for, secure in the affections of her bank clerk, Matron didn't bother to complain that the place was no better than an hotel.

Gerald was due to arrive on Friday afternoon and Pamela had said that I might have the car to go into Exeter and meet him.

Just before I left, Stephen Craig came up from the village to make a start on Henry's portrait.

Pamela wasn't pleased about it. The library, she pointed out, couldn't be turned into a studio. It was earmarked as a recreation room for the convalescents.

'But we haven't got any,' Henry said.

'There's Mrs Isaacs.' Pamela didn't want to be argued with.

'You're going to put her in there to play ping-pong by herself?'

'And Mr Butler?'

'He doesn't play ping-pong either,' and Henry had taken Stephen and Stephen's enormous easel into the library.

Friday, too, was the day on which Mrs Isaacs reappeared downstairs. Gerald and I found her in the drawing room with Pamela when we came back from the station.

Mrs Isaacs was wearing a purple hat with a dark blue veil and was as neatly rococo as when I had first met her. The creature in the pink woollen dressing jacket who had flung herself about her bed and indulged in tantrums might never have existed.

'You are a writer,' Mrs Isaacs told Gerald as they were introduced.

'I try to be,' Gerald said.

'I was brought up among writers,' Mrs Isaacs went on, inaccurately. 'I have read your books.' This was true; Mrs Isaacs had prepared herself for Gerald's visit by borrowing two of his detective stories from me and staying awake all night to read them. One wouldn't have thought that would have been good for her, but judging by her behaviour this afternoon, she had been quite soothed by them.

'So clever,' Mrs Isaacs said. 'Do you take your characters from life, or do you make them all up?'

'That's a difficult question,' Gerald said.

'It isn't at all,' Mrs Isaacs assured him. 'Either you do or you don't.'

'Well, it depends,' Gerald began and was grateful when Pamela intervened with offers of tea.

'Where's Henry?' Mrs Isaacs wanted to know.

'In the library.' Pamela sat with the silver tray and the silver kettle in front of her. She was very correct. It was a long time since she had lived in that basement flat and had had inadequate love made to her by the Hungarian.

'Anne, would you mind going and telling Henry that tea is ready.'

I got up and went along the passage which led to the library. In the passage was a Victorian weighing machine, and on a little bracket above the machine was a leather-bound book in which the thinner Pallissers had intermittently recorded their weights since the year 1881. The book started with Grandmother (9 stones, 11 pounds) and only a few pages later on there was 'Anne Pallisser, 1922 (2 stones, 6 pounds).' At this rate it would take us centuries of descendants to fill up the book.

I opened the door of the library. Stephen was standing at the easel, his back was turned to me and over his shoulder I could see the preliminary charcoal sketch for the portrait.

'Pamela says you're to come to your tea.'

Henry, who had been sitting in the window, got up and stretched. One didn't get the impression that he had been keeping particularly still.

Stephen looked round and smiled. He was a tall, rather fat, rather nice young man.

Henry came round and looked at the canvas.

'You can't judge yet,' Stephen told him.

'I wasn't going to judge, I was just looking. It isn't at all like the things you were drawing on those bits of paper.'

'It doesn't have to be. I've decided to change the pose.'

'Is the whole bunch of them in the drawing room?' Henry asked me.

I told him that Gerald had arrived.

'Oh, of course, you went into Exeter to meet him.' Henry sounded bored.

I hoped that he would be nice to Gerald.

'What have they been doing to that poor Eric?'

'Matron said he was to have tea in bed.'

'Oh, damn Matron. We give her a perfectly good drunk and she treats him as if he were an expectant mother.'

We went along to the drawing room. Both Stephen and I refused Henry's invitation to stop in the passage and weigh ourselves.

We found that we had been preceded to the drawing room by Matron who was wearing her blue afternoon. She was having a literary conversation with Gerald and I heard her ask him whether he took the characters in his book from life.

'He doesn't know,' Mrs Isaacs said.

Matron remarked that she had often thought of writing a book. One saw such a lot of things in hospital.

Pamela invited Stephen to sit beside her on the sofa. She was being gracious to her husband's friend. Perhaps she was sorry that she had been rude about the library or the recreation room or whatever it was.

'Mr Bereton-Byways on the 'phone.' Nurse Brawn appeared at the door looking flushed; how did she manage it in this cold damp house?

'You told him there was nothing to report?' Pamela was cold, formidable; one was glad not to be Nurse Brawn.

'I did, but he insisted on speaking to you personally. He sounded ever so annoyed.'

'I've spoken to him three times already today.' Pamela held out her hand for Mrs Isaac's empty cup.

'Shall *I* go?' Matron offered. 'But he's really being very foolish, his wife's not even in labour yet.'

'Tell him we don't expect her to be for another fortnight,' Henry suggested, 'and that when she is we'll send him a telegram.'

'Or a postcard,' Nurse Brawn giggled.

Matron glared and bustled out of the room shooing Nurse Brawn before her.

I went and sat beside Gerald. At least I might be able to prevent anyone else from asking him whether he took his characters from life.

It hadn't been a good idea for Gerald to come here; things were going to be difficult enough without that.

One only hoped that he would find it agreeable at Trelynt. That he would be able to work here. He had told me on the drive from the station that the water pipes in his flat had burst. 'But only this morning,' he had hastened to add, in case I might think that it was the burst pipes which had decided him to visit us.

'The plot,' I reminded him. 'When are you going to tell me about the plot?'

'Any time you like.' Gerald was pleased. 'It's in an awful mess and if I'm not careful I shall land myself with another murdered governess.'

'They murder very easily,' Stephen said, 'like those dreadfully delicate daddy-long-legs that come and practically commit suicide all over one in the autumn.'

Mrs Isaacs said that she always liked the murder to be done with an axe or something of that sort—so much more likely than pushing off a height, and she brought her fat little hands together and pushed them out in front of her.

'You don't care for poison?' Gerald asked.

'No, not poison,' Mrs Isaacs said. 'Too complicated.'

'It's funny,' Pamela said, 'but I've never really cared for murder stories.'

Suddenly there were the sounds of a scuffle and a kind of scream. It seemed to come from just outside the door.

Pamela jumped up and ran out of the room followed, after a moment of indecision, by Henry who thoughtfully left the door open. The rest of us stayed where we were, not knowing what we ought to do.

Through the open doorway I caught sight of Mr Butler who was being held on to on either side by George and Matron.

'I'm leaving,' Mr Butler shouted. 'I haven't signed anything and you can't prevent me.'

Henry darted forward and relieved Matron of her share of Mr Butler.

'You can't leave if you're only wearing your pyjamas,' George said.

'Am I wearing my pyjamas?' Mr Butler looked down at his bare feet and seemed surprised.

Pamela turned and shut the door. I saw her face. She was terrified.

We could hear George soothingly advising Mr Butler to take it easy.

'Ought one to do anything?' Stephen and Gerald spoke together.

'Better not,' I said. 'They'll call us if they want anything.

Now the sounds were going away from us. Mr Butler was being led down the passage and across the hall. He would be taken upstairs again and put to bed. Pamela would give him a sedative. Everything was all right. But Pamela had been terrified.

In the drawing room we waited for something to happen, but nothing did.

'Poor old Eric,' Stephen said. 'I didn't know he'd got as bad as that.'

Pamela was terrified. I couldn't think of anything else.

This was the end of the nursing home. Pamela knew it and I knew it as well, because I had seen the expression on Pamela's face. She no longer believed in the nursing home.

'Anne, you are always imagining things.'

But this time I wasn't imagining.

Had Pamela looked like that when they told her that her father had committed suicide?

However many philosophies Pamela studied she would always see life in two halves, good and evil.

The good was respectability and life insurance and one's own solid identity.

The evil was debts and a lack of responsibility towards others and any kind of untidiness. It had been untidy of her father to commit suicide; and it had been untidy of Mr Butler to run screaming into the hall.

'Anne, you are imagining things. Mr Butler is not important. He will be got rid of and everything will be as it was before.'

But how could it be?

It seemed to me that we had been waiting in the drawing room for hours.

But really it was only a few minutes since Mr Butler had screamed and George had told him to take it easy.

'D.T.s,' Mrs Isaacs was saying decisively.

'How interesting,' Gerald said. 'I didn't know it worked like that.'

'It can work all kinds of ways,' Mrs Isaacs said.

'Perhaps it was just that he wanted to go home,' Gerald said. 'Not that it isn't most awfully nice here.' He smiled at me reassuringly.

We were all listening for further noises, or for someone to come back and tell us what was going on; but still nothing happened.

'Tell me about your book,' I said to Gerald. I wouldn't think about Pamela any more. I would think about my own life or about Gerald's.

'It opens,' Gerald said, 'in a country house,' and he looked round the Trelynt drawing room, wondering perhaps if it would do for the scene in his book. 'It's supposed to be haunted, or do you think that would be too boring?'

It was charming this habit of Gerald's of discussing his plots with anyone who might happen to be around. Or perhaps I was prejudiced and it wasn't charming at all; perhaps other people found it tedious?

'I suppose *this* house isn't haunted?' Gerald asked.

'No,' I said, 'but there's a house in the village that's supposed to be.'

'Who by?' Gerald asked.

'Just by a ghost.'

Gerald said that there had been times when he'd thought that his cellar was haunted. 'One does hear the most extraordinary noises sometimes, people walking up and down stairs.'

'And couldn't it be people?'

'Not very well, the stairs are blocked off at the top.'

'Perhaps you ought to have a séance there,' I said and thought of Sophia. She could invite her ghosts from Crawford Street; but Sophia was sailing for Kenya.

Mrs Isaacs said it was dangerous to play about with that sort of thing; you never knew what would happen.

Stephen, who I had thought had fallen asleep, said suddenly that he believed in black magic, firmly. He looked at each of us in turn, inviting us to contradict him.

Mrs Isaacs repeated that it had always been her opinion that it was dangerous to play about with that sort of thing.

Gerald said that black magic was awfully dull when you got down to it because the whole thing depended entirely on fleas.

Still nothing seemed to be happening in the rest of the house. We couldn't go on forever like this talking to each other about black magic and anything that came into our heads.

'Do you think . . . ?' Mrs Isaacs said and got up.

'Wait,' I said. 'Please wait a minute.' I stood up—if I stood between her and the door, she couldn't very well fight her way past me.

I heard quick footsteps coming down the passage, they were Pamela's. Once they had been the governess's, she had been coming to the drawing room to tell me that it was my bedtime. I had been playing beggar-my-neighbour with mother, now I would be able to stop. The social moment of the day was over, I would be able to go up to the night nursery and relax, and take off my bronze slippers which were too tight for me.

Pamela stood in the doorway. She looked bright and efficient, the synthetic brightness of the governess or the paid companion.

'You got him quietened down?' Mrs Isaacs asked. She was triumphant; she enjoyed it when things went badly for Pamela.

'Oh, yes,' Pamela said and came into the room. 'I don't think I finished my tea.' She sat down on the sofa and picked up her cup. The tea in it must be stone-cold by now.

Pamela was quite composed; only underneath I knew that she was still frightened.

'All the same,' Mrs Isaacs went on relentlessly, 'it can't be good for the other patients having this kind of disturbance.'

Pamela shrugged her shoulders. 'The Special is arriving this evening; we ought to be able to manage all right then.'

She smiled even more brightly at Mrs Isaacs.

'When was this house built?' Gerald asked nervously.

'This part,' I said, 'in the eighteen-eighties.'

'Oh,' and Gerald relapsed into silence.

Henry came back looking self-satisfied. He had evidently enjoyed dealing with Mr Butler.

Stephen started to manoeuvre himself out of his chair. 'I must go,' he said.

'So soon?' Pamela asked.

Stephen said it was time, and Henry said he would walk down to the village with him.

They would go to the pub and Henry would probably be late for supper.

Gerald said that he must unpack.

I wondered if I might now go up to my bedroom, which had been the night nursery, and take off my shoes and lie on the bed. I was tired and I had come to Trelynt in order to rest.

ELEVEN

BY THE NEXT morning, everything was much worse. At nine o'clock Mr Bereton-Byways arrived in a Rolls-Royce to take his wife away from Trelynt. There had been a great deal of telephoning the night before between the Bereton-Byways, and this was the result.

There had been a lot of telephoning altogether the evening before. A good deal of it had been between Pamela and Henry, for Henry had not only been late for supper, he had stayed at the Pallisser Arms until after closing time. It would seem to have done him good, for this morning he was very cheerful and ready to eat an enormous breakfast. He reminded us that Lady Merton was arriving this afternoon. He would take the car into Exeter himself and meet her. It had been a long time now since his driving licence had been suspended.

Mr Bereton-Byways was perfectly furious. Furious with Pamela. Furious with the doctor who had recommended his wife to come here.

'And where do you think I can get her in now at the eleventh hour!' He had shouted at Pamela.

They were standing in the hall, where the whole life of Trelynt now seemed to take place. The hall was dark and gloomy. It had not been included in the licences for new paint. Two of the admirals hung there. They stared woodenly at each other across dim space. Their gilt frames were much dilapidated. Their pieces of sea were brown instead of blue.

Pamela had tried to shepherd Mr Bereton-Byways into the office, but he had refused to be shepherded.

He stood in the hall and roared. From the point of view of disturbance there was not much to choose between him and Mr Butler. He told Pamela that she had no right to keep drug addicts and maniacs in a maternity home. He would report her to the authorities. His face was purple and he wore old-fashioned plus-fours, which didn't become him.

Pamela stood her ground rather well. She explained that Trelynt was a nursing home as well as a Maternity Home. Mr Byways screamed that it was a lunatic asylum. He would report her to the authorities; and the whole thing began all over again.

Mrs Isaacs had come half-way down the stairs and was peering over the banisters. She clutched her pink bed-jacket to her bosom. Her large satin nightdress trailed over her feet. Seen like this and without her stays, she was more than rococo, she was indecent.

Mr Byways glared furiously up at her. And where was his wife, anyhow, he asked Pamela.

George came into the hall smoking a cigarette. He had chosen this morning to put on a very grubby pair of white trousers and he was without a coat. He trailed his broom behind him and he did the establishment no credit whatsoever.

'If you will wait in my office,' Pamela said to Mr Byways, 'I will go and see if your wife is ready. But I think you are unwise to remove her. You know her baby is already overdue.'

Mr Byways said that he would see Pamela in hell before any child of his was born in this goddamn place. And he wasn't going to wait anywhere. He was going upstairs right away. His wife had been frightened out of her wits last night, and goodness knows what had happened to her by now. He started towards the staircase.

Pamela tried to stop him, but he shook her off.

Mrs Isaacs, clutching at her bed-jacket, went into reverse.

George turned his back on them and began to sweep furiously. He didn't like Pamela, and, unless he was directly ordered to, he wasn't going to do anything to help.

'But where will you take her?' Pamela had followed Mr Byways. They stood glaring at each other each with a hand on the stair rail. Mr Byways was on the step above Pamela, which brought his face level with hers.

Watching them from the door of the dining room, I thought that he really looked very funny and too old anyhow to be going to have a baby.

He said that his child would be born at home with a qualified midwife and a qualified doctor in attendance. He had made all the arrangements and a pretty penny it had cost him. Pamela hadn't heard the last of this and neither had the authorities.

Matron came down the stairs rustling in her white apron and blue starched dress. Her newly laundered cap was trimmed with lace. Her face shone pink and wholesome. It would have been difficult at that moment to have imagined a *more* qualified person.

'Please,' Matron said. 'I cannot allow this noise.'

Mr Byways stared at her, rather taken aback.

But Matron was speaking over his head to Pamela. 'Really, Dr Merritt, it is *too* much!' Matron spoke resentfully and with authority.

'My wife.' Mr Byways recovered himself. 'Is she ready to leave?'

'She's in labour,' Matron said. 'I was just coming down to fetch the doctor.'

'But I can see her?' Mr Byways faltered. It was obvious that the situation had become too much for him, and that he had no idea what to do next.

'She's doing splendidly,' Matron said. 'There's nothing at all to worry about.' She was repeating a sentence that she had used hundreds of times before.

'If you will wait in the library,' Pamela said and passed quickly up the stairs. 'George,' she called over her shoulder, 'will you show Mr Byways the library?'

Pamela and Matron disappeared round the bend of the stairs.

'That's women all over for you,' George said. 'They beat you every time.'

Mr Byways still hesitated. He looked small and worried and his face was no longer purple.

I went into the hall. The least we could do was to offer him some coffee. It was still on the table in the dining room.

Rather reluctantly he followed me and I sat him down at the table. I poured out the coffee which was strong and black, but no longer particularly hot. I suggested that I should go and get some fresh, but he said not to bother, this would do perfectly well.

I began to clear away the debris which had been left by breakfast.

Mr Byways asked if he might smoke. He had changed a lot in the last minute and a half. He took a packet of Woodbines out of his pocket and lit a cigarette. He hesitated and then offered one to me. I accepted because now he was pathetic and I wanted to be friendly to him.

Mr Byways said that this was a bad business and I agreed.

We sat opposite to each other, our elbows on the table.

Suddenly, Mr Byways was telling me the story of his life. He was a company director. The Mrs Byways whom we had upstairs was his third wife. He had never had any children.

'But you'll have one in a minute,' I said, 'or by this evening.'

Mr Byways said that no one would ever guess it, but the wife was getting on for forty.

I couldn't think of an answer to that one and we smoked in silence.

Mrs Corwell looked in at the door. She was ready to 'do' the dining room. I pretended not to notice her. Now that I had got Mr Byways sitting down quietly I thought it would be best not to move him again. Mrs Corwell pretended not to notice *us* and started to remove the dishes.

I could hear the telephone ringing in Pamela's office. There appeared to be no one to answer it. It went on and on.

'If you will excuse me,' I said to Mr Byways. I hoped that Mrs Corwell would not menace him or sweep crumbs all over him. But Mrs Corwell was really very nice; perhaps Mr Byways would tell her about his three wives.

I crossed the hall and went into Pamela's office.

I picked up the receiver. 'Trelynt Nursing Home.'

A man's voice asked to speak to Pamela.

I said that Pamela was engaged and that I didn't think I could possibly disturb her. For I remembered that 'the wife' was getting on for forty and at this moment was probably needing all of Pamela's attention.

'Who am I speaking to?' the voice wanted to know.

I considered several answers. Finally I said that I was Dr. Merritt's secretary. Pamela had said that later on I might; help with the secretarial side. I might as well start now. But surely, if I was a doctor's secretary, I should be wearing a white kennel coat like Pamela's and the nurse at the dentist's. And white buckskin shoes? I hadn't got any, but perhaps canvas tennis shoes would do as well. I had some upstairs, left over from the pre-war visits to Cowes and Uncle George's yacht.

I asked the voice if I could take a message.

The voice said it was Dr Simpson and could it speak to Henry.

Perhaps it had guessed that I wasn't really the secretary.

I said that I would go and look for Henry.

I crossed the hall again. The door of the dining room was open and I saw that the room was empty. I wondered what Mrs Corwell had done with Mr Bereton-Byways. Perhaps she I had let him loose and he was charging about upstairs looking for his wife. But I hadn't got time now to do anything about it. I went down the passage to the library. Henry had said that Stephen was coming up to the house early to get on with the portrait. I opened the door and they were both there in the same positions they had been in yesterday. On a chair in the corner crouched the small figure of Mr Bereton-Byways.

Stephen turned round and smiled.

I asked Henry if he would like to speak to Dr Simpson.

'Who's he?' Henry didn't move.

I said that I didn't know who Dr Simpson was. 'He began by asking to speak to Pamela.'

'Oh, Lord! One of her medical friends, I suppose.' Then Henry's expression changed. 'It isn't Willie Simpson, by any chance?'

'It *could* be,' I said. I had never heard of Willie Simpson, but I felt that it was time that someone should go and talk to the doctor whom I had left dangling on the telephone in the office.

Henry slowly got out of his chair. 'I'd better go and see.'

I turned to follow him; but Mr Bereton-Byways called me back. 'Is there any news yet?'

I told him that I would try and find out. 'What you really need,' I said, 'is a whisky and soda.'

Mr Byways said that he was a teetotaller.

I glanced at Stephen's canvas. The charcoal sketch was complete now. One could begin to imagine what the picture would look like when it was finished. At least I thought that I could.

Stephen was watching me. I wondered if I ought to say anything. I liked the sketch tremendously, but perhaps if I were to say so at this point, I should be as bad as Mrs Isaacs and Matron when they asked Gerald if he took his characters from life.

'When it is finished,' Stephen said, 'I hope that it will be hung in here.'

'With the bubble admiral?'

There were quite a number of paintings in the library, but the admiral was the only one that seemed to be *of* anything.

'Please,' Mr Byways said.

'I'm just going,' I said. I shut the door of the library behind me, and ran up the back stairs. Before I got to the top, I met George who was still in his shirt-sleeves.

'Has Mrs Byways had her baby yet?' For if anybody, outside of Matron and Pamela, knew how Mrs Byways was getting on it would be George.

George took a stub of cigarette from behind his ear and lit it. 'She hasn't got beyond the first stages yet. Mark my words, she's going to have a bad time.'

'But what can I tell her husband?'

'Oh, the usual thing,' George said. 'That everything's going to be all right and there's nothing to worry about.'

It wasn't very encouraging. I went on up the stairs and along the passage which led past Mrs Byways's private ward. Perhaps if I could find Matron or Nurse Brawn I would be able to persuade one of them to go and give the message to Mr Byways. There was no one in the passage, no sounds came from Mrs Byways's room. I went on to the ward kitchen—which had once been a housemaids' cupboard. It was empty. On the table was a half-eaten rock-cake which had probably been left there by Nurse Brawn or one of the V.A.D.s. Most likely Nurse Brawn, so I was on her tracks. I heard wails coming from the far end of the passage, from the room which had once been mother's bedroom, and was now occupied by three ladies from Exeter and their week-old babies.

I remembered that nothing had been seen of Gerald since breakfast. Then Pamela had suggested that he should spend the morning in the drawing room writing his book. Had anyone thought to have a fire lit in there? I ought to have seen about it before now; but the arrival of Mr Byways had put it out of my head. I would go and deal with it right away. It would be an excuse not to go back to the library and tell Mr Byways that everything was all right when it probably wasn't.

I walked slowly down the front stairs. The red turkey carpet had worn down to the string. I hadn't noticed it before, but it must give a bad impression to patients when they arrived.

In the hall below me I saw Henry. He was whistling 'Rule, Britannia,' very gently, and he seemed to be completely preoccupied in practising golf strokes with an umbrella. He oughtn't to be doing that; if he had finished telephoning he should be posing for Stephen.

Henry heard me and looked up. 'Have you seen Pamela?'

'No, I was looking for her myself, or for Matron.'

'Amazing where people get to in this house,' Henry said. 'One minute it's so full you can't move and the next you might as well be living on a desert island.'

Henry changed from swings to short putts; but it was years since he had played golf.

'That *was* Willie Simpson on the telephone just now.'

'Oh, good,' I said.

'He's a frightfully nice chap. He was in my house at Harrow. His father was a doctor, too.'

'Oughtn't you to go back to Stephen?' I said.

'Willie is going to send us a couple of his patients. I'm glad I went to the telephone myself.'

'What sort of patients are they?' I asked.

'Just ordinary patients,' Henry said.

'But what's the matter with them?'

'Drink,' Henry said. 'But Willie told me what to do with them. I've written it down.'

'You know we're terribly full up, and anyhow, Pamela will never accept them.'

'She'll have to accept them, Willie is sending them off right away.'

'Matron said that if there were any more drunks she'd give notice and she'll probably make Nurse Brawn and the night nurse give theirs as well.'

'It couldn't matter less,' Henry said. 'Willie knows of a terribly good nurse who specialises in his kind of case, and as it happens, she's free at the moment.'

'But, Henry, Pamela will be furious.'

'I can't help that.' Henry was now practising mashie shots. 'I'm absolutely fed up with all this maternity business, and do you know it doesn't even *pay?*'

I said that Pamela had said that it was just beginning to.

'What's the good of that?' Henry said. 'It's too chancey. If we went in entirely for drunks we should make an absolutely certain profit and a much bigger one at that. Willie said so. As a matter of fact, he'd be quite keen to come in with us himself.'

'Is that what he rang up about?'

'No, he just rang up about these two patients. He'd promised their relations that he'd dump them somewhere and he'd heard about us from that doctor of Eric Butler's.'

Pamela was coming down the stairs. Henry called to her that two new patients were on their way from London. He supposed they'd be here some time this afternoon.

Pamela came into the hall without speaking.

'Is there any message for Mr Byways?' I asked quickly.

I wanted to get it in before the row broke. For there was going to be a terrible row about the new patients. One knew that.

'The baby won't be born for some time yet,' Pamela said. 'Matron is with her. Mr Byways can go up and see her for a minute if he likes.'

I almost ran down the passage to the library. I didn't want to hear even the beginnings of the scene. I threw open the door. Mr Byways, still smoking, was still crouched in his corner. Stephen was standing in front of the bookcase which contained nothing but calf-bound volumes of sermons. He and Mr Byways had evidently not found anything about which to talk to each other.

I told Mr Byways that Pamela had said that he might go up and see his wife. I asked him to follow me and even without the kennel coat and the buckskin shoes I felt like the secretary.

'What's happened to Henry?' Stephen called as we went out of the door.

'He won't be long,' I said.

In the passage I turned to the right instead of to the left. I would smuggle Mr Byways up the back stairs and we would avoid the hall. I felt a little as if we were playing hide-and-seek. I knocked on Mrs Byways's door and handed Mr Byways over to Matron. Now he would be her responsibility.

Turning, I found George at my elbow. He had appeared from nowhere, or out of the ward kitchen.

'What you need,' George said, 'is a nice cup of tea.'

I told him that I had to go and see about the drawing-room fire.

'Did it *hours* ago,' George said, 'and he's in there and typing away as merry as a cricket. If you went in you'd only disturb him.'

George and I went into the ward kitchen and I sat on the table beside Nurse Brawn's rock-cake.

'Just got the kettle on for myself,' George said. 'I don't fancy Miss Maitland's tea. Haven't for a long time.'

'I'm tired,' I said.

'I'm not surprised, I'm tired myself.' George took down a packet of tea from behind some tins of baby food.

'But it's better than when you were in that Cottage Hospital?' I wanted George to say that he was happy here. If someone was happy at Trelynt, I thought I should feel less tired.

'I'm not married to the job,' George said, and shook most of the tea-leaves which remained in the packet into a small aluminium teapot. 'Might as well make a good cup while we're at it.'

Mrs Corwell came to the door looking fat in her green overall.

'You looking for something?' George asked.

'Not particularly,' Mrs Corwell said, 'just thought you might be making a cup of tea. I've been in such a rush this morning, I haven't had time to get one yet.'

This couldn't possibly be true. I had known Mrs Corwell for years and I had never *once* seen her rush.

'Didn't even have time for one when the patients were having theirs.' Mrs Corwell brushed a strand of hair away from her forehead. 'That's a very hoity-toity V.A.D. they've got now. Starched cuffs and everything.'

'They're not *supposed* to wear them,' George said. 'It's against their regulations.'

'Oh, well.' Mrs Corwell passed a duster lightly over her face and put it back in her pocket. 'I don't expect it matters really.' Evidently she thought better of the V.A.D. now that she knew that she was going against a regulation.

George had now made the tea and he poured it out for us.

'Nice bit of excitement you had here last night.' Mrs Corwell was speaking to me. 'And do you know, I couldn't have been gone out of the door five minutes before it happened.'

'What a pity,' I said, for although the incident was regrettable, one could sympathise with Mrs Corwell for having missed it.

'It was my night for going off early,' Mrs Corwell explained. 'Trust me to miss a thing like that, and he's ever so quiet this morning. Not a murmur out of him the whole time I was doing his room. Still, I suppose they've got him doped now.'

'If it's excitement you want,' George said, 'I understand we're going to have a lot more like Mr Butler.'

How did George know? The other telephone, I supposed. Or perhaps he had listened at the top of the stairs while Henry and I had talked.

'The doctor won't ever stand for that'—Mrs Corwell stirred her tea—'and I can't truthfully say I blame her. If we *do* get any more like him, then the respectable ones will stop coming.'

'It's sad when it takes them like that,' George said reflectively. 'Too much money, that's usually the trouble.'

'Not always,' Mrs Corwell said. 'Look at old George Adams.'

Footsteps were coming along the passage; they were the kind that usually made George jump for his broom, but now he lolled against one of the cupboards and took no notice.

Pamela came to the door of the kitchen and Mrs Corwell moved a little to make room for her.

'George!' Pamela said. 'What are you doing here? You haven't finished the downstairs passages yet.'

'I've got to have my tea break, haven't I?' George didn't move.

Pamela looked at her watch. 'Not at this hour and, in any case, you're supposed to have your tea downstairs.

George said that you couldn't run a nursing home as if it were a factory. Mealtimes couldn't be hard and fast, one had to eat when one could.

I got off the table. There was going to be another row, and I didn't want to be involved in this one either.

Mrs Corwell put down her cup and began to edge herself out of the doorway. She agreed with George; but she wouldn't stay and support him.

Mrs Corwell was too large for edging. She bumped against Pamela.

Pamela stood aside, making the movement elaborate. 'I have just been into the large ward, Mrs Corwell. I think you forgot to sweep in there this morning.'

'It's got nothing to do with *forgetting*.' If Mrs Corwell was directly attacked she would give as good as she got.

'Well, perhaps you will go and do it now.' As well as everything else, Pamela didn't want to have to argue with Mrs Corwell.

'There's too much work,' Mrs Corwell complained. 'And those patients! They throw things on the floor *wantonly*.'

I was in the passage now and I could escape. But where to? This morning the house seemed to be filled with problems. I would go to my bedroom and try on my tennis shoes. Then this afternoon I would catch a bus into Exeter and buy a kennel coat. And tomorrow in glittering white I would appear as the secretary. Or perhaps I needn't bother about the bus; perhaps Henry would give me a lift when he went to fetch Lady Merton. Lady Merton, when she arrived, would be another problem.

I got to my room. The bed had not been made. That was because, wanting to be helpful, I had told Pamela I would do it myself. I started slowly and thoroughly to make the bed. I have never been quick over housework; but I am extremely thorough. I tried to remember if it was the day for dusting or the day for sweeping the floor. I should have liked to do *both* every morning, but there never seemed to be time.

There was a tap on the door. It was Mrs Isaacs; she asked if she might come in.

'Yes, do.' I swept some things off the armchair. The faded chintz cover was the same which had been here when the room was the night nursery.

Mrs Isaacs lowered herself into the chair. She was still only partly dressed. She wore a purple satin dressing gown; but you could tell from her general outline that she had found time to put on her stays.

'I want to talk to you. I'm worried.'

Here it was again. Mrs Isaacs was always wanting to talk to me. Usually it was about Pamela.

'I am not disturbing you,' Mrs Isaacs said. So I sat on the partly made bed and was sorry about the creases I was making in the carefully smoothed sheet.

'You remember the pantomime,' Mrs Isaacs said.

I remembered the pantomime very well. Gloria and Cinderella and the rest of them. And I remembered the look on Mrs Isaacs's face when she had told me that Pamela's father had committed suicide.

'I heard from Rose Denton this morning.'

Rose Denton—that was Cinderella and she had been at school with Pamela. Mrs Isaacs had arranged that we should go backstage in order that Pamela and Rose should meet. She had done it deliberately so that Pamela should be discomforted.

'Rose hasn't been very well,' Mrs Isaacs was saying. 'I thought it would be nice when the run is over if she were to come here and pay me a little visit. I should pay for her, of course.'

'I thought it was the other one, Gloria, who was your friend.'

'I have a great many friends,' Mrs Isaacs said.

Surprisingly, this was true. I looked at her, wondering if she wanted to have Rose Denton here for the sole purpose of introducing further trouble into the house, or whether she was genuinely worried about her and wanted to give her a holiday. You couldn't tell with Mrs Isaacs, she was such an extraordinary mixture of kindness and cruelty, of subtlety and stupidity.

'Don't you think Pamela has enough to cope with?' I said.

Mrs Isaacs looked directly into my eyes and smiled.

It was ludicrous. What did Rose Denton matter one way or the other?

'The nursing home's starting to be quite a success, isn't it?' Mrs Isaacs said. 'I do hope, for Pamela's sake, it will go on all right. It's such a pity that she and Henry don't pull more together.'

I got up. I would get on with making my bed. I had already wasted too much time on Mrs Isaacs.

Henry and I waited on the platform for Lady Merton's train. Under my arm I held the parcel containing my new white overall. I had had only enough money for one. I hoped that it wouldn't get dirty too soon.

Luncheon had been an uncomfortable meal. Pamela and Henry spoke to each other stiffly, as people do who have just had a terrific row. It might have been less embarrassing for everyone else if they had simply not been on speaking terms.

Eric Butler had been allowed to come down to luncheon. He sat beside the newly arrived 'Special,' a swarthy woman with a moustache and a hare-lip. We all talked to him much too heartily.

Mr Byways was at luncheon, too, fortunately *not* sitting next to Eric Butler. He had looked up inquiringly when Matron had come in, and she had whispered to him not to worry. Nurse Brawn was holding the fort. Mr Byways had resumed his attack on the rissoles, and I had wondered if he liked having Mrs Byways referred to as a fort, a round Martello tower.

The only person who had seemed not to mind the rissoles was Gerald. He told us that he had had a splendid morning's work.

Mrs Isaacs said was he going to be typing in the drawing-room this afternoon as *well*, because if not she had thought of sitting there.

Gerald said that he could type equally well in his bedroom.

One doubted it; the bedrooms were so terribly cold.

Henry and I paced up and down the platform with our hands in our pockets. We had tried the waiting rooms, but they were crammed with babies who had lost their tempers.

'Stephen says that when he has finished my portrait he wants to do you.' Henry was peering at me over his coat collar. 'He says that your face has got good lines, too.'

I was pleased. It is nice to have somebody think well of your face.

'Pamela's in rather a state about taking the new patients,' Henry said.

All the way into Exeter we hadn't mentioned the new patients.

'If I'd known she was going to make such a scene over it, I'd have told Willie we couldn't do with them.'

'Couldn't you have put them off?'

'Not very well. I'd have looked such a fool.'

We stood beside a case of dead rabbits and a perambulator which was filled with unhealthy-looking cushions.

'Willie's coming down himself this evening; he rang up just as we were starting.' Henry kicked at the perambulator. It rocked a little on its springs.

'Have you told Pamela?'

'Not yet; while you were in that shop, I rang up and got him a room at the pub. I thought it would be more tactful.'

People were coming out of the waiting rooms. Porters with barrows stood around in groups of two or three talking to each other. The train had been signalled. The mothers of families and the old men who had been sitting on the benches stood up. People pressed forward, then as the train thundered into the station they drew back again. Immediately the platform was a confusion of passengers alighting, of welcoming relatives, of passengers trying to board the train, of porters who shouted at us to mind our backs.

There was no sign of Lady Merton; but how could there be? This whole scene could not have been painted as a back-drop, there was no place in it for individuals. A youth wheeled a bicycle into my legs; I had omitted to mind my back. The scene cleared a little. A few yards away, I saw Henry and Lady Merton. I hurried up to them. Lady Merton was wearing a fur coat made out of some animal which had been dyed to look like some *other* animal.

She swung round as I approached. 'Ah, there you are.' Henry picked up Lady Merton's two suitcases and I picked up a brief-case.

We went up the steps, covered as usual with filthy pieces of paper.

Walking behind Henry and Lady Merton, I wondered if we were going to tell her about Eric Butler. I wondered what was going to happen this evening when Dr Simpson and the new patients arrived.

We got into the car. Lady Merton and Henry in front, me and the luggage at the back.

'You look a bit peaked,' Lady Merton said, glancing at me over her shoulder.

'It's cold,' I said defensively and remembered that Stephen wanted to paint me.

'It's too early for a drink,' Henry said. 'We could try to get some tea somewhere; that *might* warm you up.'

I said that it wasn't as cold as all that, and that in any case we should soon be home. But now that Henry had thought of it he was determined that we should have tea in Exeter. Quite probably he wanted to delay the return to Trelynt. He hardly consulted Lady Merton; he must have forgotten that she had come down especially to see Eric.

We went to an hotel which specialised in being Old World. A lot of the furniture was made of oak and the walls were hung with Zulu weapons.

We were told by the hall-porter to go and sit in the lounge. In a corner two old ladies read aloud to each other alternatively out of a guide-book. In another corner an old gentleman with asthma was asleep. The tea was a long time in coming.

'Well, and how are the bodies?' Lady Merton asked brightly.

I said that the patients were all right.

'They're not, they're perfectly terrible,' Henry interrupted.

'And how's Eric?' Lady Merton was asking me.

'He has to be given sedatives,' I said, 'but he was down to luncheon today.'

'It seems funny to think of Eric in a maternity home.' Lady Merton was taking off her fur coat.

'He kicked up such a row last night, that I doubt if it *will* be a maternity home very much longer,' Henry said.

Lady Merton laughed.

Henry laughed.

Lady Merton turned to me. 'You don't think it's funny?'

'Not particularly.'

'Don't be silly,' Henry said. 'You know all this maternity business is awfully boring. Pamela might just as well face it, and we can get on with something else.'

'But it's just beginning to be a success, you can't take it away from her now. I was defending an unpopular point of view and I felt inadequate and rather foolish.

Lady Merton smiled indulgently, and I was furious. She didn't see that there was anything to smile about in her canteens. How dared she laugh at Pamela's nursing home. Pamela at least didn't dress up in a silly uniform with quasi-military buttons and tabs.

I should have liked to say something sharp and fairly disagreeable to Lady Merton, but at this moment tea arrived. It was brought by an old cross waiter. All the cups and sawdust cakes and bread and butter were piled together on a small tray. The waiter put the tray down on an oak table and left us to do our own unpacking.

Lady Merton and Henry were very gay about it all. I sat opposite to them and went on disliking Lady Merton. I was really being very silly, for in a way Henry was right: the nursing home was becoming a bore and it was not really a success. Perhaps it was better that Pamela should face that now and get it over with.

But perhaps it was a failure because Henry was so very unco-operative. *Nobody* could run a business with Henry hanging about the place, either sulking or finding everything so excruciatingly funny.

Henry told Lady Merton about Willie Simpson.

'He's got a home for inebriates somewhere near Radlett, hasn't he?' Lady Merton asked.

'That's right,' Henry said. 'He was saying something about it on the telephone just now.'

Lady Merton said that she believed it was an absolutely wonderful place.

'Then why didn't you send Eric there?' I asked.

'My dear, they've got a waiting list about a yard long. You can't get in there under six weeks.'

'Then it wouldn't be a bad idea if we joined up with him?' Henry asked.

'I wonder,' Lady Merton said. 'He couldn't be both here and in Hertfordshire, and so much of his work depends simply on his personality.'

Lady Merton should know, because so much of her own work was done purely on personality. Without it she would have been merely a silly woman playing at soldiers, and she ought to have got over that during the war when everyone else was doing it.

I remembered the women officers I had met during the war, looking elegant in their uniforms or bulging shapelessly. I thought of their signet rings and their gold wristwatches. They had sat at desks and pretended to be young lieutenants, or hard-bitten commanders, and now, in the remnants of their uniforms, they were taking the dog for a walk. Most of them had nothing but their belief in their organising ability and their pieces of uniform.

'Ex-Officer, W.R.N.S. Ex-Officer, W.A.A.F., organising ability, strong personality, used to responsibility, seeks work here or abroad, reply Box No.—' And did anyone ever reply? I had begun to doubt it. In Lady Merton's office we received hundreds of applications from these organisers, who were used to numbers, and who wanted to go on endlessly organising. There were too many people in the world who wanted responsibility; it left nobody to do the washing-up.

Lady Merton had been lucky, but then she really *had* personality. She had fought her way into her present job; she had bullied and cajoled the heads of Service Departments and charitable organisations. The Sir Andrew Merton Canteens were a memorial to her late husband, who had given his life for his country, whose splendid record of devoted public service had been ended by his death. (Sir Andrew hadn't been killed suddenly in a battle, his health had broken down in 1940 and he had lingered on as an invalid until almost the end of the war. Lady Merton, who was a great deal younger than he was, had had to give up being a lady officer in order to nurse him.)

'Their name liveth for evermore.' Usually their names don't. They are remembered only by their immediate relations; but Sir Andrew's name would live, anyhow for a little while, because of the canteens. Lady Merton was right and she was desperately wrong.

She would have been shocked if it had been suggested to her that her choice of a memorial was influenced at all by her wish to sit at a desk and pretend to be a young lieutenant. But in her way she was a remarkable woman. Perhaps she did know what had influenced her choice, but thought that nobody else did. I looked at her and immediately rejected the idea that she should know anything at all that lay below the surface. She had a remarkably stupid face. So to have a personality it wasn't necessary to be clever.

'If we joined up with Willie,' Henry was saying, 'Pamela could look after our end of it. It's only a question of making her see reason.'

'It's unusual for a woman to run an inebriates' home,' Lady Merton said. 'Besides, Pamela isn't the type.'

Lady Merton had terrific driving force and—again—personality, and she recognised these qualities, or the lack of them, when she met them in other people. Pamela hadn't got them.

'Of course, it was different your taking in Eric,' Lady Merton said. 'All he needed was a bit of rest and supervision, and then I knew you both, you didn't have to sell me the idea.'

Lady Merton was really wonderful! When one thought of the way in which, less than a week ago, she had forced Pamela into accepting Eric as a patient, and now she could say that Pamela hadn't had to sell her the idea!

'Excuse me.' One of the guide-book ladies was standing beside us; she looked nervous but determined. 'Excuse me, but are you staying in the hotel?'

'No,' Lady Merton said, and Henry got up.

The lady was looking more nervous than ever, but she stood her ground.

'Oh,' she said. 'Oh, I thought perhaps you were and that I'd better have a word with you about the baths.'

'Aren't they all they should be?' Henry asked.

'Oh, yes, yes,' the lady assured him. 'Only if you *had* been staying, I thought I'd better tell you that I generally have mine at a quarter *to* eight in the morning and my friend has hers at a quarter *past*, but if that hadn't been convenient to you we could have changed.'

'But it's an enormous hotel,' Lady Merton said. 'There must be heaps of bathrooms.'

The lady said that there weren't as many as we'd think, and that we might all have been given rooms on the same landing. This time none of us answered her and she drifted away.

'Then, you don't think it would be a good thing,' Henry asked Lady Merton, 'for us to go in with Willie?'

'If you want to know what *I* think,' Lady Merton said, 'I think you're crazy to try and run a nursing home at all.'

Silently I agreed with her. The nursing home was fine for Pamela, but as a way of life for Henry it made no sense at all.

'We ought to have stuck to market gardening,' Henry said, 'or training horses. One might do quite well training horses at Trelynt.'

'Do you know *how* to train them?' Lady Merton asked.

'I ought to,' Henry said. 'I worked in a training stables for quite a long time.'

I hadn't known that, but perhaps it wasn't true. Perhaps Henry made it up in order to impress Lady Merton.

I looked at Henry slouched in his chair and realised that he might never succeed at anything. I realised it with something of a shock. He was no longer young. In youth there are always possibilities. Nobody can point to a child of ten and say for certain that it is a failure. A young man of twenty may be wild and dissolute and a mediocrity; there is still time for him to settle down or pull himself together and become a serious politician or a writer of detective stories.

'Anne, if you don't get on with that foreground it will go streaky.'

I was in the schoolroom, painting a classical still-life—Iceland poppies and a paper fan. The background was the blue cover of an old drawing book. Mother had come in to speak to the governess. It must have been a few months before Miss Hills left to get married. They stood together in the window, mother and Miss Hills; I watched them and I was very sorry for them. Mother and Miss Hills had had it. They would never be rich or famous or beautiful; the future held nothing for them but death and old age.

'Anne, get on with your work. If you let the foreground get dry it will go streaky.' I dipped my brush in the water. I hadn't mixed enough dark green and I was having to eke it out with water, so the foreground would be streaky anyhow.

I was very lucky, I still had years and years of my life ahead of me, I wasn't even grown up yet. It was open to me to imagine that I would be another Shakespeare, or a great actress in a musical comedy. 'Lord, open thou my lips.' If only he would, so that I wasn't continually singing on one note, or anyhow on the wrong note. Or I might be a famous artist? I looked doubtfully at the picture before me. Never mind, I was still quite young. I had time in which to improve, and when I was grown up I could paint in oils and there wouldn't be this difficulty about the splodging.

I was sorry for mother and Miss Hills, because they knew now that they would never be anything important, they knew for certain that they were failures, a wife and mother, and a governess who was leaving to be married.

'Anne, will you get on with your work. . . .' I had taken it for granted that mother and Miss Hills must, in their time, have been ambitious. I believed that everyone was ambitious, and that those who were young enough dreamed of a splendid future. Everything lay in the future, when you would be rich and famous. It would be terrible when you came to the place where the future wasn't there any more. Daydreams were comforting and exciting, but there would be no point in them if you weren't able to believe that one day they would come true.

I knew now that it was too late for me to be a famous actress, but I jealously collected stories of writers and artists who had not published a book or painted a picture until they were in their thirties or, better still, their forties.

I had not yet reached the place where I denied the future to myself; but now, sitting in this hotel in Exeter, I was denying it to Henry. He would never be famous; it was improbable that he would ever succeed at anything.

Come to think of it, most of the people one knew were failures, but their failures weren't so all-embracing as Henry's. Pamela, for instance. Before she had met Henry, Pamela had been a mildly successful doctor. Anyhow she hadn't been a dead failure. She had passed her examinations, she had had her clinics and she had been assistant to the woman doctor in Fulham.

'But what will your life *be*?' I was older now, going on for twenty. Mother stood by the window in the schoolroom, which was now used as a sewing room, and Sophia brought her Girl Guides here on Thursday afternoons to do handicrafts.

I had just returned from Cowes and there had been a letter of complaint from Aunt Emily. I had refused the invitation of some friends of hers—crashing bores—to go and stay with them in Hampshire. It had been kind of them to ask me and I had been ungracious in not accepting.

Mother had just pointed out that if I didn't go anywhere, I wouldn't meet anybody. I had been sulky and said that I didn't want to meet people. 'But what will your life *be*; you want to get married don't you?' I said that I didn't want to get married. As nobody had asked me, mother's question seemed to be pointless, as well as impertinent.

'You none of you even *try* to make anything of your lives.' Mother continued to stand in the window holding Aunt Emily s letter, and in a detached way I felt some sympathy I for her. But I couldn't remain detached for I was one of the chief reasons for mother's exasperation. I fiddled with Sophia's sewing machine and hoped mother would go away. And surely she was being illogical if she expected her children to make something of their lives. What had she ever made of her own?

Success is a quality. Sophia and Henry and I hadn't got it. Well, anyway, Henry hadn't.

I looked again at Henry lying back in his chair and smiling at Lady Merton. He was charming and delightful. But he was a failure.

'Poor Millicent, always so unlucky, and that son of hers, nothing but a waster.' Now it was Aunt Emily who stood in the schoolroom window, or in the window of her own rich drawing room.

But it wouldn't have mattered about Henry's being a waster, if he hadn't also been charming, and it was noticeable that people coming much into contact with Henry quite often cease to work hard and struggle for their small successes.

'You know what's the matter with me, I'm manic-depressive.' Henry had said that when he was in the hospital last summer. He had been rather pleased with the words.

But he had been thinking of those times when he knew that nothing was worth while, because nothing he did would ever amount to anything. Faced with despair, he would get deliberately drunk and then he would forget.

But in spite of everything, there would always be people who would be charmed by Henry, and people who would fall in love with him. For a time life would be bearable again.

The sequence would go on endlessly repeating itself.

'You're in a bit of a trance, aren't you?' It was Lady Merton; she was standing up and Henry was helping her on with her fur coat, so we must be going.

I got quickly to my feet.

'Aren't you taking that parcel?' Henry said.

I bent down and picked up the paper bag which contained the kennel coat. I wondered if I should ever bother to wear it.

'So Pamela isn't keen on this partnership idea?' Lady Merton said to Henry.

'I haven't exactly told her yet.'

We were leaving the lounge with its Zulu weapons and the ladies who had their baths at a quarter to and a quarter past eight.

'That's a bit tough, isn't it?' Lady Merton said. But I don't suppose she really minded much about Pamela.

We got into the car.

On the way home we stopped at several pubs. Henry's mood and his attitude towards Pamela and the whole situation at Trelynt underwent a change.

On the platform at Exeter he had been nervous because Pamela was so upset about the arrival of the new patients. He had been frightened that this time he had gone too far, and mixed up with that was consideration for Pamela's feelings. By the time we reached the last pub he was no longer frightened. He would do what *he* wanted, and Pamela could go to hell.

The pub was in a village only a few miles from Trelynt. We went into the private bar. Two countrymen sat on stools at the far end of it. The publican with his elbows on the counter read the evening paper. Henry addressed him as Arthur and ordered four double whiskies. Arthur put the paper aside and said that it was a bit early still, so if Henry didn't mind, he'd just have a half of bitter. I said that if Henry didn't mind, I'd just have a single gin. That left Henry and Lady Merton drinking whisky.

'Here's to the blasted nursing home.' Henry raised his glass, Arthur drew his beer from one of the casks which stood in a row at the back of the bar.

'How are things with you?' he asked. He put his filled glass down on the counter. He was a thin man with a red face and looked as if he suffered from indigestion. Maybe he oughtn't to drink anything but milk.

'Everything's fine,' Henry said. 'Couldn't be better.'

I looked at him and saw that he really believed what he said.

Lady Merton was beginning to be uneasy. I suppose she realised that Henry ought to be at Trelynt coping with Pamela and the new patients who had probably arrived by now. (And then there was Eric Butler.) She suggested to Henry that we should get cracking.

Henry said that there was plenty of time. He ordered another round of drinks and drank to the health of his partner, Dr Simpson.

The bar began to fill up. There were one or two retired Colonels with their wives, and several chicken farmers who had once been in the Hussars, and some real farmers and the local grocer. Henry seemed to be well known to nearly all of them.

'Well, and how are things with you?' A chicken farmer wearing an old regimental tie came and stood just behind Henry.

Henry said that everything was fine, and began a long explanation of how he was going to make a fortune by curing everyone of drink.

The chicken farmer thought that extremely funny and so did quite a lot of other people.

Thus encouraged, Henry told them how Trelynt was absolutely *crammed* with rich drunken patients. 'We've got a waiting list about a yard long.'

The chicken farmer looked rather impressed.

Henry bought him a drink.

I tried to catch Lady Merton's eye. It was really getting terribly late. If we stayed here much longer we shouldn't be in time for supper. But Lady Merton was deep in conversation with a retired Colonel. The Colonel's wife, obviously not pleased, talked brightly to a lady-friend.

'Oh, good *evening*, Mrs Holmes, how nice to see you. What are you drinking?' Henry smiled warmly, obviously pleased to see her, pleased to see everyone.

Mrs Holmes smiled back and repeated that Trelynt was on the 'phone.

'Tell them to go to hell,' Henry said. His voice was pleasant and friendly.

'I could tell them you're not here.' Mrs Holmes was going towards the door at the back of the bar.

'I'll speak to them,' I said, and got up.

I started to crawl through the opening under the counter. One of the chicken farmers lifted the flap for me. I followed Mrs Holmes through the door which led to the private part of the house. The telephone was at the end of the passage. It stood on one of those rather complicated pieces of furniture which have inserts of looking glass, and hooks on which to hang foxes, brushes, and cages at the sides for umbrellas and walking sticks.

I picked up the receiver, prepared to placate Pamela, to tell her that we were just on our way, that the car had, most unfortunately, broken down but was now mended, and we would be home within a few minutes, and that everyone was dreadfully sorry.

But the voice which was monotonously intoning 'Hullo' at the end of the line was not Pamela's. It belonged to George.

'Hullo, George.'

'Who's that?' George asked suspiciously. He didn't like talking on the telephone; he preferred to listen to other people's conversations on the extension.

'It's me,' I said. 'Henry's in the bar, what's happened?'

"Well, thank God one of you's sober.' George paused to reflect, or perhaps to get a better grip on the receiver.

I restrained myself from reminding him that I was always sober. The conversation was going to take long enough as it was.

'I've had a frightful time getting you,' George complained. 'I've been on to every blasted pub between here and Exeter, and half of them aren't even connected to the telephone. Would you believe it? I mean, you'd think they'd have to be from a business point of view, wouldn't you?'

'What's happened?' I asked.

'Everything.'

There was another pause. I could hear the sounds of heavy regular breathing. I wanted to scream at George to get on with it, but it wouldn't help at all to get him flustered. I tried to be patient.

'Everything's happened,' George repeated. 'And it's about time somebody came back and did something about it. I've been on to every blasted pub . . .'

I interrupted him. I didn't think I could bear to have that part all over again. 'Have the new patients arrived?'

They had, but that was nothing. Mr Butler, who had been put in his bedroom to rest after luncheon, had escaped. The Special had been off duty, of course. If there was one kind of nurse that was worse than another it was a Special. . . .

Again I tried to interrupt. I thanked George for telephoning and said that we'd be home within a few minutes. 'Here, don't go so fast, you haven't heard half of it yet.'

'It's enough,' I said, 'we'll be right back.'

'But he's disappeared,' George said urgently. 'Roaming the woods killing people, I shouldn't be surprised; and Mr Byways back on the boil, carrying on something shocking, and all the women in the house having hysterics.'

'You're exaggerating,' I said coldly and hung up the receiver.

I stood in the little passage trying to gather up enough I force to deal with all the things which would have to be done. Of course George had exaggerated, but even so, it was bad enough.

First, I must get Henry out of the bar. Even that mightn't be very easy. But there was Lady Merton. For a moment I had forgotten her. Lady Merton was conscientious and perhaps she was good in emergencies. Anyhow it was *her* friend who had escaped and who was now presumed to be roaming about the woods killing people; so it was up to her to help.

Lady Merton, once I could persuade her to listen to me, was co-operative and decisive. She said good-night to the retired Colonel, got off her stool and strode in amongst the chicken farmers. She collected Henry and we were outside and getting into the car before he had quite realised what was happening.

I was relieved to see that it was Lady Merton who was in the driving seat. Henry made a few feeble protests, but Lady Merton opened the near-side door and told him to hop in, and look sharp as we were in a hurry.

We drove off very fast. Lady Merton shouted to me that I was to give her sailing directions. I sat at the back leaning anxiously forward and telling her when to turn left or right. Fortunately it was a fairly straight road. When we came to the drive gates, I got out and opened them.

TWELVE

THE HOUSE was a blaze of light. I jumped out of the car and ran into the hall. It was deserted, so was the office, so was the dining room. I ran down the passage to the drawing room. There, sitting in front of the fire, was Gerald. He was reading his manuscript.

'You seem very excited, dear.'

'Where is everybody?' I said. 'And have they found Mr Butler?'

'I hope *not*,' Gerald said. 'He's most disturbing when he's in the house. Much better to let him go.'

Gerald wasn't being helpful.

I shut the door of the drawing room behind me. Mrs Onslow, the night nurse, was in the passage. She never came on duty till eight o'clock, so it must be later than I had thought.

'This is terrible.' Mrs Onslow wrung her hands. 'Such a disgrace, and that Special, she ought to be ashamed of herself.'

'Have they found him yet?'

'They're out looking for him,' Mrs Onslow said. 'But *where* can you look?' And she gazed round despairingly, appalled perhaps by the size of Devonshire. Or, indeed, of England.

'Did Mrs Byways have her baby?'

'Oh, yes.' Mrs Onslow brightened a little. 'A girl, nine pounds two ounces. She came through it very well, better than I expected.'

So *that* was all right. It would have been too much if Mrs Byways had died or even needed an emergency Caesarian in the middle of all this.

'And the new patients?'

Patients! Mrs Onslow sniffed. 'I'm not going to be responsible for them, and I've told the doctor so.'

'What are they like?' I asked.

'I haven't seen them,' Mrs Onslow said, 'and I don't *intend* to see them. I've enough to do as it is, without battling all night with a lot of drunkards,' and she limped away down the passage.

'Pallisser!' It was Lady Merton. In the excitement of the moment she must have forgotten that we were now on very friendly terms and that she was supposed to call me 'Anne.'

I ran back to the hall. Lady Merton was in the office. She sat in Pamela's chair, her elbows on Pamela's desk. Henry was in the armchair by the fire. He was smiling weakly, concentrating on appearing to be perfectly sober.

'Where is the search-party?' Lady Merton rapped out the words.

Wearily, I realised that we were playing at soldiers.

'I don't know,' I said. 'I can't find anybody who's making any sense.'

'There's no need to panic, Pallisser. Have the police been informed?'

There were the sounds of quick footsteps in the hall. Lady Merton and I turned our heads to see who it was and I noticed, with some resentment, that I had been standing to attention.

Mrs Isaacs came briskly into the room.

'I'm so sorry, I didn't hear the car, I was upstairs with those poor men.'

So Mrs Isaacs, as well as Lady Merton, was now in charge of Trelynt. I introduced them to each other and waited to see what would happen.

Lady Merton repeated her question about the police. Mrs Isaacs said that everything was under control and that Lady Merton wasn't to upset herself.

'You have shown this lady her room?' Mrs Isaacs was speaking to me. It was obvious that she wished to take Lady Merton's place at the desk.

'Would you . . .' I began, but Lady Merton shook her head impatiently.

'It's that poor Pamela I am sorry for,' Mrs Isaacs said. 'Such a disgrace, and if it gets into the papers! Well, the place is completely finished.'

'And you'd be delighted,' Henry said.

'Really!' Mrs Isaacs was outraged.

The telephone rang. Lady Merton put out a hand to pick it up; but Mrs Isaacs was too quick for her. She sprang across the room on her little high heels and grabbed the instrument.

'Trelynt Nursing Home. No, we have no news at present. Everyone is out searching, the doctor is with them. We think definitely that he was not wearing any shoes. Thank you so much.' She put back the receiver.

'I suppose that was the police,' Henry said gloomily. He had become suddenly quite sober.

'Yes,' Mrs Isaacs agreed, 'they are stopping all the cars on the main roads.'

'You told them, I suppose.' Henry was very angry.

Mrs Isaacs hesitated.

'You couldn't leave it alone for a minute. He'll turn up under a bush, and we'll have a scandal on our hands for nothing. You're a blasted interfering old bitch.'

'He's been gone at least three hours.'

Mrs Isaacs was retreating towards the door. 'There was no one to do anything. Pamela was running about like a mad woman. You were out, God knows where. It was my duty to tell the police. If he is found there will be nothing in the papers.'

Henry jumped up. I thought for a moment that he was going to strike Mrs Isaacs a smack on either side of that plump face. She deserved that, but he turned away.

'Perhaps you were right,' he said flatly and subsided into the armchair.

'I can't understand it,' Lady Merton said. 'He wasn't as bad as this when we brought him here.'

'He's very unstable,' Mrs Isaacs said, 'and he'd been drinking.'

'But how did he get it?' Lady Merton looked at Henry.

Henry said that he didn't know, but he must surely have known that it was George. George believed in getting people what they wanted, and he could always put his hand on a bottle of whisky. No one had ever known him to fail.

Henry got up. 'I'm going to help look for him. Where's he supposed to have gone?'

Mrs Isaacs didn't know. Mr Butler had been missing from his room when the Special had come back from her tea at five o'clock. They thought that he was probably completely dressed except for his shoes.

The front door opened and Pamela came into the hall with Nurse Brawn clattering at her heels. They were both wearing mackintoshes.

'You haven't any news?' Pamela came to the door of the office. She was looking wild and dishevelled; her cheeks glowed from the cold.

'Not yet,' Mrs Isaacs said.

Lady Merton stood up.

Pamela was staring at Henry.

'I hope that you're satisfied?'

It was the sort of thing that a child might have said.

'You're not going to start blaming *me*?' Henry was defiant. 'I wasn't even in the house.'

'You insisted that this man should come here.' Pamela's voice broke on the last word. 'And now he's ruined us.'

But it was Lady Merton who had insisted. Pamela must have forgotten that.

'Don't be silly,' Henry said, but he was uneasy.

'*You* brought that man here, and those others who arrived this afternoon; *you* weren't even in the house, you didn't *dare* stay in the house.'

Nurse Brawn stood behind Pamela, her mouth slightly open, an expression of incredulity on her face.

'Steady,' Lady Merton said. 'You want to get a hold on yourself.'

'You never *meant* this place to succeed, you tried to destroy it from the beginning.'

'And it's been fun for me, hasn't it?' Henry, too, was very angry now. 'You fill my house with all these bloody women. You're "running a nursing home"; you think you're important. Why didn't you stay in Fulham with your birth-control clinics and your blasted lady doctors? Why *didn't* you?'

'How dare you,' Pamela said. Her voice was hard and furious, but it was controlled.

'I'll tell you why you didn't,' Henry said. 'Because it wasn't grand enough. You weren't able to kick people around, "Matron bring me this"—"Nurse Brawn, this ward is a perfect disgrace."'

At the sound of her own name Nurse Brawn started violently.

'I say, steady on.' Lady Merton tried to lay a hand on Henry's arm.

'How *dare* you,' Pamela repeated. 'How dare you, when you're *absolutely* worthless.'

Mrs Isaacs said nothing, but she was smiling.

'Absolutely worthless'—the words hung in the air, terrifying because we all believed them to be true.

The telephone was ringing again. This time no one tried to prevent Mrs Isaacs from answering it.

'Trelynt Nursing Home.'

'But how splendid! But that's perfectly wonderful.' Mrs Isaacs, the receiver held tightly against her ear, beamed reassuringly at Lady Merton, at Pamela or anyone who would look in her direction.

'But that's splendid, no need to worry, of course, of course, only a question of time. Yes, most relieved'—and here she smiled very particularly at Lady Merton. 'You'll ring again the moment that you've actually got him? Well, no, perhaps better just to bring him straight home.'

She put the receiver back on the stand.

'What on earth was all that?' Henry said crossly.

'Everything is perfectly all right.' Mrs Isaacs held up her hand for a silence which already existed. 'That was that dear Stephen. So thoughtful of him, and Mr Butler's been found, or practically found.' For a moment Mrs Isaacs sounded less confident. 'That is to say, he's been seen in the Drewston Quarry by one of the farm labourers; and now Stephen and George and a lot of the labourers are looking for him under the bushes; and Stephen just went back to the farm to telephone; so that we shouldn't worry any more,' she finished triumphantly.

'So he hasn't been found?' It was Pamela.

'Well, very nearly,' Mrs Isaacs said. 'I mean, there can't be all that amount of bushes, and he can only be asleep under one of them.'

'But I don't understand,' Nurse Brawn said. 'If they've seen him, why has he got lost again?'

'I suppose who ever did see him didn't know he was lost,' Mrs Isaacs said impatiently. Which, of course, was a perfectly reasonable explanation.

'But whatever would Mr Butler be doing at the quarry?' Nurse Brawn still didn't appear to be satisfied.

'Trying to chuck himself over the edge perhaps,' Henry said.

'Oh, no!' Lady Merton started up dramatically. 'He *couldn't* do that; I couldn't bear it if he had done that.'

'I think we ought to go out there,' Pamela said.

'Oh, for God's sake,' Henry said, but he was looking worried.

'Of course we must go,' Lady Merton said. 'Nothing must be left undone, nothing at all.' She sounded as if she were reciting.

Mrs Isaacs remarked that there was no need for anyone to become hysterical again.

Pamela repeated that we might as well go to the quarry; anyhow she would go.

'And I,' Lady Merton said. She had now allied herself to Pamela. Together they would go into the night and rescue Mr Butler.

Mrs Isaacs settled herself comfortably in Pamela's chair and looked superior.

As there was nothing else for Henry, Nurse Brawn and me to do we followed Pamela and Lady Merton. When we got out to the car Pamela and Lady Merton were already sitting in the front and we got into the back. Pamela started the car.

'If anything has happened to him, I shall never forgive myself.' Lady Merton's voice was tense; she was leaning forward staring into the darkness.

'Ooh, isn't it frightening,' Nurse Brawn said, but so far it wasn't frightening at all, merely rather boring.

The Drewston Quarry was about three miles from Trelynt. It was 'ornamental' and it belonged to old Colonel Ingram. Sometimes when we were children we had gone there for picnics and permission had always to be asked beforehand.

We passed Colonel Ingram's home farm, from which Stephen had telephoned; we drove another few hundred yards along the road which was little more than a cart track and then, just before we reached the entrance to the Quarry, Pamela stopped the car.

'There's a fork in the road; someone ought to stay here in case he comes back this way.'

'Why should he?' Henry said. 'He's supposed to be asleep under a bush.'

'We don't know that that's true.'

They wrangled about it a little.

'Oh, for goodness' sake, do let's get *on*,' Lady Merton said, and, 'If anything should have happened to him, I should never forgive myself.'

Eventually Pamela decided that I should be left here while the others went to the quarry. If Mr Butler was to come down either of the roads I was to arrest him. Reluctantly, I got out of the car; I wished now that I had stayed at home with Mrs Isaacs. At the last moment Nurse Brawn thrust her torch into my hand.

'If it doesn't go on properly, you just wiggle it at the side.'

I was left alone. It was very dark and very cold. And I remained alone for hours and hours. Sometimes I walked up and down in an effort to restore the circulation, and sometimes I sat in the hedge and smoked. The only sounds I heard were disagreeable ones, such as the cry of a nightjar or a banshee. From the quarry itself, supposed to be filled with eager searchers, I could hear nothing at all; perhaps it was too far off; perhaps the wind was in the wrong direction; or perhaps they had all gone home by some other road and had completely forgotten about me.

Several times I was tempted to desert my post; but that would be pusillanimous, unworthy, and faint-hearted. Besides, there was always the hope that in a few, a very few, minutes, I should hear the sounds, see the headlights of the car, and the others would have returned to pick me up. If I were to desert my post, I should have to start walking home, and it was a very long way, at least three miles, perhaps even farther.

I had begun by hoping that, whatever else happened, Mr Butler would not appear in the road. I ended by longing for him to do so. He might be raving mad, he might be homicidal, but at least he would be company.

But Mr Butler never did appear, neither did the car. The first sign I had that the whole world had not died this night was the sound of hurried footsteps coming down the lane. My heart misgave me, but I stepped out from the hedge, vainly trying to operate Nurse Brawn's torch. No amount of agitated wiggling seemed capable of making it light. Now I hoped very much indeed that the footsteps did not belong to Mr Butler—'Roaming about the woods killing people, I shouldn't wonder'—and the footsteps were running, and no one but a killer would run by night, and I had nothing with which to protect myself, nothing except a torch which would not light.

'Who's there?' Who, indeed, and my voice, even to myself, sounded thin and panicky.

'That you? No need to get the wind up, it's only me.'

So, after all, it was not a killer, not a homicidal maniac who advanced towards me down the lane, but George.

'What the hell are you doing here?'

'Just waiting for Mr Butler,' I said, and tried to sound as if I had not been frightened.

'Oh, him,' George said. 'But come on, there's been an accident. I'm going down to the farm to telephone for an ambulance.'

I fell into step with George.

'It isn't Mr Butler, it's Henry. Blinking fool, might have broken his blinking neck.'

'What do you mean? What's happened?'

But George was running again now, and had no breath for conversation, or for the answering of questions.

'It's Henry, it's Henry, it's Henry.' The words were being pounded out by our footsteps. 'It's Henry.'

But now we had arrived at the farm. The telephone. Torness Hospital. The Ambulance Station. An accident at Drewston Quarry. Mr Pallisser. As quickly as possible.

But what happened? What can have possibly happened?

Right the other side of the quarry. Didn't know a thing about it till we heard him scream. Must have slipped and fallen over the edge. Dark as hell in those woods. Dark as night.

THIRTEEN

THEY WERE KIND to us at the farm; kind, but inevitably rather ghoulish. And while we waited they told us stories of men who had fallen to their deaths from the tops of hayricks; and of men who had been gored by bulls and who had never walked again. Men who had come right through the war with never a scratch and then . . .

Better, the farmer's wife had said, not to go back to the quarry, better to wait here for the ambulance; and then when it came George could intercept it and go with them to the exact spot where Henry lay at the far end of the quarry.

'But they'll never be able to drive right inside, the ground is gone all boggy,' the farmer's mother had said.

'Not on a night like this there won't be a bog, the ground is as hard as iron.'

And all this time we sat with cups of tea in the parlour which was warm and cosy and filled with the photographs of their relations and of Colonel Ingram and his relations.

The ambulance came, stopped to pick up George and then drove on. In a very short space of time we heard it coming down the lane again.

'It won't be long now before they have him in the hospital.' The remark was meant to be reassuring, but there was no comfort in the old woman's voice, for the hospital was where they took you to die.

'I must go.'

'Stay where you are until they come for you with the car.' And then George was at the door again, and I was getting into the back of a car which appeared to be filled with strangers.

'How is he?'

'As right as rain.'

We arrived at Trelynt; George and I went in but there didn't seem to be anyone about.

'What you need,' George said as we crossed the hall, 'is a good stiff drink.'

'What she needs is to go straight to bed.' It was Matron, who had been standing in the shadows of the staircase.

'You've heard about what happened?' George said.

Matron nodded.

'Has there been any news from the hospital yet?'

Matron said that there hadn't been any time for that and that I must go straight to bed; as well as everything else she didn't want the whole house down with pneumonia.

'But Henry?'

'If there should be any news I will let you know. Now if you go to bed, I will bring you a sleeping tablet.'

'I don't want a sleeping tablet.'

But by this time Matron and I had reached the door of my bedroom.

When Matron came back with the sleeping pill she said that Dr Simpson had arrived; and as she left the room she said that Mr Butler had never been anywhere near the quarry.

'He was at the pantomime the whole time,' and Matron turned off the light and shut the door.

It was very late on Sunday morning when I woke. Nurse Brawn was coming into the room with a breakfast-tray.

I shot up in bed. 'You shouldn't have bothered, I'll get up.'

'No point in that now that I've carried it here,' Nurse Brawn said sensibly and put the tray on the bed. She walked across the room and drew the curtains.

'Is there any news?'

'He's just the same. Nurse Brawn turned back from the window. 'As far as I can make out, it's the internal injuries that they're worried about.'

There was nothing more to be said, and Nurse Brawn was about to leave the room when she turned on me and said, 'Mrs Isaacs!'

'What's the matter with her?' I asked, although I couldn't feel that I cared.

Nurse Brawn sniffed. 'There's *nothing* the matter with her. Carrying on as if she owned the place. As if we hadn't got enough to do without running backwards and forwards looking after her. And keeping that Cinderella person here all night, because she was upset. *Cinderella* upset!'

'Cinderella,' I said. 'What's she doing here?'

'I don't mind that King Rat or Demon, or whatever he calls himself,' Nurse Brawn said, 'he's quite a nice chap; but *Cinderella*! I didn't care for her the night we met her after the panto; *nor* when they all came traipsing over here, but she's a thousand times worse this morning.'

It was all very confusing. I suggested that Nurse Brawn should have a cigarette.

'I oughtn't to, really. I've ever such a lot to do.' But Nurse Brawn was already feeling in the pocket of her apron for her matches and sitting down on the edge of the bed.

'What's Cinderella, I mean Rose Denton, doing here anyway?' I asked again.

'They brought Mr Butler back here last night,' Nurse Brawn said. 'This Rose Denton and King Demon and the rest of them. Ever so jolly I believe they were, quite pleased with themselves. Of course, they didn't know then what had happened.'

What with letting her cigarette go out and having to relight it, and having to remember to be tactful about Henry, it took Nurse Brawn some time to tell the story as she had picked it up during the morning from different people.

But in the end I was able to gather, more or less, what had happened. Eric Butler had, as we all knew, left the house just before five o'clock. He was probably already fairly drunk. That none of his shoes were missing was explained by the fact that when he returned he was found to be wearing a pair of Nurse Brawn's. The pair that she always kept under the sink in the ward kitchen.

On leaving the house, he had walked to the main road, and then caught a bus into Torness.

Why? We didn't know. Perhaps he was running away from the Special, or perhaps he thought that the bus would take him into Exeter where he would be re-united with Lady Merton. But once in Torness he forgot all about Lady Merton and only remembered he must go to the pantomime, which had been described to him, at various times and in glowing terms, by Nurse Brawn.

From then on the whole expedition might well have been called, 'In the footsteps of Nurse Brawn,' for he remembered that after the performance she had visited the cast back stage and he decided to do the same. When he got there he had introduced himself as a guest who was staying at Trelynt and as a friend of Mrs Isaacs. No one had suspected him of being an escaped patient, why should they? For until a few days ago Trelynt had been a maternity home, not an asylum for inebriates.

They had had a party in Cinderella's dressing room. It was all very gay. It was unthinkable that they should part. Mr Butler begged them to return with him to Trelynt. There, they could have an even bigger party. There would be a great deal to drink— George would see to that. A taxi was ordered. Mr Butler would pay for it. He would pay for everything.

Cinderella, Dandini and Buttons, a couple of chorus girls and the Demon King, and, of course, Mr Butler. Gloria couldn't come, she had an appointment with a gentleman friend.

When they got to Trelynt, they found only Mrs Isaacs, installed in the office. She was the liaison officer between the police and the search-party, a sort of amateur 999.

She told them that the whole household, probably the whole neighbourhood, were searching for Mr Butler. It had seemed an excellent joke.

The police were supposed to be stopping all the cars on the main road. But they hadn't stopped the taxi in which Mr Butler had returned from Torness. That showed you what the police were like.

All the same, Mrs Isaacs thought perhaps she ought to let them know that Mr Butler had turned up, but it was more than they deserved. The police ought not to expect to have their work done for them by the public.

In the meantime they would carry on with the party here in the office. George was out, but Mrs Isaacs knew where the drink was kept. Upstairs in her bedroom she even had some champagne. They would open some of that, for this was a celebration.

Perhaps she ought to telephone the Drewston Home Farm. They would take a message to the searchers in the quarry. But it wasn't likely that we were still in the quarry. It was hours since the car had driven away with Pamela and Henry and the rest of us.

Cinderella and the Demon King were sent upstairs to fetch the champagne. Mr Byways was seen to be wandering about in the hall. He must join the party, for hadn't he too got something to celebrate? Mr Byways was a teetotaller.

He must forget it, for this afternoon the wife had presented him with a daughter weighing nine pounds two ounces.

Mrs Isaacs started to telephone; but she had difficulty in getting through. All the lines seemed to be blocked. From the police station she got the engaged signal, and it was the same when she tried Drewston.

Dandini would like to see the baby. Couldn't she and Mr Byways just go and peep at it in the nursery? There was a notice on the door of the nursery saying that no one was allowed to go in; but, surely, they could just 'peep.'

The Demon King was asked to open the champagne. It would be rather warm, but when Mrs Isaacs had finished telephoning, she would go to the kitchen and get some ice. There were some glasses in the corner cupboard. Matron was still about somewhere. Perhaps, if she was asked to join the party, she would see about the ice. Matron wasn't a bad sort when you got to know her, and surely at this time of night Mrs Onslow and the hare-lipped Special could safely be left to deal with the patients? But the Special hadn't been seen since just after tea. As her patient had escaped she had probably gone off duty.

What *was* the matter with the telephone? How delighted and surprised we would all be when we got back to find this party going on. It seemed a shame that those poor men who had arrived this afternoon couldn't come down and join in. But they were probably asleep by now, and anyhow Mrs Isaacs wouldn't care to take the responsibility.

The telephone was ringing, probably the police to say they couldn't find Mr Butler.

Mrs Isaacs picked up the receiver.

'I don't know exactly what happened after that.' Nurse Brawn stubbed out her second cigarette. 'It was the message about the accident, you see, and Mrs Isaacs screamed out that Mr Pallisser had been killed, and rang off before anyone else could get at the telephone and make any sense of it. Of course, there was a frightful to-do, with no one knowing exactly what had happened, and I suppose most of them must have felt a bit ashamed of themselves, especially Mr Butler, who was the cause of it all really, because, say what you like, if it hadn't been for him it wouldn't ever have happened.'

'That isn't fair,' I said.

'Anyhow'—Nurse Brawn got up off the bed—'Cinderella went and fainted, or pretended to faint more likely. The Demon King did the best, from what I could hear. He got them all out of the office and into the library. They couldn't go away, you see, because they hadn't kept the taxi. And he lugged Cinderella off upstairs somewhere and got hold of Matron. He's still here, as a matter of fact; he sort of stayed on to help. Somebody with a car drove the others back to Torness. And of course, Cinderella's here. Mrs Isaacs kept saying that she was too upset to be moved, and all the doctors were too busy to say it was nonsense.'

'How's Pamela?'

'Calm,' Nurse Brawn said, 'wonderfully calm. She didn't get back from Torness until about eight o'clock this morning. And she's been round the wards just as if . . . well, just as if it was an ordinary day. By the way, I believe your mother's arrived; she came on the early train and went straight out to the hospital.'

I was sorry for mother. I wondered if I ought to go over to Torness in order to be with her; or would I only be in the way?

'They say that Dr Merritt never broke down at all,' Nurse Brawn said wonderingly, 'and she's in the office now seeing to everything. Of course she's got that Dr Simpson to help her, and he's been making a lot of the arrangements. And one of his own nurses has arrived to take over those two patients of his. She seems rather a nice girl. Heavens!'—she looked at her watch—'it's terribly late, and I've got another couple of babies I should have seen to before eleven o'clock.' She darted out of the room.

I had finished my breakfast while Nurse Brawn talked, and now I must get up.

There were a great many other things I should have liked to have asked Nurse Brawn.

I wondered if Lady Merton and Gerald were still here. If Trelynt had been just a house, people would have left as soon as possible after the accident in order not to be in the way. But most of the people at Trelynt couldn't leave. They had a reason for being here, or, like Mrs Isaacs, they had nowhere else to go.

By the time I had had my bath and dressed, it was twelve o'clock. The house was very quiet. I went down the back stairs.

I hesitated by the door of the library. Should I go in? But the unfinished portrait of Henry would still be on its easel, and somehow I didn't want to see the portrait again until it was certain that it could be finished.

I thought I could hear voices coming from the drawing room, but probably they belonged to Cinderella and Mrs Isaacs, and I wasn't in the mood for Mrs Isaacs. Only I must make a start somewhere. There were things to be done and I ought to help.

I still hesitated, standing beside the weighing machine. The door of the library was opened by Stephen.

'Why don't you come and sit in here? There's quite a good fire.'

He held the door open for me and I went into the library. I avoided looking at the easel. I wondered why Stephen was here. Surely he couldn't have been painting this morning. Probably he had come to collect his things; for whatever happened it would be a long time before he would be able to continue with Henry's picture.

I looked up at the bubble admiral. All you could really see of him were his face and hands. His clothes and the conventional seascape, and the draped curtain behind him, had fused together into a dark mass.

I sat down in an armchair on one side of the fireplace, my back to the windows.

Nurse Brawn had been wrong when she had said that Pamela was behaving as if this were an ordinary morning. On an ordinary morning, Pamela would not have allowed a fire in the library.

Stephen sat in the armchair opposite mine. I began to feel a little as if I were a visitor.

We neither of us spoke, but the silence was pleasant and friendly, not strained as it might have been.

Stephen was looking at me intently. 'You are extraordinarily alike, you and Henry, and you have the same quality of remoteness.'

'Have we?' I was surprised, for I had not thought of it before.

I think you have,' Stephen said, 'but the physical resemblance is astonishing. Especially the eyes. And the mouth, only his is weaker.'

Yesterday on Exeter platform Henry had said that Stephen liked the lines of my face and wanted to paint me. I had been pleased then, but now I didn't care.

'He is weak,' Stephen said, 'but there's nothing else the matter with him.'

'Pamela said he was worthless.'

'That isn't true,' Stephen said.

It was as if we continued a conversation, but Stephen and I had never had a conversation about Henry.

Stephen stood up, his foot on the fender. He stared into the fire.

'I know it isn't the right time to ask you, but will you marry me?'

I looked at him in amazement. I hardly knew him.

'Don't answer if you'd rather not,' Stephen said, 'but I wanted you to know before, well, before anything else happens.'

I stared at him; I was incapable of saying anything at all.

'It's only happened like this because of last night,' Stephen said. 'Otherwise, there'd have been the usual sort of preliminaries. I would have painted you, we'd have spent a lot of time together. I'd have asked you out, if there is anything to ask someone out to down here. A cinema and supper in Exeter, perhaps. It would have gone along gently according to the rules. I'd got it all worked out.'

'According to the rules.' There were rules. A set form of pre-arranged words and a set behaviour for everything.

'It would have come to the same thing in the end,' Stephen was saying. 'Only now all that mayn't be possible. We don't know *what's* going to happen.' Was he hinting at the possibility that Henry might die?

I continued to stare at him, only half understanding what he was saying. For a solid-looking, normally rather silent young man he was behaving extremely oddly.

'You don't have to answer,' Stephen said. 'I only wanted you to know.'

He was gone; I was alone in the library.

A few minutes later Dr Simpson came and found me there.

Would I be so kind as to type some letters for him? They were fairly urgent; there would probably be time to get two or three of them done before luncheon.

I got up, glad of the diversion. Dr Simpson handed me some pencilled notes. I put them on the table and then went along to the office.

Pamela was at her desk with Matron standing beside her.

I said good-morning and asked if I might take the type-writer.

Pamela nodded. She was speaking to Matron about a prescription which hadn't come from the chemist's. Her voice I was cool and impersonal, and she didn't even look tired.

Dr Simpson's letters were very dull. Just as I was starting on the second one, Gerald came into the library.

'Oh, there you are, dear, I was wondering what had happened to you.' He picked up a book which lay on the table.

'Is there anything I can do to help you?'

'I don't think so,' I said, and smiled at him.

Gerald was turning over the pages of the book. 'I'm going back to London this afternoon. I offered to go this morning but Pamela wouldn't hear of it.'

'I wish you didn't have to go at all.'

'So do I.' He hesitated and then went on. 'You don't have to worry, you know, everything's going to be all right.'

He was very sweet; it was understandable that I had thought I was in love with him.

He patted my shoulder reassuringly and then went and sat on one of the window-seats, the book held open on his knees.

I went back to Dr Simpson's letters.

Gerald remarked that there was after all a lot to be said for Jane Austen.

I tried to get on with my work. I tried not to think too much about Henry. I glanced across at Gerald, now completely absorbed in *Persuasion*.

'What a pity you have not got nicer friends.' But mother didn't know Gerald—she had met him, but that wasn't the same thing.

George came in to say that luncheon was ready.

During the afternoon there was a great deal to be done; there was very little time in which to think.

Lady Merton was looking after Eric Butler now, the Special must have been dismissed; or perhaps the whole thing had been too much for her and she had thrown up the case.

Rose Denton was still upstairs in bed. Mrs Isaacs insisted that she was really ill.

At various moments during the day I came across the Demon King being quietly helpful. He had attached himself to George. They went about together performing the same duties. George had become a sort of double act.

Mr Byways was up at the house nearly all day, either sitting with his wife or waiting patiently outside her room. Today the wife was not so well and there was some anxiety about her.

A reporter arrived from the local paper. The London papers were on the telephone.

It was tea-time, it was supper-time and then, almost immediately, it seemed that it was bedtime.

Tonight in spite of a sleeping draught, I couldn't sleep.

But Henry wasn't going to die. It was unthinkable that he should die. Other people, perhaps, but not Henry. Today had passed in a nightmare of anxiety. Everything that one did, everything that one said, had been accompanied by this dark background of fear and uncertainty; and how many more such days would we be called on to endure?

I thought about Stephen and the extraordinary conversation we had had in the library this morning. But it must be morning again now, so it had been yesterday when I had sat in the chair, looking at the bubble admiral, and Stephen had asked me to marry him. Would we ever be married? It was something which would have to be thought about later.

During the day someone, probably Mrs Isaacs, had hinted that if Henry had been perfectly sober he would never have fallen over the quarry. 'Your brother was a heavy drinker.' But what did that amount to when you put it against his gaiety; or his depressions; his charm; or his gay inconsequence.

'It doesn't seem right that he should go and marry a lady doctor, not when you think what a dear little boy he used to be,' that was Mrs Corwell. And Daphne had hidden in the coal hole for love of him. 'That woman' had lived with him for a whole year and gone with him to race meetings although she had no interest in racing. His first wife had been devoted to him. Lady Merton had been flattered by his notice.

Pamela had fallen desperately in love with him. She must have or she wouldn't have married him. And Pamela had continued to love him. The quarrel just before the accident had been exasperation. She had been frightened and worried by the disappearance of Mr Butler, and by the sudden arrival of Dr Simpson's patients.

The quarrel had not been important. Quick impatient words were often spoken between husbands and wives. 'You're absolutely worthless.' At the time the words had seemed terrible because we had all believed them to be true. Even I had believed them. Probably I had been the only person in the room who had not compared myself to Henry and been a little set up by my own superiority. Nurse Brawn, for instance. *She* was aware of the dignity of her profession, and the solid worth of her certificates. And Lady Merton, the chain of canteens spread across Europe, and the men so grateful for what you did for them. And Pamela. She might, as Henry said, kick people around, but she was a doctor. Even Mrs Isaacs had been complacent.

But Pamela hadn't *really* meant what she said, she couldn't have meant it.

I turned over again in bed. Should I get up and go and make a cup of tea with Mrs Onslow? There must be a lot of people in this house who were not asleep.

Pamela, for instance. Was she lying alone in the dark and worrying about Henry? But surely Pamela was in Torness, sitting with mother beside Henry's bed, or would that not be considered good for the patient? Perhaps mother and Pamela sat together in a waiting room, disliking each other.

When I awoke it was still dark, and mother was coming into the room.

'I'm not disturbing you.' It was an announcement, rather than a question.

'What time is it?'

'Five o'clock,' and mother switched on the top light. It shone directly into my eyes.

I turned my head on the pillow and discovered I had a headache.

Mother stood at the foot of my bed, holding the rail.

'He's going to be all right.' But her voice was unhappy and she looked old and tired.

'Won't you sit down?'

Mother sat on the hard chair near my bed. I thought perhaps she was going to cry.

'It was a terrible accident.'

'An accident,' I repeated, and wished that my head would stop aching.

'You didn't think it was anything else?' mother asked.

But I hadn't been thinking. Only I was so very relieved about Henry. I had almost forgotten that at one moment during the night I had wondered if Henry had tried to commit suicide, but that, of course, had been ridiculous, as well as wicked.

'An accident,' mother repeated, 'and a very stupid one; he knows perfectly well that he hasn't got a head for heights.' She sounded extremely cross.

FOURTEEN

'EVERYONE ought to live abroad,' Henry said.

The girl with the rat-trap mouth nodded sympathetically; although, as she was an Australian, she presumably, from our point of view, lived abroad permanently.

What she was doing in this Devonshire public-house one wouldn't know. She was seeing Europe? But for that she would have had to be an American. Australians 'come home,' and Colonials, or what used to be Colonials, 'go on leave.' Lady Merton would have preferred to go on leave, so nice and military.

Henry finished his drink and called for Arthur, who was busy. Mrs Holmes came to our end of the bar and leant over the counter. Her pink blouse bulged even more largely than it had two years before when Henry and I and Lady Merton had stopped here on our way from Exeter. 'Trelynt's on the 'phone,' and it had been George to say that Mr Butler had escaped and was most probably roaming the woods killing people. Tonight, Trelynt was not yet on the 'phone; but if I didn't succeed in taking Henry away it soon would be, and it would be Pamela demanding his immediate return.

'Three double whiskies,' Henry ordered.

'Don't be silly.' Mrs Homes reached for our glasses. 'You know there hasn't been a drop in the house for months.' She put three small gins on the counter and waited for the money, knowing she wouldn't get it.

'On the slate,' Henry said, 'and you might just as well have made it doubles. What are you having yourself, a port?'

'Might as well,' Mrs Homes said resignedly. 'Not that I really care about it nowadays.'

Henry slumped further forward in his chair. 'I'm thinking of going abroad this winter.'

'Why don't you come to Melbourne,' the girl invited. 'You'd have a wonderful time.'

'I'd come next week,' Henry said, 'only I can't think of anywhere to stay on the way.'

'You wouldn't have to stay anywhere,' the girl said—what was her name? Janie or Maidie or something?—'The ship brings you to within a quarter of an hour of our door.'

'Handy,' Henry said. He had swallowed his gin in one go and was looking round for another. He said that he had once known an Australian horse which was branded with a wine-glass.

Maidie said that that was a terribly famous mark with them, and taking a pencil out of her bag she drew a picture of it on the back of an envelope.

After looking at the envelope for a while Henry said, no, *his* horse had had a champagne glass.

He called for Arthur, ordered another round of whiskies, and was given gin by Mrs Holmes.

I smiled at Maidie, half-rose in my chair and said that really we ought to be going now. I didn't think it would be as easy as all that to get Henry away, but as Pamela had sent me out in the car to fetch him, I thought that I ought to do my best.

'How are you off for drink in Australia?' Henry asked Maidie.

Maidie said that they could get anything they wanted, but that the pubs shut at six o'clock.

'What an extraordinary country,' Henry said.

A chicken farmer who was standing quite close agreed with him and Henry bought him a drink.

'How are things with you?' the chicken farmer asked.

'Perfectly splendid,' Henry said untruthfully. 'Place absolutely crowded with patients. *I* don't know why people want to have so many children.'

'Gives them something to do?' the chicken farmer suggested.

Maidie looked away, afraid, perhaps, that the implications of the remark might be improper.

The chicken farmer cautiously suggested that as it was getting on for Christmas we should have another drink.

We were immediately joined by another chicken farmer who was Maidie's uncle. He explained to us that she came from 'down under,' and was over here seeing the old country.

We looked respectfully at Maidie who had come so far to see us, and we all became a little self-conscious. 'I met some terribly nice people when I was in England.' Would she tell them that when she got back to Melbourne, or would she say that the country was shabby and the people uninteresting? And what had she expected us to be like anyhow? Ought we to be making lace, or doing folk dances—or were we supposed to be terribly sophisticated Europeans?

'We must go,' I said, but nobody took any notice.

Henry wasn't very drunk yet, but all the same, I ought to take him away. It was the least I could do for Pamela, who had invited me to Trelynt for Christmas. She had invited Gerald, too. He was spending this evening in the drawing room struggling with a detective story. At least, I hoped he was being allowed to struggle, but it was more than possible that Mrs Isaacs was interrupting him; asking him whether he took his characters from life; or sitting in an armchair rustling a newspaper, exercising her right to be by the fire. And nowadays, no one at Trelynt had a greater right to be near a fire, for now Mrs. Isaacs was Henry's and Pamela's only certain source of income. Maternity cases were becoming increasingly rare, and the day-dream of a partnership with Dr Simpson had faded away when he had removed the two patients who had so inopportunely arrived on the terrible day that Mr Butler had decided to go to the pantomime.

'Trelynt on the 'phone.' Mrs Holmes was leaning towards us across the bar.

'Tell them to go to hell,' Henry said; and Maidie's uncle, whose turn to order a round of drinks was long overdue, reluctantly asked us if we would have the same again.

Two years ago I had crawled under the bar and gone to the telephone; but tonight I couldn't be bothered. If Henry wanted to tell Pamela to go to hell it was his own affair.

Mrs Holmes disappeared through the door at the back of the bar and Arthur served us our drinks. I didn't want one, but it was too much trouble to protest. If I left it for long enough on the counter somebody else, probably Henry, would drink it for me.

* * * * *

Two years ago Lady Merton had sat in this corner and flirted with the retired Colonel. I wished she were here now, for she was fun, but it was a long time since I had seen Lady Merton. She and Eric Butler had left Trelynt as soon as it was known that Henry was going to recover. Back in London Lady Merton, with her usual energy, had arranged for Eric to go into some other inebriates' home. After that, I believe, he became involved in rather a round of them, and that at some time during his progress he disappeared, apparently permanently, from the world. Perhaps someone had taken the trouble to have him certified; or perhaps he liked one of the homes and decided to stay on; or perhaps it was that Lady Merton forgot about him. In any case, it was only a few months later when we read of her marriage to a Wing-co (Retired). On marrying Lady Merton he retired still further to somewhere in the tropics, where it was rumoured that he grew something at a dead loss.

So Lady Merton didn't marry Eric Butler and *I* didn't marry Stephen. How could I, when all the time I was in love with Gerald? Only now I knew that it was unlikely that Gerald would ever marry anyone. All the same, I went on being in love with him, for how could I help myself? And I went on hoping that one day, somehow, we would spend the rest of our lives together. Stephen didn't seem particularly surprised or even to mind very much when I told him that I wasn't going to marry him, and quite soon he left Devonshire; he was an incident which might have turned into my whole life.

After Henry's accident, mother had stayed on at Trelynt for several months; then she had gone back to London and taken me with her.

'Of course you can't remain with them as the secretary. You would only be living on your brother and he can't afford it. It's perfectly obvious that the place is hardly self-supporting.'

It was true, of course it was true; but it was galling to be told so by mother, and naturally I shouldn't have remained and been a burden to Henry and Pamela.

'Are you any good as a secretary?' mother had asked me on my way up in the train.

'Medium,' I said. 'I type much better than I did to begin with, and I don't lose my head.'

The last part of the sentence was a quotation from Lady Merton, but mother didn't recognise it. She only said that she should hope *not*. Just before we reached London she said that she thought she knew of a suitable job for me. 'Five pounds a week and the hours are nothing very much.' Mother was really extraordinary. 'Social secretary,' she was saying, and, 'Lady Labenham, you're to go and see her next week.' Mother pulled on her beige fabric gloves, 'quite good enough for travelling.' 'Why she thinks she needs a secretary I *can't* imagine; and all that Dockland settlement business is very foolish.'

Five days later I had been engaged by Lady Labenham. She was very different from Lady Merton, elderly and grey-haired, and she didn't wear a uniform or expect me to wear one. Our mornings were spent in writing one or two letters, and then I would take the dog for a walk in the park. Once a week we would drive to the East End. There were also accounts connected with the East End, but they weren't very complicated ones. When Lady Labenham had saved up her meat ration she would decide to ask someone to dinner and I would have to get them for her on the telephone. She always stayed in the room while I did this; she liked to hear that it was Lady Labenham's secretary speaking.

I had been with her two years now and I was quite fond of her.

Maidie's uncle was telling a story about a jungle in which he had run over a leopard. 'Hell of a bump it was, damn nearly broke the back axle.' It wasn't very interesting, but it made a change from the jungles in which the other chicken farmers had shot leopards between the eyes.

The door of the bar opened and it was Pamela. She wore her mackintosh and she looked flushed and excited. The chicken farmers hadn't noticed her, but Henry and I had been aware of her from the moment she opened the door. She came over to us and I got off my stool.

'Mrs Holmes told me you weren't here.' Pamela was looking at Henry.

'Silly mistake for her to have made,' Henry smiled.

'Want a drink?' But he didn't wait for her answer. Suddenly he had become interested in the leopard which had been run over. Pamela was isolated; the chicken farmers appeared not to have noticed her. For a moment it was as if she wasn't there, and it would have been so much better if she had not been.

'Why don't you come home? You're half-drunk as it is.'

And I couldn't be sure if she had spoken loudly or very softly.

'Just one for the road,' someone said; but he hadn't included Pamela in the general invitation.

Mrs Holmes announced that that was the end of the spirits anyway; automatically she began to draw pints of beer.

Someone was offering Pamela a glass. She hesitated, but she accepted it. Perhaps after all everything was going to be all right this evening.

They were talking again about Australia; in Melbourne at this moment it wouldn't be tonight, it would be early tomorrow morning.

'Or *this* morning,' somebody suggested. But apparently that wasn't right; Maidie and her uncle were certain about that. Anyhow it would be the morning and it would be the summer.

Henry repeated that everyone ought to live abroad. He turned to Pamela. Didn't she agree with him? His voice was rather thick, otherwise you might have thought he was completely sober.

There was still a moment during which I thought that perhaps *tonight* it might be all right; but the moment passed. Pamela's voice rose high above the general noises of the bar. There was no doubt now that she was speaking loudly. Pamela was tired of hearing of *where* Henry would like to live. She was tired of being always in the wrong. Surely I must realise that they couldn't afford to live anywhere. There were so few patients, and whose fault was that but Henry's? Her voice had dropped, but she directed it towards the back which Henry had turned on her. It was his drinking which kept patients away. No one would stand for it, and there he sat, the last of a family which had once been respected, a family which had 'stood' for something—her voice rose again on the preposterous words.

Didn't I know that if something didn't happen soon she and Henry would be bankrupt? It was true, but the horrible thing was that her words made no impression on anyone; they made no impression on me. The standards had been removed. We no longer had any standards; it was shown by the indifference of the people who surrounded us. Only Maidie was looking at Pamela, and Maidie was clearly appalled; she had never heard Pamela before.

'I think,' Henry was saying, 'I shall definitely visit Australia, even if the pubs *do* shut at six o'clock. I suppose one could always get in a bottle or two beforehand.'

Maidie nodded, trying to simulate her previous enthusiasm.

We were indifferent now to so many things. This was what life had done to us or what we had done to each other.

'And it would be peaceful,' Henry said, 'and comparatively safe. At least they wouldn't push one over the edge of quarries.'

Maidie smiled uncertainly; this must be a joke, but she hadn't seen it.

'Because that's what my wife did.' Henry was becoming confidential. 'Two years ago, pushed me over the edge of a quarry— amazing, wasn't it? She wanted to kill me.'

Maidie was edging away, looking round for her uncle, feeling in need of protection. But no one else took any notice. At a certain stage of drunkenness Henry *always* said that Pamela had pushed him over the edge of the Drewston quarry. It was true and once it had been very terrible; but now it was merely boring. And I could see that with endless repetition it would become even more tedious in the years to come.

Our glasses were empty. No one ordered another round. Suddenly Henry got up.

'I'm going home.'

He walked out of the bar. His footsteps were not quite steady, but that might be because he walked with a slight limp and with the help of a stick.

Pamela and I followed him. At the door I turned back. Maidie was staring after us, staring at Henry.

But tomorrow morning Mrs Corwell would not find Maidie in the coal hole, as once she had found Daphne. Henry was no longer attractive enough for that to happen.

THE END

FURROWED MIDDLEBROW

CPSIA information can be obtained
at www.ICGtesting.com
Printed in the USA
LVHW040726271218
601879LV00012B/100/P